TRUE LOVE

"You work for the Foreign Office?" she asked in a small voice.

He eased his grip on her arms, and pulled her a bit closer to him, so they were almost embracing. "Yes. That's how I found out you're an heiress." Blackmoore gently took her chin in his hand and forced her to look up at him. "And yes, I know you're Welsh and your family is in trade. And Castlereagh didn't tell me, you did," he concluded mysteriously.

Jane frowned. "No I didn't. Aunt Lydia would banish me from London if I ever admitted that I was from Wales. How did you find out?"

His smile was as gentle as a summer breeze. "I deduced it when you told me your brother is marrying Pembroke's daughter."

She broke away from him grip, and crossed the room, sitting back down on the chair. "Aunt Lydia told me Society would undoubtedly reject a spinster from Wales who was connected to trade. I had no choice."

Once again, Blackmoore amazed her. He walked over to Jane's chair and sat down next to her, his hazel eyes glimmering with something she couldn't define. "I wouldn't care if you were a demi-rep with a child born on the wrong side of the blanket. Your status in Society means nothing to me."

She looked up into his golden hazel eyes and really wasn't sure if he leaned toward her or not. Once again, she found herself entwined in his arms, his lips moving fervently over hers . . .

Books by Sharon Stancavage

EMILY'S CHRISTMAS WISH

AN ENCHANTING MINX

Published by Kensington Publishing Corporation

AN
ENCHANTING
MINX

SHARON STANCAVAGE

ZEBRA BOOKS
Kensington Publishing Corp.
http://www.kensingtonbooks.com

ZEBRA BOOKS are published by

Kensington Publishing Corp.
850 Third Avenue
New York, NY 10022

Zebra and the Z logo Reg. U.S. Pat. & TM Off.

First Printing: September 2004
10 9 8 7 6 5 4 3 2 1

Printed in the United States of America

CHAPTER ONE

Richard Hughes, the eminently eligible Marquess of Blackmoore, was bored. Not just the simple "Should I go riding or should I go wagering?" boredom, but a boredom that enveloped him like a thick fog. In the country, nothing was interesting—he knew, having spent an interminable time at his estates for a few months after returning from France following the incident that forced him out of the Foreign Service. Now he was in London, and once again everything and everyone was drab and lackluster. He stared moodily into his drink, not really paying attention to anything his companion was saying. What was even worse was that he was bored with everyone, even Roger, his best friend. It was common knowledge around Town that Roger Wyndmere, Earl of Stockmorton, was a most entertaining and congenial companion. However, Richard didn't find Roger particularly entertaining and congenial of late.

It's been six months, he thought, sipping his port leisurely. *Six months since I returned from France and resumed my ever-so-proper place in English Society,* he mused. Cyprians, actresses, and opera singers were vying for his attention as they knew he would be generous to them. For once, he wasn't interested. His broad, muscular shoulders looked rigid and unyielding.

The Cyprians weren't nearly as annoying as the match-making mamas that had descended upon him like a veritable flock of vultures. Every mother in London with a young, brainless chit to marry off was certain that her daughter was just the one to cure the eligible marquess of his doldrums. On a good day, the mindless daughters of the ton bored him. On particularly bad days, he pondered putting a period to their existence. Blackmoore sighed. The life of the apparently rich, single man about Town was utterly dull and meaningless.

He surveyed the room with a jaundiced eye. Jillian was drunk again, and telling another off-color story at the top of his lungs. Milbury was there with his son, both clad in the most ridiculous striped chartreuse and magenta waistcoats. Wilford was in the corner, trying to entice a young buck into a game of cards. The same wastrels sat at the same tables and were having the same discussions they had every night. *Gads, London couldn't be more tedious,* he concluded, shifting his gaze back to his glass.

"Richard, you're not attending again," Roger Wyndmere pointed out, studying his friend intently. "And your valet, you're ignoring him again, aren't you? You really should think about combing your hair before you appear in public, you know," he said with a slight smile.

Blackmoore snapped out of his reverie and focused on Roger. "Sorry, what were you saying?" he said, draining his glass of port and motioning to the waiter for another.

Roger laughed heartily. "Before I gave you a dressing-down for looking like a gypsy, I mentioned my cousin. She's coming into Town and is going to be staying with us," Roger commented.

"A cousin? How many cousins do you possess, Roger?" Blackmoore asked in a voice tinged with sarcasm.

Roger frowned. "There aren't so many," he said a bit defensively.

"And does this unknown cousin of yours have a name?" Blackmoore asked, trying to appear interested, but not really succeeding.

"The unknown cousin of mine is Miss Jane Ravenwood. Mama says she has been reared somewhere in the country and is five-and-twenty years old. She is the daughter of Mama's sister," Roger finished.

"Have you ever met this cousin before?" Blackmoore asked, not really interested.

"No. It appears that branch of the family tree enjoyed languishing in the country," Roger replied.

"So, an unknown relation appears. Is your mother launching this little chit—no, she wouldn't be a chit now, would she?" Blackmoore mused, running his hand through his unruly dark hair. "Is your mother sponsoring this undoubtedly homely ape leader in society or is she just doing your uncle a favor?" he asked sardonically.

Roger lifted his eyebrows in mock horror. "You're doing it up a bit too brown, my friend. As a rule, my family is undeniably attractive, so I don't doubt Cousin Jane is passable. And yes, I think Mother means to take her about some, but at her age she can hardly be presented, now can she?" he concluded.

"So when is the cousin supposed to arrive?" Richard asked, gazing around the room at all of the other bored Corinthians in White's.

"Her name is Jane, and she is arriving sometime today," Roger replied, still a trifle defensive.

"I suppose I'll have the pleasure of meeting the paragon sooner or later, since I'm taking Charlotte to the theater later in the week," Blackmoore remarked unenthusiastically. He fully expected this unknown cousin to be insipid as well as homely. And, since he was apparently courting Roger's sister Charlotte, he would more than likely be honor bound to be polite to the cousin. Life in London was getting more tedious by the moment for the Marquess of Blackmoore.

* * *

"Has your father spoken with you about your situation?" Lydia Wyndmere asked, her jewel-encrusted headdress bobbing as she spoke.

Jane looked up and suppressed her laughter. Aunt Lydia stared at her from across the dinner table, wearing the most ridiculous outfit Jane had ever seen in her admittedly very sheltered life. Jane wasn't even sure what to call the tiara-like headdress. It had several unbelievably huge stones, possibly fake, along the front and the most ridiculous pea-cock feathers on the side that bobbed as she spoke. As if the headdress weren't enough, Aunt Lydia chose to wear a brilliant green gown that almost glowed in the dark, along with a very impressive necklace of gigantic emeralds that were probably real.

"Well?" Aunt Lydia demanded, and Jane's sun-kissed cheeks turned a bright red.

"Do you mean the fact that I shouldn't speak about being Welsh?" Jane asked, her green eyes large and innocent.

Aunt Lydia frowned, which made her look rather fright-ening and formidable. "You're in England now, my dear. Therefore, if anyone asks, tell them you're English. It's not quite the thing to be from Wales, of all places, and we cer-tainly wouldn't want anyone to know you live in that horrid medieval Abbey. If anyone presses you, just say that you live in the country. That will quiet any gossipmon-gers," Lydia finished, taking a large forkful of cold poached fish.

"Do you think it will be that much of a hindrance, Mama?" Charlotte asked softly.

Charlotte was everything that Jane knew she herself was not. At eighteen, Charlotte was the famous English Rose. Her long blond hair glistened like the sunlight, and Jane was certain that armies of men had written odes to her cornflower blue eyes and her porcelain skin.

Jane looked at her own reflection in her dinner plate. Her hair was short, curly and black, while her tan made her glow like the sun. No one in London had black hair or golden skin. At least no one she had seen on her visit to Aunt Lydia's. Worst of all, she was as tall as her cousin Roger. *I'm probably the tallest woman in London,* Jane lamented to herself as she sipped her sherry.

Before Aunt Lydia could voice her oracle-like opinion regarding Jane's unfortunate situation, Roger decided to have his say. "Mama, it's true that Jane is from Wales, but she is the granddaughter of a Duke. And you're rich as the Golden Ball, aren't you Jane?" he asked cordially.

"Yes, yes, her Papa is fabulously wealthy. But we certainly don't want to advertise that fact or every fortune hunter in London will be at our door, and that most certainly won't do," Lydia concluded aristocratically.

Roger frowned and apparently decided to try a different tack. "Do you ride, Cousin Jane?" he asked curiously.

"Of course she rides, Roger. Every well bred woman in Society can ride," Aunt Lydia answered, as if her son were a simpleton.

Roger ignored his mother and glanced over at Jane.

"Of course I ride," Jane replied. "We have a rather extensive stable at home. Papa keeps a few stallions for racing that are a bit of trouble for my brother to handle, but they're a bit more cooperative with me," she said.

Roger gave her a broad smile, now more at ease with his newfound relation. "Well, feel free to ride any of our mounts. Charlotte usually rides Buttercup; she's an easy goer. If you feel up to a challenge, take Diablo out. I race him occasionally, and he's a bit spirited, so you have to keep him on a tight rein," he finished cheerfully.

"Roger, Diablo is half wild! Jane most certainly could not ride him," Charlotte scolded, her disapproval quite apparent.

Roger grinned boyishly. "The offer still stands, Cousin Jane. Diablo is a handful, but if you have a way with horses, he should behave for you."

Jane favored him with a bright smile. "I certainly look

forward to meeting this wild beast of yours," she said, her eyes dancing mischievously.

Jane sat atop Roger's massive black stallion Diablo and surveyed Hyde Park. Dawn was just creeping over the horizon, and the Park was blissfully empty.

A sigh escaped her full, red lips. All she really wanted to do was have a good run on Diablo to help clear the cobwebs that had been plaguing her brain. She glanced around the Park again. Far off in the distance was another rider, but he didn't see her. Turning to the young groom, Jane managed a wistful smile. "I'd really like to take Diablo for a run," she said simply.

The groom, a lanky youth, frowned. "Diablo needs a strong hand, miss. That mightn't be a good idea."

Jane gave him a persuasive smile. "But I'm prodigiously good with horses, and Diablo and I fancy each other. And I'd only go up to that group of trees."

The groom looked at the group of trees that seemed very far away indeed. "I don't know, miss," he muttered, shaking his head.

"If I fall off or lose control of Diablo, I promise I'll tell everyone you couldn't stop me," she said with a smile.

The groom finally gave in. "I don't see any harm then, but be careful, will you, Miss Jane?"

"Of course," Jane said, spurring Diablo on. Diablo responded instantly, and they flew across the deathly quiet park as if the hounds of hell were after them.

Jane clung to Diablo's back, feeling more alive than she had in weeks. Her favorite maroon riding habit clung to her slender form, and Jane could feel the wind against her face. Her blood pounded through her veins, and her heart beat as if she were the one doing the running. Yes, this was most certainly what she needed.

Then suddenly, as if out of nowhere, she noticed that

someone was riding up alongside her. This was somewhat amazing, since Diablo was faster than some of her Papa's racehorses. She glanced over quickly, and determined that it was a tall gentleman dressed in black on a very respectable looking chestnut mount. He seemed to be gesturing and shouting something. Jane glanced quickly over at him, frowned, then switched her focus back to Diablo, who was having the most wonderful exercise.

Before Jane realized what was actually happening, a large, powerful male hand seized her reins and forced Diablo to a rather unpleasant, grinding halt. Both the girl and the stallion were breathing hard when they faced him.

"Why have you accosted me, sir?" Jane demanded in her haughtiest tone, hoping to intimidate the very handsome man that was now scowling at her.

Actually, handsome wasn't the correct word for the gentleman who could ride like the Devil. He wore an aura of authority like other men wore hats and his eyes were a hypnotic golden hazel that sparkled dangerously in the morning mist. His skin was dark and his hair was jet black and wavy, like a gypsy's. In a city filled with polite gentlemen who had never experienced hardship, here was a man who had experienced everything and lived to tell about it. A man who knew of all of life's sensual pleasures.

"Why have I *accosted* you?" the gentleman began angrily, eyeing her as if she were the veriest schoolroom chit. "I have certainly not accosted you," he proclaimed arrogantly, straightening in his saddle to an enormous height, even taller than Jane herself. "You obviously don't know any better than to let your horse run wild in Hyde Park. I was simply trying help a fellow rider who lost control of her mount," he finished, his hazel eyes turning a dark gold in the early morning mist.

Jane blushed furiously. The devastatingly attractive rider was absolutely right. She was running wild on Diablo, and this rather arrogant peer might very well have thought that she couldn't handle the beast.

"I was in complete control of my mount, sir," she said, casually glancing around for her groom. "He simply wanted a good run, as did I," she said, hoping to sound confident and worldly.

To Jane's utter amazement, the handsome man actually began to smile at her, a boyish grin that quite transformed his harsh features. "In the future, my lady, you might remember that London is not the place to give any animal his head, no matter how early in the morning," he said, calmly, his eyes traveling over Jane's lithe form.

Once again, Jane blushed, transforming her into a delicate yet alluring woman. "I'm sure you're right, sir. I haven't been riding for a few days, and I suppose I've been missing the country," she finished lamely, looking anywhere but at the very handsome gentleman who was wearing black from head to toe. *If I could only have an introduction to him,* Jane thought wistfully, but knew that it wasn't proper. London was always dreadfully proper, and, because of that simple fact, Jane would never know the name of the dark-haired man that made her heart pound wildly.

"That's quite all right, I certainly understand that," he said, his eyes never leaving Jane. If any of the London tabbies had been about, they would have claimed that Jane had made a conquest.

Then, a voice out of nowhere instantly spoiled any plans that Jane or the unknown gentleman might have been pondering. "We'd best be going, miss," the groom said with all the authority that someone not nearly one-and-twenty could muster.

Jane gazed intently at her rescuer, sadness suddenly engulfing her. She wanted a proper introduction, and wanted to find out what he was doing in Hyde Park at dawn. Now that her groom appeared, all the dreadfully dull formalities must be followed. "Thank you so much for your help, sir,"

Jane said softly, her disappointment echoed in her enormous green eyes.

"It was my pleasure, miss," the gentleman said in his most cultured tone, looking increasingly handsome in the misty morning light.

Jane thought she could see regret in his eyes, but there was nothing she could do. "Good day," she finally said in her soft voice, the one that held a very faint trace of a lilting musical accent.

As Jane and the groom left the park, she turned to see him one last time. He was still there, his eyes transfixed on her receding form.

"Of course you need new clothes, Jane," Aunt Lydia said seriously. "You can't be seen around London looking like a provincial," she proclaimed, as she emerged from the Stockmorton carriage.

Jane, Charlotte, and Aunt Lydia bustled into Madame Mimette's, Charlotte's dressmaker. In Jane's mind, her clothes were perfectly fine. But her father told her to go along with Aunt Lydia's suggestions. So it appeared Jane would be getting a new dress or two.

When Madame Mimette, who was more English than Aunt Lydia, appeared and laid eyes on Jane, she uttered the words Jane had learned to hate. "Your niece, she is quite tall, no?"

Jane winced, and to her absolute horror, Madame Mimette actually noticed.

"Miss Ravenwood, please pardon me, tall is good, you see, you can wear more daring fashions," Madame Mimette said quickly, and Jane smiled a little. It was obvious that Madame Mimette was trying to be helpful.

"Yes, yes, she's a bit on the tall side," Aunt Lydia commented. "But she needs clothes. Everything. She's visiting from the country you see and, well, you know how country fashions look in London," Aunt Lydia concluded, smiling at Madame Mimette.

Madame Mimette nodded. "She needs everything? Gowns, riding dresses, morning dresses, walking dresses?"

Lydia nodded. "Everything."

Madame Mimette actually glowed. "Very good. I hope Miss Jane will find something she likes in the fashion plates," she said, nodding toward the books of the latest designs for ladies.

Aunt Lydia and Charlotte are very skilled and experienced at buying clothes, Jane decided, as they offered their very definite opinions on dozens of dresses. In the end, the ladies decided on several ball gowns, a few evening dresses, a few carriage dresses, a half-dozen walking dresses, each one complete with matching pelisse and spencer. After placing this rather large order, Jane sighed in relief.

"Are we done shopping, Aunt Lydia?" Jane asked innocently.

Lydia threw back her head and laughed heartily. "Finished? We've hardly begun, child!" she exclaimed exuberantly.

They went to store after store, and, when they were finally finished, Jane had a half-dozen pairs of gloves, a dozen of the most intricate and delicate fans, a full selection of footwear for every occasion known to man, and, finally, bonnets to match each and every ensemble. Jane decided that she had purchased more clothes in one afternoon than she had in all of her five-and-twenty years combined.

By the time dinner was ready to be served, Jane begged to be excused to her room. After all, Jane was a mere spinster from the country. She wasn't used to Town hours.

"You have the luck of the Devil himself," Blackmoore's opponent growled at him as he lost another hand of piquet to him.

Blackmoore sighed as he threw the cards across the table. "It's probably because I'm not in my cups," he replied sardonically. Haversham, his opponent, had consumed a prodigious amount of port. He was also notoriously let in the pockets. *Any moment now, he's going to tell me he doesn't have the blunt to settle our bets,* Blackmoore thought, his eyes scanning the group of gambling wastrels that frequented Waiters.

"Need to speak with you alone," Haversham mumbled, practically falling out of his chair.

Blackmoore sighed. Life in Town was getting old very quickly. He led the hapless young Haversham to a corner where they could be private. Haversham had all the elegance of a drunken chimney sweep. Blackmoore, on the other hand, rivaled Beau Brummel for understated elegance. His strong and muscular form was clothed in black from head to toe, giving him a look of power amid a room full of preening peacocks. All eyes in the room were on the pair, expecting a violent confrontation.

"Blackmoore, it's just that, well, my sister has just come out, and I've had to pick up a new carriage and well . . ." Haversham muttered, staring a bit fuzzily at the carpet.

Blackmoore sighed. London was getting so utterly predictable. "I'll accept your vowels, Haversham," he said simply, and saw the man let out a great sigh of relief. "You might be careful next time to watch your play, since you might run into someone who isn't so agreeable about your situation," he warned, hoping the young man wasn't going to drive his family into debtors' gaol.

Haversham tried to meet his eyes but could not. "Thank you," he said simply, and slunk off into the crowd, mortified.

Blackmoore turned to leave, disgusted with the useless young bucks surrounding him, when he felt a hand on his shoulder.

"So, I hear you've had a run of luck tonight," Roger

commented cheerfully, his lighthearted demeanor quite a contrast to Blackmoore's moodiness.

"I suppose. Haversham was in his cups, so the game wasn't truly equitable. He couldn't pay me, of course," Blackmoore finished, wondering why Roger seemed to be so damnably cheerful.

"Well, your prediction regarding my cousin turned out to be completely inaccurate," he began, as they made their way to an empty table. "She isn't some old quiz, though she is rather on the shelf. Quite attractive in a foreign way though, and a bit on the tall side. Not your pocket Venus at all," he said, as they sat down.

"So she's freakishly tall but passable?" Blackmoore commented, a bit bored with the talk of Roger's cousin.

"Don't be so hard on her, she's actually quite acceptable."

Blackmoore sighed and resigned himself to another talk about the cousin. "So, what does this cousin look like?"

"Well, she's on the tall side, has dark hair, that sort of thing. Didn't pay much attention to her looks, she being a relation and all of that. I hear she rides like the Devil himself, and even took Diablo out this morning and had a wonderful time from what my groom says," Roger reported.

Once again, Blackmoore wasn't attending. In fact, as he gazed at the dandies gambling in front of him, his mind replayed the encounter with the Goddess: the sight of her lean and well-formed thighs hugging the sidesaddle of the enormous black horse she rode; the sparkle in her green eyes as she dared to argue with him; the curve of her milky white breasts under the horribly serviceable riding outfit she wore. *She's undoubtedly lovely but heartless,* he thought cynically. *It's probably best that I didn't manage a proper introduction,* he decided with a slight sigh.

"Richard, what has gotten into you? Are you let in the attic?" Roger demanded, trying to snap the spell his friend was under.

Blackmoore smiled a bit hesitantly. "Sorry. It's just that I ran across the most enchanting minx in the Park today and I have no idea who she might be," he said, a bit embarrassed to admit a mere woman might be on his mind.

Roger grinned at him. "You're actually interested in a woman who isn't an opera singer or a Cyprian? I'm shocked," he said, teasingly, trying to lift Blackmoore out of his blue devils.

"She was quite magnificent. Rode like Diana of the Hunt and had the most lilting voice," Blackmoore replied.

"Well, I hope we run across this paragon. You certainly need something to liven up your life, and I don't think taking your seat in Parliament is quite the answer," said Roger, finishing his glass of port.

"I doubt that I'll ever see her again," Blackmoore said with a sigh.

"And the opera? You've attended the opera before, haven't you, Jane?" Aunt Lydia asked, her face pinched with anxiety.

"No, Aunt Lydia," Jane answered wearily. Aunt Lydia was quizzing her as if she were one of Boney's men, rather than simply a provincial relation. Aunt Lydia wanted to know every detail of Jane's life at the Abbey so she could prepare her for "proper society," as she put it.

Lydia sighed and glanced toward the heavens, her frustration very apparent. "So Jane, you've never attended the opera, the theater, or any rout larger than a country dance. However, you can dance, play pianoforte, and recite poetry. Are there any other accomplishments you possess that I should be aware of?" she asked, pacing the room nervously.

"Well, I can ride, I speak several languages, I do my Papa's accounts, and manage our tenants," Jane added, certain that Aunt Lydia would not appreciate any of her skills.

Aunt Lydia frowned, her brow wrinkling. "I'm sure in your rustic little town, those skills may be seen as useful. But you're in London now, my girl, and we don't need to make any of those facts common knowledge," Aunt Lydia proclaimed.

"Of course, Aunt Lydia," Jane said obediently, not feeling very obedient at all.

"Just remember, it's really not proper for you to spend any time alone with any gentleman, not until he declares his intentions. I'm rather a high stickler about this, and I won't have it being said by the gossips that my niece is fast," Lydia concluded, gazing intently at her.

"Yes, Aunt Lydia," Jane intoned blandly, still gazing out the window into their small garden. All she could think of was the handsome stranger dressed in black that she had met on her ride in Hyde Park.

"And you mustn't tell anyone you're from Wales. That would certainly put a pox on your stay in Society," Aunt Lydia commented. "If your Mama was still alive, she would have sent you to me ages ago," she added, with a sigh.

Jane was still staring out the window, not really attending to Aunt Lydia's lecture. *If Mama were alive, I would be here with her, not Aunt Lydia,* Jane reasoned, her spirits lowering considerably.

"And try to watch your Cousin Charlotte," Aunt Lydia continued. "She's the model of how a young lady in Society should behave. She doesn't contradict any of the young bucks and simply smiles at them. That's what men like, ladies who smile and don't show any sign of intelligence. If you want to do well in London, you'll have to mind your tongue, Jane, for you're a bluestocking and that isn't the least bit fashionable," she concluded with her natural authority.

Jane smiled blandly, all the while thinking of her handsome rider. "Of course, Aunt Lydia."

"And by the by, later in the week you're going to the theater with Charlotte and her beau, the Marquess of Black-moore. Roger will escort you. I expect you to be on your best behavior, especially in front of Blackmoore. He can be rather difficult," she finished ominously.

"Yes, Aunt Lydia," Jane recited for what seemed to be the millionth time. *Papa was all wrong,* she thought. *London isn't going to be quite so much fun after all.*

CHAPTER TWO

"You look all the crack, Miss Jane," Jane's lively maid Gwen announced as she fussed with the plethora of buttons on the back of Jane's gown.

"I really don't know how I let Aunt Lydia convince me to get this dress," Jane said. "It shows more of my . . . um . . . bosom than I even knew I possessed," she finished, smiling at Gwen in the mirror.

Gwen beamed back at her, tossing her blond curls. "I think your Aunt Lydia wants you to be rigged out properly. And you are a granddaughter of a Duke, if you'll pardon me for saying so," Gwen concluded in her sage voice.

Jane shrugged. "The Duke stuck his spoon in the wall years ago, and everyone in London is related to someone important," Jane replied in a disheartened voice. *Maybe I'll claim I have a megrim. Then I won't have to go to the theater and worry about embarrassing Aunt Lydia,* she thought traitorously.

"There, you're all ready, Miss Jane," Gwen announced, and led Jane over to the cheval glass mirror.

Jane was stunned at her reflection. She was no longer the dowdy Welsh spinster that had arrived in London with no real expectations. The diaphanous green silk practically caressed her lithe form, cloaking her in an aura of elegance and sophistication. Her green eyes sparkled magically against her dress, and her short curly black hair was arranged in what Gwen called "a fashionable disarray."

The sum of the whole was that Jane was quite unrecognizable, at least to herself.

Jane's reverie was interrupted by an insistent knock on her bedroom door.

"May I come in?" Charlotte asked from the other side of the door.

"Of course," Jane called out, stunned by the sight of her younger cousin Charlotte.

Charlotte was an angelic vision in her modestly cut white gown, embellished with dozens of tiny seed pearls and gold embroidery. Her long blond curls were done up around a large comb embedded with larger pearls. Delicate white kid slippers covered her dainty feet and a demure yet impressive string of pearls graced her classical neck. Charlotte was the image of the English beauty that every man desired, and Jane knew that at her age, she couldn't hope to compete with a Diamond of the First Water like Charlotte.

"You look lovely, Jane!" Charlotte exclaimed with a heartfelt smile.

Jane blushed delicately. "Thank you. I just hope I don't embarrass anyone tonight," she said, trying to pull up her disgracefully revealing bodice.

"I'm sure everything will go well," Charlotte said. "But before we go downstairs, I thought I had better warn you about Richard, Lord Blackmoore, my escort tonight," she added a bit cryptically.

Jane frowned. "What do I need to know about Lord Blackmoore?" she asked. *Is Blackmoore some sort of tyrant? Or possibly old enough to be Charlotte's grandfather? Or pock-marked?* Jane's curiosity was piqued.

"Well, he's a friend of the family, and we saw quite a lot of him before the war. Then he left for the Continent for a period, and when he came back, he was different. He seems to be suffering from a bad case of the blue devils, and he can be a bit prickly. So if he offends you, please don't take it to heart," Charlotte finished breathlessly, playing absently with the magnificent string of pearls dangling into her creamy bodice.

Jane tried to appear confident. This was, after all, her younger cousin. If she could cope with Lord Blackmoore, then Jane most certainly could. "Your Mama has given me quite a few lectures on my behavior lately. I'll be as demure as a schoolroom miss and politely unobtrusive," Jane finished, walking toward the door, Charlotte trailing after her.

Each step closer to the staircase made Jane more apprehensive. *I hate to simper,* her mind wailed, but she was determined to follow Aunt Lydia's rules. *If men in London want well-behaved, mindless beauties, then I'll do my best,* she thought as she reached the top of the stairs.

As Jane watched Charlotte descend the staircase with the grace of a gazelle, her heart began to fail her. Charlotte was obviously the beauty in the family, and she radiated grace and charm.

Jane trailed behind her, feeling rather like the crow that followed the peacock. Instead of even looking at Roger and Lord Blackmoore waiting below, she kept her eyes downcast, concentrating on the staircase. *I don't need to fall like a sapskull on my first night in public,* Jane thought, unconsciously looking quite graceful herself.

As Jane reached the bottom of the stairs, her eyes immediately sought reassurance from Roger, who gave her an encouraging smile. "Good evening, Jane," he said cordially, lightly kissing her hand.

Jane blushed, and as she looked over at Charlotte's beau, her mouth dropped open.

It was he! The rider in Hyde Park. Now he looked even more devastatingly attractive. His expressive golden eyes met hers, boring into her very soul. Once again, he was dressed in black from head to toe, and made poor Roger look like a veritable dandy. Jane could feel her hand trembling as she waited patiently for an introduction. The most handsome man she had ever seen was involved with her very beautiful younger cousin. Her heart sunk into the pit of her stomach like a ship letting down an anchor that would never, ever be retrieved.

"Lord Blackmoore, may I present my cousin, Miss Jane Ravenwood," Charlotte said smoothly, staring expectantly from one to the other.

Jane didn't know where to look as the supposedly disagreeable Lord Blackmoore took her gloved hand in his and kissed it gently, murmuring huskily, "The pleasure is mine, Miss Ravenwood."

Charlotte and Roger gaped at him like a pair of idiots. Blackmoore was acting so . . . cavalier with a complete stranger.

Jane transfixed Blackmoore. Jane, in turn, responded by staring intently at his shiny black Hessians. Roger, thoroughly confused by the situation, coughed politely and brought their attention back to the matter at hand.

"Well, we'd best be off. Mama won't be joining us tonight since she's abed with a megrim," Roger announced, and began to move out of the hall, a puzzled expression on his face.

Charlotte wore the same confused look. As Blackmoore and Jane walked out of the door, she whispered to Roger, "What's wrong with Richard? He's practically slavering over Jane."

Roger shrugged his shoulders and followed her outside. "I have no idea. Maybe he's making an effort to be polite," he said, then added with a grin, "or else he's run mad."

Charlotte grinned at her brother, but wisely said nothing. As Blackmoore led her to his very impressive carriage, all of Aunt Lydia's lessons on proper conduct flew from Jane's mind.

"What magnificent animals!" she exclaimed, staring at the matched pair of chestnuts. Then, to the horror of everyone present, Jane went over to the pair that Blackmoore owned and began to stroke the neck of the nearest one.

"You are a beauty, aren't you?" she said softly to the horse, who began to nuzzle her very expensive silk gown.

Luckily, Charlotte was already in the carriage, so she was spared the embarrassment of seeing her country cousin actually speaking to a horse. Roger and Blackmoore both stared at her in dismay, as the horse continued to nuzzle her and nickered softly.

"I'm sorry, I don't have any treats for you," she said quietly, suddenly aware of Blackmoore standing beside her. Charlotte's suitor, she thought, dejected. *No one who would ever be interested in me,* she decided, with an imperceptible sigh. When she looked up, she found Lord Blackmoore staring down at her with the oddest expression on his face. She turned an even deeper shade of red and said in her soft lilting voice "You certainly have excellent taste in horseflesh, my lord."

Blackmoore smiled and replied "Yes, they're one of the few luxuries I allow myself. It's nice to see that someone of the gentler sex can appreciate them." Then, much to Roger's and Charlotte's amazement, Jane and Richard gazed at each other like mooncalves, unaware of how utterly ridiculous they appeared.

Taking command of the situation, Roger casually said, "We are ready to leave, aren't we, Richard?"

So Jane and Blackmoore got into the carriage, which was more than fashionable and a far cry from the mail coach she had traveled in from Wales. Jane decided to try and salvage her manners, since Roger was giving her a fairly telling look. *I shouldn't have noticed the horses,* she thought with dismay. So, to prove that she could fit into London society, Jane applied everything that Aunt Lydia had quizzed her with, and was the picture of the demure spinster. She never looked up from her hands, which were neatly folded in her lap, and answered every single question with a bland and respectful "Yes, my lord" or "No, my lord" as dear Aunt Lydia had fervently advised. She was as simpering as any schoolroom miss and despised every moment of the charade.

If Jane had looked up from the less than fascinating view of her hands, she would have noticed that Blackmoore looked completely and utterly confused. Unfortunately, she kept her eyes downcast, and was the picture of a demure young lady.

The fashionable members of London Society filled Drury Lane, and the entire scene fascinated Jane. The women were dressed extravagantly, in every color of the rainbow, and the more daring even dampened their petticoats, a look that Jane knew was considered fast. The gentlemen were in various modes of dress, some quite outrageous, with wildly complicated cravats and their shirt points so high they could barely move their necks. Jane smiled at them in amusement, noticing how elegant Lord Blackmoore looked next to these preening, effeminate dandies.

As they made their way to the Wyndmere box, a wave of nervousness swept over Jane. *What if Blackmoore singles me out? But that's impossible. He's Charlotte's suitor and doesn't even remember me from the Park,* she realized.

Jane settled herself next to Roger in the box and as far away from Lord Blackmoore as possible. Her eyes darted around the ornate theater, observing the ladies and gentlemen swarming below them. When she noticed an area filled with particularly beautiful (but a bit overdone) ladies, she quietly asked Roger "Who are those ladies below us?"

Roger followed her eyes and was dumbfounded for a moment. Before he could answer, Blackmoore leaned over and announced, ever so casually, "The 'ladies' you are referring to are Cyprians, Miss Ravenwood."

Jane's face turned a charming shade of bright red and Blackmoore smiled mischievously.

"Richard, you know that it is not proper to speak of Cyprians to Cousin Jane," Charlotte scolded, playfully swatting his arm with her fan.

"Charlotte, I certainly don't need a schoolroom miss to dictate my manners," he commented in a brittle voice. Something about Charlotte and Lord Blackmoore didn't make sense, but then what did Jane know? She was from Wales and proper society was almost a complete mystery to her.

Instead of thinking about Lord Blackmoore and Charlotte, she focused on the play unfolding before her. Jane had never seen a production so grand, and Kean was wonderful in the role of Shakespeare's *Othello*. The costumes, the scenery, and the whole ambiance of Drury Lane enthralled her and she sat thoroughly transfixed until intermission.

As the curtain closed and intermission began, Blackmoore immediately turned to Jane and asked "Would you favor me with a turn about the halls, Miss Ravenwood?" in his most congenial voice.

Jane's expressive green eyes widened, and her mind raced through her new catalog of proper behavior, courtesy of Aunt Lydia. It didn't seem quite proper that Charlotte's beau wanted to be alone with her, but she was certain that she couldn't refuse his escort either. Not that she wanted to refuse.

"Jane, Lord Blackmoore has asked you a question," Charlotte prompted as Jane stared blankly into space, the thoughts racing wildly through her head.

"Oh, I'm so sorry," Jane said in her meekest voice, and added, "Of course I'd be delighted to join you, Lord Blackmoore," rising and taking his arm.

A faint scowl marred the face of Lord Blackmoore as he strolled through the halls of Drury Lane with Jane on his arm. More than one gossipmonger took note, since Jane was utterly unknown in Society. In fact, the sight of Blackmoore with any female who wasn't the charming and docile Charlotte Wyndmere was rare, and caused quite the stir. Everyone knew Blackmoore was dangling after Charlotte, and the world was awaiting their betrothal announcement.

As Blackmoore ushered Jane through the throngs of theater goers, he hissed to her, "That was a wonderful performance, my dear, but you can save the simpering for your relatives."

Jane turned red once again, and stopped in her tracks, unaware of the attention they were attracting. Blackmoore and Jane were the play-within-the-play and many eyes were on their not-so-private performance.

"Pardon me, my lord?" she said ever so properly, her eyes flashing fire.

Blackmoore, nodding to a few passing acquaintances, forcibly grabbed her arm and lead her to a fairly secluded area off the main corridors. He made it very clear that he was not in a congenial mood.

When they finally stopped, Blackmoore turned to her, his eyes wild with anger, and whispered. "Why are you acting as if we are complete strangers? We did meet in Hyde Park, you may recall. Or perhaps you don't, since your mental capacities seem to have diminished considerably since then," he added sarcastically.

To his utter amazement, she simply stared at the floor and said absolutely nothing. Her beautiful, full red lips were pursed tightly shut, and she was playing the role of wet goose to the hilt. "I demand an answer now, Miss Ravenwood," Blackmoore said between gritted teeth, his extreme irritation obvious to all of the gossips studying the pair.

Jane slowly lifted her head up, her anger very apparent. "Lord Blackmoore," she began, her eyes all but spitting fire. "I have spent a week listening to lessons from Aunt Lydia. As you are well aware, we were not properly introduced in the Park so I couldn't very well claim an acquaintance with you. I'm terribly sorry if I've offended your sense of consequence, but I'm certain that your ego is healthy enough to survive this inconsequential incident," she finished recklessly, her passionate anger making her radiantly beautiful.

Blackmoore stood in front of her in disbelief, his jaw open. A myriad of expressions passed over his handsome face, but none of them were pleasant. He took a long, calming breath and said, "You think you've offended my sense of consequence? I think not, Miss Ravenwood. In the scope of Society, you're the one who's inconsequential," he finished angrily.

Blackmoore could see the struggle that was going on inside her. The chit was obviously playing some sort of game, and he caught her in the act. Jane's hands were turning white as she grasped her wonderfully expensive fan, and all the color had drained from her face. He half expected another setdown, which was a rare occurrence indeed for Blackmoore.

To his obvious amazement, Jane's natural resolve took over and she straightened to her full height before announcing, "Polite Society holds no interest for me. I'm here simply to please my papa. Nothing would make me happier than to be sent home," she finished, her eyes daring him to question her.

Her devil-may-care attitude stunned him. For a moment, Blackmoore gaped at her, unsure of a response. Miraculously, his composure returned, although he continued to glare at her. "You will take my arm and accompany me back to the box," he commanded, unaware of the fact that a handful of the worst gossips in London were practically gaping at them. On that night, Blackmoore and Jane actually gave a more entertaining performance than had Kean.

The rest of the performance was utterly magnificent to Jane, who had technically never been to a proper theater before. She somehow managed to put the whole disagreeable incident with Lord Blackmoore in the back of her mind and fully concentrated on the unraveling of the familiar Shakespearean plot. Of course, it wasn't easy with Blackmoore staring daggers at her. Of course, she was determined to maintain a distant and cordial relationship with Blackmoore, even though he was disagreeable. And unerringly dashing. And Charlotte's beau. So she fixed her attention upon the stage and by the time the curtain closed, Jane had quite forgotten all of her worries and was actually enjoying herself.

As they began their journey home in the chilly night air, Roger suddenly became a very attentive escort, much to Jane's surprise.

"So, Cousin Jane, how did you enjoy your first night at the theater?" Roger asked as he leaned back into the upholstery of Blackmoore's luxurious carriage.

Jane rewarded him with a brilliant smile, which lit up the inside of the carriage. "I enjoyed the performance immensely, Cousin Roger. Of course, they were a bit liberal in their interpretation, but I suppose one does have to make allowances," she finished, in her lilting voice, the one that held a faint trace of her native Welsh tongue. Her eyes locked with Roger's and she purposely ignored Blackmoore, afraid he would try to goad her into another unpleasant scene.

Charlotte chuckled a bit. "Dearest Jane, you do have to watch your tongue! Lord Blackmoore is apt to think you the veriest of bluestockings!" Charlotte said, and gave Jane a slight kick with her kid leather shoe. Obviously Jane was treading into dangerous territory.

Before Jane could think of a suitable reply, Blackmoore focused his golden eyes on her and sardonically asked, "I suppose you mean to tell us that you've actually read Shakespeare, Miss Ravenwood?"

Jane stared at her hands in her lap, and quietly said, "In my part of the country, everyone has read Shakespeare my lord, be they male or female."

Charlotte and Roger exchanged looks, waiting for Blackmoore's reaction. Jane didn't quite contradict him, but she did put him in his place, something neither of the siblings ever attempted.

To their utter astonishment, Blackmoore laughed sardonically. "And, in your part of the country, do women ride astride, wear breeches, and compete in prize fights? Do tell us what other notable feats women are capable of performing, Miss Ravenwood," he finished sarcastically, making Jane turn a bright shade of red.

He thinks I'm a fool, she thought, her heart plunging. *If only I wasn't from Wales and I was a proper lady,* she mused, hating every moment of this deception.

Before Jane could reply, the carriage came to a rambling halt, and Jane thanked the heavens that they were on their way back to the Stockmorton residence. Lord Blackmoore, as dramatically handsome as he was, had a tendency to be disagreeable and disliked and insulted her for some unknown reason. It was all a bit mystifying. And horribly depressing.

As the group left the carriage, Blackmoore smiled at Charlotte, but Jane noticed that it was a false smile that didn't reach his vibrant hazel eyes. "Thank you for your company Charlotte," he said in a silky voice, adding, "Will you still be able to join me for a drive next week?"

Charlotte gazed up at him in what looked like abject worship. "Nothing pleases me more than the time we spend together, Richard," she cooed in her most seductive voice.

Jane felt a lurching in her stomach as Blackmoore, the most handsome and interesting man she had ever met, practically slavered over the vibrantly beautiful Charlotte. It was as if someone had given her a blow to her chest and she couldn't breathe. Blackmoore kissed Charlotte delicately on her gloved hand, and turned to Jane. The expression he wore made the hair rise on the back of her neck. When he spoke to Charlotte, his eyes softened like a man deeply in love; when he looked at Jane, it was as if his eyes were diamonds, glittering in dislike. His mouth was set in a firm line and his body was rigid with tension. "It was a pleasure to make your acquaintance, Miss Ravenwood. I'm sure you'll find your time in Town to be . . . educational," he finished, staring at her as if she were a lame animal that needed to be put out of its misery.

"It was my pleasure, Lord Blackmoore," Jane replied in her most simpering voice, detesting every word that came out of her mouth. *I have to remember my place,* Jane thought as she walked up the stairs. *I'm not a beautiful lady of the* ton. *I'm just a vulgar Welsh heiress, and I certainly can't let anyone know that,* she thought, sinking deeper into the blue devils.

They proceeded into the house and Jane almost fainted when Charlotte took off her wrap and quietly said, "All in all, I think things went rather well tonight."

As they bid Roger good night and mounted the stairs to their bedchambers, Jane stared at Charlotte in disbelief. "Charlotte, I spent most of the evening at loggerheads with Lord Blackmoore. I behaved atrociously," she concluded, completely embarrassed.

"Nonsense. Blackmoore was baiting you. You had no choice. And, to be honest, you didn't create any sort of scene, so I shall report to Mama that the evening was a success," Charlotte concluded, reaching her room.

As Jane gaped after her in amazement, Charlotte turned and smiled again. "You'll see, you'll get used to Richard. He's been rather prickly since returning from France. But he's really the most wonderful man," Charlotte concluded with a dreamy look in her eyes.

Jane managed a weak smile. "I'm sure he is, Charlotte,"

she said as she walked in to her room. She hated talking about Blackmoore and just wanted to retire for the evening.

Unfortunately, her maid, Gwen, had other ideas. As she helped Jane out of her diaphanous gown, she quizzed Jane relentlessly about the evening.

"Gwen, I've told you every detail I can recall," Jane lamented, in awe of the bulldog-like tenacity of her long-time abigail.

"When you was leaving, I saw the way that man looked at you. He's sweet on you, Miss Jane," Gwen pronounced, helping Jane into her dainty cotton nightgown.

Jane frowned. "Roger? Cousin Roger isn't interested in me. Or at least I don't think he is. He is a very congenial companion though," she concluded.

"Not your Cousin Roger. The other one. The tall swell with the long wavy black hair," Gwen concluded, hunting for Jane's hairbrush.

Jane stared at her reflection in the mirror. Her hair was too short; she was too tall, too old, and didn't have the slightest idea of how to become Aunt Lydia's version of a paragon of propriety. Blondes were all the crack; her hair was as black as the night. The perfect lady was demure and quiet. She was as well educated as her brother and had a tendency to be outspoken. If she had any common sense, she would take all the pin money her papa gave her and bolt out of the city on the instant.

Gwen saw her frowning at herself in the mirror and tried to cheer her up. "You'll see, Miss Jane. You'll learn to get on in London and probably have dozens of suitors here, more than Miss Charlotte, since you're much more beautiful than she is," Gwen concluded, readying the warmed brick for her minuscule bed.

Jane smiled at her servant. Gwen might not be the most intelligent ladies' maid but she couldn't be faulted for her loyalty, Jane mused. "Thank you, Gwen. I do appreciate your optimism."

When the lights were out and Jane listened to all of the noises of the city at night, she realized with a stunning insight that she didn't want dozens of suitors. Only one. The man who was devoted to her cousin and heartily disliked her. Lord Blackmoore.

CHAPTER THREE

Lord Blackmoore squirmed a bit in the straight-backed lacquer chair in his mother's drawing room. It wasn't very elegant or manly to squirm like a jackanapes, but he couldn't help it. His mother had kept him waiting well over a quarter-of-an-hour and he despised waiting. Even more unpleasant was the fact that they were going to discuss Mother's ball. He was less than enthusiastic about the ball.

Blackmoore downed his port, shifting uncomfortably in the chair. But the immediate discomfort of his posterior was the least of his problems. Each time his mind wandered, it wandered to one Miss Jane Ravenwood. Her behavior was completely inconsistent, which made him suspicious of her motives. One moment, she was a strong and powerful woman, the next, a simpering school miss. *Which makes no sense at all,* he thought irritably. True, she was undeniably lovely, not a bland commonplace lovely like every single blond English girl in the country. But a rare, exotic beauty that she didn't even know she possessed. Rather like Yvette, the scheming whore.

He squirmed in the chair more, and checked his watch. His Mother was being dashed inconsiderate. Invariably, his mind returned to the mysterious and alluring Miss Ravenwood. He knew she was far from stupid, so why the act? Every young woman born in polite society knew how to behave in public, so she couldn't be playacting for Lydia's sake. He tapped his long, elegant fingers on the crystal glass, trying to figure out the motives of the mysterious Miss Ravenwood.

He was so preoccupied with his thoughts that he didn't even notice his mother walk into the drawing room. The Dowager Marchioness of Blackmoore practically glided into the drawing room, her carriage still straight after too many years to remark on. Her gray hair was fashionably piled atop her head, and her Clarence blue silk gown suited her figure admirably.

She smiled at her wayward son, and gently said, "Yes, I know I've kept you waiting, Richard. You were always impatient, even as a child and you're no better at four-and-thirty."

Blackmoore looked up quickly, rose to his feet and managed a half-hearted smile. He gave his mother a peck on the cheek and replied, "I know I'm a constant trial to you, Mother."

Mother and son sat on one of her very fashionable yet dashed uncomfortable settees, and Blackmoore tried to concentrate on what she was saying. Which was difficult, since his thoughts constantly returned to the intriguing Miss Ravenwood. And her emerald eyes. And the soft lilt in her voice. The lilt that sounded almost . . . French.

"Richard?" his Mother said softly. "Is something bothering you?"

Blackmoore snapped back into reality. "No, not at all. What were you saying?" he said, trying to retain some semblance of his manners.

"I wanted to inform you that the ball was going to be on the twenty-fifth of May. I was hoping to make it a betrothal ball," she said, cautiously.

Blackmoore's eyes almost popped out of their sockets and he fell into a fit of coughing. "Betrothal Ball? I think not. I'm certainly not in any position to get leg-shackled right now," he claimed, tugging at his expertly tied silk neck cloth. It suddenly seemed that the room was getting much warmer than usual, and he was dashed uncomfortable.

The Dowager Marchioness shrugged, and replied, "You know you should be setting up your nursery soon. You wouldn't want the title going to your awful Cousin Aubrey would you?"

Blackmoore immediately had a vision of his mutton-headed cousin Aubrey and his termagant, hellcat wife, who weighed as much as two draft horses. And their passel of thoroughly unattractive runny-nosed children that ran wild through the house like demented puppies. *Damnation, I'd rather give my title to someone in trade,* he immediately thought with a frown. No, Aubrey wouldn't make a suitable Marquess of Blackmoore, by any stretch of the imagination.

"You're right, Mother, Aubrey would certainly not do. But I'll wed when I'm ready, and not a moment before," he declared, hating the whole topic.

"Of course." She reached over to one of the tables and produced a sheet of paper. "This is my invitation list. Is there anyone you'd like to include that I've missed?"

Blackmoore perused the list of the most eligible Upper Ten that his mother presented him, and smiled. His mother had made sure that almost every single eligible and beautiful young lady in London was invited. "As usual, you've outdone yourself, Mother," he commented dryly, wondering if he could scare up a duel to keep him from her infernal ball. "Only the best of Society is being invited," he noted.

"If you'll notice, I also included the Kinley girl. As well as the Hanron girl, the Bradford girl, and the Lumley girl. You have shown interest in all of them at one time or another," his mother reminded him gently.

The Kinley girl was insipid, Blackmoore decided. The Hanron girl was beautiful, but had an annoying laugh, rather like the bray of a donkey. The Lumley girl, a Diamond that rivaled Charlotte Wyndmere, was as dumb as a post. He paused for a moment then casually, almost too casually, added a request. "There is someone that I would like you to include, a houseguest of Roger Wyndmere's, Miss Ravenwood," he said, surprised at his own words.

The Dowager Marchioness stared at him, her hazel eyes causing him to tug nervously at his neck cloth again. "Who is this Miss Ravenwood?" she asked, jumping on the topic like a starving dog on a bone.

Blackmoore sighed. He needed another drink. Immediately if not sooner. "Miss Ravenwood is Charlotte and Roger's cousin from the country. I met her a few nights ago when I escorted Charlotte to Drury Lane. I don't believe she has many acquaintances around Town," he explained, hoping that he wouldn't have to say more on the topic of Miss Ravenwood.

As he gazed into his mother's eyes, he knew that his wish was in vain. He knew his mother suspected his courtship of Charlotte was a Banbury tale, which he proved by dismissing the idea of a betrothal ball. His mother wasn't a gossip, but he knew what was coming next. It wouldn't be pleasant, especially since he didn't want to talk about Jane. Miss Ravenwood.

"What is Miss Ravenwood like, Richard?" the marchioness asked innocently, a smile hovering on her lips.

"Miss Ravenwood is a spinster from the country. I understand that she is five-and-twenty, and she is the daughter of the Dowager Countess of Stockmorton's sister," he answered ever so correctly, clearly not saying anything of interest to his mother.

"So the girl is well connected enough. Is she an antidote?" she asked curiously.

"I suppose she's attractive enough. She's a veritable giantess compared to Charlotte, and has the most unfashionable short black hair. I suspect she's a bluestocking, but should be able to behave herself at our rout," he concluded, wondering if this interview would ever end.

The Dowager Marchioness was silent for a moment, then calmly said, "Of course I'll invite your Miss Ravenwood."

Blackmoore winced. Mother was already calling her "your Miss Ravenwood." "In fact, I seem to vaguely remember Lydia's sister Sara. She passed on quite a few years ago. It will be interesting to make her daughter's acquaintance," she concluded calmly.

Blackmoore's eyes rolled to the ceiling. *Gads, now Mother actually wants to meet the chit,* he thought, thoroughly vexed with the situation. *With my luck, Mother will probably adore her,* he decided, still tugging at the neck cloth that was suddenly choking him.

"Oh can't we take them for a run, Roger?" Jane implored, certain that Charlotte's docile mount Buttercup wanted a good, hard run alongside of Diablo.

Roger smiled at his cousin, his sandy brown hair glowing like gold in the afternoon sun. "Jane, you know the rules. We're here to socialize, not to exercise the horses. I'll introduce you to any of my friends that we happen upon, and you'll pretend to enjoy meeting them," he said with a broad smile.

"All right," Jane acquiesced, smoothing her new kerseymere riding habit.

Roger, Jane found out, was quite well known around Town. In fact, it appeared that he knew almost everyone who was in the Park. She met scores of "eligible" gentlemen that, in her mind, weren't eligible at all.

First, there was Lord Milnor, a strapping young man who was more interested in talking about Diablo than Jane. Then Lord Roarkston. He was a widower well past his prime, who was all but bursting out of his magenta and white striped waistcoat, and once again, showed no real interest in Jane. Instead, he chatted with Roger about White's. Then there was Lord Foxworth. He was everything that Lord Blackmoore wasn't. He was about the same age as Jane, and had thick, blond hair and the looks of a Greek god. Lord Foxworth was apparently in the petticoat line, because after his introduction to Jane, he virtually ignored her and gave Roger some rather indelicate details of his latest amour, a Lady Wilkerson. To round out Jane's acquaintances around London, Roger also introduced her to several spotty youths, a military man, and a well-known fortune hunter.

After almost an hour, they were on their way out of Hyde Park when a gentleman approached them and Roger muttered "Damnation," under his breath.

Jane looked at him curiously, since the gentleman approaching them seemed respectable enough. He looked about eight-and-thirty years old, sat quite tall in the saddle, and had what Jane usually thought of as an air of dissipation about him. He wore his black hair a bit longer than usual, in almost the same style as Lord Blackmoore, but didn't resemble him in any other way. As he approached them and Roger very reluctantly introduced her to the Earl of Wilford, Jane noticed that his weak blue eyes were too close together, and he was rather pale and slightly bloated.

Jane, for what seemed like the millionth time that afternoon, found herself automatically saying, "It's my pleasure, Lord Wilford." She could tell that Roger didn't like him, and wondered why, since Wilford seemed cordial enough.

Wilford favored her with a dazzling yet somewhat false smile that had obviously charmed many females. "The pleasure is undoubtedly mine, Miss Ravenwood. Obviously you've stayed out of Society or you couldn't ride alone in the Park without being pestered by swarms of adoring admirers," he said smoothly, ever the polite dandy.

Jane blushed prettily and replied, "I'm not taken in by your flummery, sir."

Wilford gave her another smile that didn't quite reach his eyes. "It's not flummery, Miss Ravenwood," he said smoothly. "By the by, are you related to the late Earl?" he asked ever so casually, flicking a piece of lint from his blue jacket.

"Not at all. My mother was the Lady Stockmorton's sister," she replied, trying her best to be cordial and polite and proper.

A strange light came into Wilford's eyes and he leaned toward Jane, intently interested in her. "Is your mother in Town with you?"

Before Roger could release Jane from the conversation with Wilford, Jane cut him off and answered directly. "No, my mama died quite a number of years ago."

Wilford reined in his dappled gray mount and could barely contain his excitement. "Will you be in Town for the Season?" he asked politely, suddenly intensely interested in Miss Jane Ravenwood.

"We expect Jane to be with us this Season," Roger answered curtly, then added "You'll have to excuse us, we're expected home," and all but grabbed Jane's reins to get her away from Wilford.

As they rode off, Jane was quite miffed. "Why did we leave so abruptly, Roger?" she asked, completely confused by his actions.

Roger stared straight ahead, and simply answered, "He isn't quite the best ton, Jane. I wouldn't encourage you to further your acquaintance with him."

Jane frowned and wondered what exactly was wrong with the Earl of Wilford. He seemed respectable enough to her. Instead of making trivial polite conversation, like almost all the other men she met, he actually asked about her family. She liked that. In fact, she liked Lord Wilford. He wasn't handsome or exciting, but at least he didn't stare at her cleavage when she spoke to him. Lord Wilford was definitely a worthwhile acquaintance, she decided.

* * *

"Aunt Lydia, I refuse to do any more shopping," Jane declared, her natural stubbornness showing itself to her relations for the first time.

Lydia stared at her in stunned silence, her mouth gaping open like a dying fish. "But don't you enjoy shopping, Jane?" she asked tentatively, amazed that Jane didn't want to go shopping, which Lydia considered life's most important activity. The most important activity after going to balls and routs, that is.

Jane began to pace around the sitting room, staring at the richly flocked wallpaper. "That's practically all I've done since arriving in London! Surely I have enough dresses by now," Jane said, completely disgusted with shopping, London, and Aunt Lydia.

Lydia rustled her voluminous magenta satin dress and adjusted her chartreuse turban. "Of course, most of your ball gowns haven't been finished yet, but the rest of your wardrobe seems to be coming along nicely. Is there something you particularly want to do while you're here, Jane?" she asked as if she were talking to a small child.

Jane stopped at the window, and looked into the small garden behind the house. The flowers were coming along nicely, but someone really did need to go outside in the balmy spring air and actually weed the garden. *Of course, Aunt Lydia will probably swoon if I suggested something that outrageous,* she thought.

"I'd like to see some of the sights in London. Like the British Museum, perhaps. Or the Tower of London. Or Astley's," Jane concluded, thinking of how glorious spring was in Wales. Her Father owned a medieval Abbey that just came alive with flowers of all colors as far as the eye could see, making the outside more fragrant than any perfume. Not drab and colorless like most of London.

Lydia absently toyed with the large ruby on her finger, considering the request. "I'll speak to your Cousin Roger to see when he can escort you," she finally said, still frowning.

Jane gave her a sincere, brilliant smile and sat down next to her aunt. "Thank you so much, Aunt Lydia. I knew you would understand," she said, feeling somewhat better about the next few days.

Lydia smiled a bit at her. "That's all right, Jane. I'm sure it's not easy getting used to life in Town. I did want to let you know though, about an invitation we received. The Dowager Marchioness of Blackmoore has specifically invited us to her ball. In fact, your presence was specifically requested," Aunt Lydia announced, much to Jane's surprise.

"Why would I be invited to a rout being given by the Dowager Marchioness of Blackmoore? Lord Blackmoore doesn't seem to find me particularly . . . agreeable," Jane said cautiously. "There must be a mistake," she concluded nervously, hoping she didn't have to see Lord Blackmoore again.

Frowning, Lydia answered, "Of course you're invited. Blackmoore has been a bosom bow of Roger's since they were both in Eton together. Obviously, they don't want you to feel that by attending you're imposing on them, so your name was included on the invitation. Roger probably talked to him about it."

"Do I have to go?" Jane asked candidly, even though she knew the answer.

"Of course. The Dowager Marchioness always has the most splendid crushes. You'll meet quite a few eligible young bucks. Don't even think of succumbing to a fit of the vapors and crying off," Lydia said, stalking out of the room, the feather on her turban bobbing as she walked.

Jane smiled to herself as she sat alone in the Stockmorton library, a few afternoons later. Roger was the best of cousins, and when they began discussing the family home in Cornwall and some of the bookkeeping problems he was having, Jane offered to look over his steward's books.

"A female? Look over my financial books? I think not, Jane," he said, thoroughly offended at the idea.

After several glasses of port, Roger became a bit more congenial, and after Jane explained her father's extensive mine holdings, Roger was quite impressed. When Jane mentioned that she had handled all of her Father's accounts because she had a knack for numbers, his mouth dropped open. After another glass of port, he handed over his books and admitted that he would be more than grateful for her help. As long as his mama didn't find out. Or anyone else for that matter.

Jane sat at the enormous mahogany desk, a smile on her face because she was actually doing something useful, rather than whiling her day away on fripperies. Luckily, Aunt Lydia was spending the day in bed, so she could work uninterrupted.

This actually turned out to be harder than she anticipated. Every time she turned a page, and there were many, she thought about the irritating Lord Blackmoore. *I wonder if he does his own books,* she mused as she jotted down some numbers. *Probably not,* she decided. Blackmoore didn't strike her as the type of man who would like to spend the day locked indoors.

As the sunlight spilled into the library, forming a delightful halo behind Jane's raven colored hair, she thought she heard some sort of commotion in the hall. More than likely it was some sort of crisis belowstairs, she mused, and continued staring at the numbers in the ledger in front of her. *I bet Lord Blackmoore has perfect servants,* she thought, and began to frown. *What's wrong with me? I'll never get any work done at this rate,* she decided, flipping to the next page, willing herself to focus on the inked numbers staring her in the face.

She was concentrating so deeply that she did not hear

the door to the library open. Moreover, she most certainly didn't notice Lord Blackmoore, once again resplendent in the finest black clothes from Weston no less, walk in.

Lord Blackmoore, a very sophisticated man about Town who had experienced his share of adventures, stood in the brightly lit library in shock. Miss Ravenwood was hunched over what seemed to be ledgers, making calculations with an ink pen. She was deep in concentration, which wasn't a look he often saw on a female.

Before he could say anything, she looked up, exclaimed "Oh," in a startled voice, and jumped up from behind the desk guiltily, almost knocking over her chair in the process.

How many times did I find Yvette looking through my papers, he thought immediately, frowning at Jane. *Once? Twice? Or was it a dozen before I realized she wasn't as innocent as she seemed? How long did it take me to figure out she was selling me to the French,* he wondered, instantly transported to that horrible time in his life.

"Lord Blackmoore?" Jane said in soft voice, the one that sounded French. The one that had to be French.

Blackmoore instantly regained his composure, determined to find out what Jane was doing in Roger's library. "I'm sorry to interrupt you, Miss Ravenwood, but Jeffries asked me to wait for Charlotte here. I'm taking her for a drive," he said patiently, trying not to alarm her. But all he could see was the slight swell of her milk-white breasts encased in a fashionable cream muslin gown. *She's so lovely,* he thought, before willing the vision of a barely clothed Miss Ravenwood out of his mind.

Jane's cheeks turned a guilty shade of red. "Oh, you're driving with Charlotte," she stuttered, covering up the ledger. "Jeffries wasn't aware that the library was occupied."

Curiosity consumed Blackmoore. Occasionally, Roger

did some clandestine work for the government, so there was a chance that she might be looking at some sensitive documents. The type of documents that one of Boney's men would pay good money to obtain.

He ever so casually walked over to the desk, and asked, "Does Roger know you're prying into his private papers?"

Predictably, her demure, schoolroom-miss manners were gone. Jane's eyes flashed fire. "Of course! Roger has given me permission to look at his ledgers, as long as I don't inform Aunt Lydia," she replied, her temper starting to rise.

Blackmoore's eyebrows raised. "You've got to be bamming me. Roger would never give you permission to do that."

"Roger most certainly did give me permission to look over his ledgers," she insisted passionately, her breasts heaving very alluringly. "He's having some problems and he wanted to see if I could sort things out for him."

Blackmoore was highly insulted. She obviously thought he was stupid enough to buy her blatantly false explanation. "You are obviously adept at telling tales, Miss Ravenwood. What could any woman know about accounting?" he said, certain he was fully in the right. He had caught Miss Ravenwood prying, and now she was making up some Banbury tale to cover up her digression.

"My lord," she began in a clipped voice, "I personally run my father's household and have been doing so since I left the schoolroom. My father discovered that I have a talent for numbers and has encouraged me. I'm sorry if you don't believe me, but that most certainly is the truth," she finished, her cheeks flushed delicately.

Blackmoore strolled over to the other side of the desk and stood next to her, uncovering the ledger. His eyes were riveted to the page she was working on, and the two stood in a tense silence that hung between them.

Time seemed to stand still for them, as Blackmoore studied the ledger and Jane waited for some sort of proclamation from him. After a very long pause, he commented, "You seem to have a grasp of the numbers after all."

When she didn't say anything, Blackmoore frowned. Had he actually offended her? That didn't appear to be likely, so he found himself asking, "Are you all right, Miss Ravenwood?" in a worried voice.

Before Jane could reply, the door to the library swept open again.

Charlotte burst into the room like a messenger from the goddess Venus. This afternoon she was clad in a Pomona green walking dress decorated with yards and yards of Belgian lace.

"I'm sorry you had to wait, Richard," Charlotte said, favoring him with a smile that would melt stone and ignoring Jane.

Blackmoore smiled adoringly at Charlotte, which was what he was supposed to do. Even though he really wanted to find out why Jane was so quiet all of a sudden. Instead, he simply turned to her and said, "I enjoyed speaking with you, Miss Ravenwood, and look forward to seeing you at my mother's rout."

Jane smiled weakly at him and said, "Yes, certainly."

Blackmoore frowned at her once more, as he ushered Charlotte out of the room. Jane utterly and completely confused him. *Chits from the county don't understand the financial workings of a large estate.* So why did she understand them? And why did she always have to look so damnably attractive, he wondered, but didn't have any clue to the answer.

CHAPTER FOUR

As Charlotte and Blackmoore sat in his sporty new phaeton pulled by a perfect pair of matching grays, he forced himself to concentrate on the matters at hand. It wasn't natural for his thoughts to keep going back to Miss Ravenwood, no matter how intriguing she might be.

"So, Richard, are we going to the Gallery today?" Charlotte asked brightly, nodding to several acquaintances they passed on the street.

Blackmoore frowned. Was she still interested in the artist? If she was, then why was she flirting outrageously with him? "You still want to go to the Gallery?" he said in an incredulous tone, maneuvering the phaeton with the expert skill that made him one of the most respected members of the Four-in-Hand Club.

It was Charlotte's turn to be confused. A delicate frown appeared on her brow and she stared at him, her mouth dripping open. "Richard, we always go to the Gallery to see James. That's the only reason I go out driving with you," she explained patiently, as if he were a simpleton.

He unconsciously let out a deep sigh and headed toward the Gallery. "Then you're still interested in James?"

She stared at him as if he had lost his mind. "Of course I'm still interested in James. I told you I intend to marry him. What exactly are you about today, Richard?"

"You've been acting a bit different since your cousin has come to Town. I thought perhaps your feelings toward your artist had changed," he said simply, thanking the heavens that she really wasn't interested in him.

"I was just teasing you, Richard," she answered airily, slapping him gently with her fan.

They drove a bit longer in companionable silence, the noise of London surrounding them, until he casually remarked, "So, how is Miss Ravenwood getting along?"

Once again, Charlotte frowned, something she didn't do often, since it caused wrinkles and Mama told her it marred her perfect features. "Jane is doing just fine. I don't know if she particularly enjoys society though," Charlotte finished calmly, smoothing an invisible crease out of her dress.

"Has she fixed her interest on anyone?" he asked in a deliberately uninterested tone. *Gads, why am I asking that,* he wondered, shocked at the audacity of his own tongue. *If Miss Ravenwood is involved in some sort of deception, I should know—before she entangles some poor, aging roué who is taken in by her obvious charms,* he reasoned.

"Not that I know of. She did mention meeting Lord Wilford and found him rather charming. Roger doesn't approve of him, but that doesn't seem to have changed Jane's opinion of him."

Blackmoore was frowning when the pair arrived at the small gallery where Charlotte's artist worked and showed some of his paintings. As Blackmoore helped her out of the vehicle, he was flooded with relief when she said, "I'll meet you in the vestibule in a half hour," and rushed into the modest building alone.

Therefore, Blackmoore had some time to cool his heels while helping Charlotte and her wayward suitor. *It's unfortunate,* he thought, *that James is a mere mister and has no solid potential or wherewithal. He'd make Charlotte an admirable husband,* he decided, shaking his head in regret. Lydia was a high stickler for that sort of thing, and would disown her for such an association.

As he sat by the banks of the Thames and watched the school children with their nannies playing in the sunshine, many flying brightly colored kites, he wondered what was wrong with Miss Ravenwood.

A giggling blond boy ran by, and Blackmoore smiled at him for a brief moment, thinking of the joyful days of his youth. That seemed eons ago, before he learned how traitorous people could be. Especially women.

For the life of him, he couldn't logically explain Jane's behavior in the library. It was dashed strange, he mused, picking at a blade of grass. One moment she was practically a hellcat, the next she looked as if she was going to cry—like Yvette, he realized with a shock. *When I caught her in a lie, Yvette always tried to squirm out by crying. It usually worked,* he concluded grimly.

Charlotte paced the room, her beautiful complexion flushed in vexation. "Oh James, what are we going to do? I don't care that you have no expectations. We can live off my dowry, you know that," she said passionately, feeling as if the small cluttered office was going to swallow her whole.

James Clayton, the very talented artist of two-and-twenty years that Charlotte worshipped, gave his beloved a frown. "Charlotte," he began, his brown eyes staring imploringly into her fair blue ones, "you know we cannot marry until I find myself in a better situation."

"Tosh!" Charlotte exclaimed, throwing her small beaded reticule on the desk to emphasize her point. "I don't want to wait until your finances are in better shape. I have enough money for both of us," she said, her breasts heaving in agitation beneath his steady gaze.

James moved to the other side of the large, well-worn desk and took her hands in his. "Charlotte dearest, if we were to marry, you most certainly would be disowned and shunned by society. My meager salary and my rare commissions couldn't support us both," he said gently, staring into her sea blue eyes.

For that instant, time stopped for Charlotte. When James held her small, delicate hands in his, all of her problems seemed to fade away into the bright spring sunlight. *James is all I ever want in a man,* she thought passionately, her heart melting under his fiery gaze. "James, I don't care what I have to do," she said in a rush, winding her arms around his neck. "I'll get a job. As a governess. Or a companion," she said, her desperation to be with the man she loved apparent in every move of her dainty frame.

James smiled indulgently at her. "My little widgeon, you know you're not suited for work, and I would never ask you to give up your way of life for me," he said passionately, wrapping his paint-stained hands around her tiny waist.

Charlotte just frowned even more. "Then what are we to do?" she said in a hopeless voice, her flawless ivory skin becoming a bit paler as the moments passed. The thoughts of her family and her comfortable way of life meant nothing to Charlotte when she was with her beloved.

James sighed. "Yes my dear, what are we to do?" he replied softly, despair clouding his eyes like a winter storm.

"So tell me Roger, why haven't any of your friends come to call on Jane?" Lydia quizzed, not looking up from her needlework.

Roger quickly got up from the striped settee and walked over the cabinet where he kept his brandy. "I don't know, Mama," he said, pouring the dark liquid into a cut glass snifter.

"Tosh. Of course you know. What's wrong with the chit?"

Roger walked over to the window and gazed outside. "What isn't wrong with Cousin Jane? She's too tall, and that puts them off. She's taller than almost all of my friends."

Aunt Lydia never looked up from her needlework. "Well, we certainly can't do anything about that."

"And she's dashed old. She's just five years younger than I am. You know men like their wives right out of the schoolroom," Roger complained.

"Well, we can't do anything about her age."

"And her looks are . . . irregular," Roger commented, sipping his brandy.

"Irregular in what way?" Aunt Lydia quizzed.

"Well, blondes are all the crack. She isn't blond. And her hair is short. Everyone knows that men prefer long hair. And her skin isn't milky white. She just doesn't look English. Or even French. She just looks different," he concluded.

Lydia sighed and put down her embroidery. "Is that all?"

Roger frowned. "I like Cousin Jane prodigiously, but she's just not self-effacing. Looks at a man like she knows what he's thinking and it scares them off."

"Has anyone shown any interest in the girl?" she asked curiously.

"No one except Wilford. And he's not good ton."

That bit of news seemed to perk up Aunt Lydia. "Wilford—he is an earl. And I believe that his father was once connected to Jane's mama," she added.

It was Roger's turn to frown. "That may be, but I don't like him hanging about Cousin Jane. I just don't," he said firmly.

Dinner with the family was becoming a trial for Jane. Every time they sat down to eat, Aunt Lydia used the time as an opportunity to instruct Jane in all of her character faults. Which were considerable and varied. And to make Jane aware of the rules of proper behavior in London Society, of which there were many.

Jane stared at the congealing pigeon pie in front of her, not hungry in the least. *I wonder why so many people in*

*London are inclined to be on the corpulent side. They can't
be eating the same food I'm eating,* she decided with a sigh.

"And another thing Jane, we can't hope for a peer for you,
you're quite on the shelf, but there is always a possibility of
a very respectable country squire, or possibly an older gentleman. Someone who needs a young woman to look after
his needs," Aunt Lydia lectured, somehow managing to eat
a large quantity of food and talk at the same time.

Roger practically shoveled the food into his mouth, and
remained blissfully silent.

"Mama, Jane could certainly do much better than a
squire," said Charlotte. "She's an heiress, for goodness
sake. And the granddaughter of a Duke. I think she could
at least attract a baronet. Or even a military man."

"We can't be too ambitious, Charlotte. Lately, it seems
that everyone is a granddaughter or grandson of a Duke.
Our Jane has more than a few faults, and it will be a challenge to find an eligible partner for her," Lydia said, filling
her plate with another portion.

It was as if Jane wasn't even there, a sensation she didn't
care for in the least. In fact, she was getting very angry and
was ready to tell the entire family what she thought of their
ideas on some impending marriage. Or the lack of one. "I do
hope you know I don't plan on marrying anyone I don't
love."

Aunt Lydia stared at Jane as if she had grown a second
head. "You're hoping for a love match, child? You've been
spending too much time reading those Minerva Press novels. When you're in Society, you don't marry for love; the
whole idea is horribly vulgar! You marry wisely and provide your husband with an heir. After that you have all
the freedom you could wish for," Aunt Lydia explained, as
if Jane were a flat.

Strangely enough, Charlotte came to Jane's rescue. "I'm
sure Jane understands what you're saying, Mama. I'm cer-

tain she'd like to make a love match, as would I, but knows that isn't likely to happen."

Jane didn't mean that at all. *I won't marry without affection and I'd rather be a spinster than marry for position,* she thought rebelliously. *And I won't marry some fortune hunter that's after my dowry. Life in London is very tedious indeed,* Jane decided, still picking at her grayish pigeon pie.

The rain poured down in veritable sheets, washing some of the grime off London. Morning calls were kept to a minimum, and those prone to illness were more than likely to stay at home. Luckily for Jane, Aunt Lydia felt she herself was prone to illness and stayed inside during the torrential downpours. Even better yet, most of Aunt Lydia's friends didn't like going about in the rain, so there were virtually no callers at the house.

That left Jane to her own devices. She thoroughly investigated the library, surprised that it was so extensive. She also finished going over the accounts at the estate for Roger. Charlotte was also her constant companion, and while Jane read, Charlotte worked on her watercolors, which were quite good, in Jane's opinion. For the moment, Jane was out of the social loop.

That situation suited her fine. Aunt Lydia's constant lectures on her behavior and her numerous character flaws were becoming more than a trifle tedious, and she welcomed any relief from them.

The third day of torrential rain found Jane and Charlotte alone in the parlor playing an amiable game of piquet. Jane, attempting to turn the conversation away from fashion, ever so casually asked, "How was your ride with Lord Blackmoore?"

Charlotte played her trick and frowned a bit, an expression that was becoming quite commonplace. "It was all right. Richard asked about you," she said finally, her eyes fixed on Jane.

For some unexplained reason Jane turned red as a currant and said, "Why would he ask about me? Lord Blackmoore doesn't even like me."

Charlotte shrugged. "I wouldn't say Richard dislikes you. In fact, he did specifically ask if you had fixed your attentions on anyone."

Jane dropped her hand of cards in embarrassment. As she rushed to pick them up, she nervously said, "I'm sure he was just being polite."

"Richard is rarely polite," Charlotte declared.

Jane studied her cards. "How long have you been involved with Lord Blackmoore?" she asked curiously.

Charlotte glanced towards the open door and softly said, "I'm not really involved with Lord Blackmoore. Richard is just a friend of the family. He's letting everyone think he's coming up to scratch to help me with a difficulty."

Jane frowned, her green eyes studying Charlotte seriously. "Is there something I could help you with, Charlotte?" she asked in a grave voice, hoping nothing was wrong. Charlotte rose quickly, went over to the door, and quietly closed it. She then walked back over to her seat and sat opposite Jane, her beautiful features marred by another frown.

"About six months ago, I met a gentleman at a Gallery I was visiting with Richard. The gentleman and I started talking, and became friends. Then I started visiting the Gallery myself, to talk to him about his painting, and his ideas on my artwork," she began softly. "I know my watercolors can't compare to his paintings, but he . . . understands about my painting. After a while, we both realized that we had become . . . attached to one another," she confessed, taking a deep breath. "The problem is that James is a mister and an artist. I know Mama won't ever approve of him, so I asked Richard to help me continue seeing James. He agreed, and that's why everyone thinks

Richard is courting me," Charlotte finished quickly, her blue eyes large and worried.

Jane stared at the cards on the table, wondering what to say to her cousin. Charlotte was beautiful, graceful, and fully capable of attracting a handsome and wealthy peer. Yet, she was love with an artist with no expectations. "Is there anything I can do?" Jane asked softly, knowing the answer.

"Not right now. But please don't tell anyone. Mama would exile me to the country if she had an inkling of what I was doing," Charlotte finished melodramatically.

"Of course I'll keep your secret. And I'll try to think of a way for Aunt Lydia to get to know James so it will be easier to accept that you have feelings for each other," Jane pledged silently. Although Charlotte was a Diamond of the First Water, Jane found it comforting to know that Charlotte was prone to misadventures of the heart like everyone else.

"Try some of the pigeon pie, Richard, it's done to perfection tonight," Roger recommended, washing it down with some claret.

Blackmoore looked at his friend with awe in his eyes. The way Roger ate, it was a wonder that he didn't weigh three stone more than he did. Blackmoore knew for certain that if he ate as much as Roger he would most definitely resemble the very corpulent Prince Regent. "I'll just have another glass of claret," Blackmoore said, draining his glass.

Roger frowned a bit and commented, "The only person who eats less than you is Cousin Jane. I don't think I've ever seen her eat a complete meal since she's been staying with us."

Once again, the topic of Cousin Jane came up and Blackmoore frowned. The lady was no good, and it was time that Roger and the rest of the family knew that she was gulling them. He took a languid drink from his elegant glass and remarked, "You know, your innocent spinster cousin was nosing into your estate books."

Roger looked up from his plate. "Why are you always so suspicious? Never used to be," Roger commented.

Blackmoore frowned. "Of course I'm suspicious, especially when I see a female nosing into your books."

"Asked her to. Knows everything about running a large establishment. She's going to help me find a new steward," Roger finished, sipping his claret.

Blackmoore stared at him as if he were a candidate for Bedlam. "You're letting some female advise you on choosing a steward? Is that wise?" he finally asked, a deep frown etched on his striking features.

Roger signaled for some more pigeon pie and glanced at Blackmoore as if he had a screw loose. "Richard, she's my cousin, she's not out to bilk me. And she does know what she's about. I discussed quite a few issues with her, and she has a better grasp on certain things than I do," Roger explained patiently.

Leaning back in the mahogany chair, Blackmoore resolved to show Roger that his charming cousin was pulling the wool over his eyes. But not at the moment. *Roger is obviously too involved in his own life to see what's happening around him,* Blackmoore thought acidly.

"If you say so. Has your cousin, the veritable genius, managed to lure some poor sapskull into the parson's mousetrap yet?" he asked sardonically.

Roger continued eating, immune to Blackmoore's sarcasm. "From what Jane tells me, she has no interest in marrying, and wants to go home. She's simply here to appease her father. Wanted her to have a London Season. She's met a few eligible men, but hasn't remarked on any of them," he said, digging into his second helping of pigeon pie. "Oh, she did converse at length with Lord Wilford. I told her he wasn't the best ton, but she appeared to find him interesting."

Blackmoore snapped to attention at the mention of Wilford's name. Perhaps the cousin's home was near Dover. It would be no stretch of imagination to see Cousin Jane meeting Wilford, a known spy, in that part of the country. Could he be using her in some sort of plot? Why would she find him charming, above everyone else in Town? Obviously, something was amiss. Blackmoore decided immediately to consult Castlereagh at the Foreign Office. He was always interested in the comings and goings of the traitorous Earl of Wilford.

Blackmoore also had one simple question for Roger to answer, if he could. "By the by, Roger, you mentioned that Miss Ravenwood has spent her life rusticating in the country," Blackmoore began casually.

"Umm," Roger said, nodding his head.

"Where, exactly?" Blackmoore asked, almost challenging Roger to answer.

Blackmoore saw a hint of panic in Roger's eyes, before he masked it. Instead, he just shrugged and said, "Not quite sure, I'm deuced awful at geography. You'd have to ask Mama."

An evasive reply that didn't tell him anything. Blackmoore was sure that Roger didn't want him to know where his long lost cousin actually lived. What did he have to hide, Blackmoore wondered. What was she hiding?

Fortunately, the rest of their dinner was a bit more congenial, and Blackmoore let Roger tease him about setting up a nursery before his dreadful Cousin Aubrey inherited the title. In fact, Roger even coaxed him into a good mood by the time they walked out onto the darkened street.

Blackmoore frowned as he noticed the most unusual event taking place across the street from the Club. Lord Wilford was standing in the shadows talking with some man who looked rather shabby and slightly disreputable.

"Roger, look to your left. Isn't that Wilford over there?" he wondered, taking in the details of the unknown man.

Roger glanced over towards his left curiously. Wilford was standing in the shadows talking to what looked like an impoverished, yet deuced handsome man of about one-and-twenty. The shabbily dressed man had short, light-colored hair that was fashioned in the Brutus cut, which was popular with the blades around London. He was of medium height, but carried himself well, and didn't have the air of poverty about him that many suffered from. In fact, outside of his shabby clothes, he could have passed as a gentleman.

"Yes, that's Wilford all right. I wonder what he's up to," Roger commented, unconcerned.

Wilford and the unknown man talked for a bit more, then Wilford got into a nearby carriage, and his associate began to walk confidently toward the more unsavory part of London.

"I wonder what that was all about," Blackmoore said, staring after the departing young man.

"I'd venture a guess that it was no good," Roger answered. "I wish Jane didn't find him so charming." Blackmoore was frowning all the way back to his town house.

Jane waited eagerly at the bottom of the steps, smoothing the fabric of her pastel yellow walking dress. It was a simple dress, as were all of Madame Mimette's creations, devoid of all bows and ruffles. "I do hope Cousin Roger shows up soon. I do want to get to the Museum as soon as possible," Jane commented to Gwen.

Behind her, Gwen adjusted her mob-cap. "I've never been to a museum before and it sounds ever so nice," she said in a bubbly tone of voice. Jane smiled at her. Gwen had learned so much in the four years that she had been her abigail. She could read, write her name and, most important, she purposely lost her pronounced Welsh accent, so she could work in a proper establishment in London if she ever wished to. Of course, Gwen was much too friendly with the male servants in the household, but Jane adored her and her good-hearted nature.

Roger appeared a few minutes later, looking like the proper Corinthian in a buff-colored pair of breeches, light stockings, and the most impressive Spanish blue waistcoat. "Are you ready to leave, Jane?" he asked cordially, heading towards the door.

Jane smiled brightly, just as excited as Gwen was, if not more. "I've been ready to see the British Museum since I first read about it," she answered, almost bouncing out of the door in her eagerness.

The legendary British Museum was everything Jane hoped it would be, and, as a result, she was in a wonderful mood. In fact, the visit to the museum, filled with the Egyptian artifacts and the Elgin Marbles was the high point of her trip to London. Their bespeckled, elderly guide had been ever so interesting, and Jane decided she could visit the museum a dozen times and not get bored. In fact, she was so wrapped up in her thoughts that she bumped into Lord Wilford outside of the Museum.

"Lord Wilford! Do pardon my clumsiness!" She exclaimed, blushing from head to toe.

Wilford smiled indulgently at her. "It was my fault, Miss Ravenwood," he said, and nodded to a frowning Roger. Wilford's manners were flawless, as usual.

"Are you planning to visit the Museum?" Jane asked politely, noticing how his bottle-green colored coat was rather snug and that the numerous fobs he wore looked rather ridiculous.

"Why yes, I am. Did you enjoy your visit?" he asked, giving her a radiant smile.

"Oh, yes. It was everything I hoped for," she answered eagerly, her face glowing in the afternoon sun.

"How nice to hear. Are we going to be graced with your beauty in public soon?" he asked, his blue eyes narrowing.

"Jane will be out and about soon enough," Roger answered, moving down the steps.

Before Roger could lead Jane away from what he considered an undesirable person, Wilford quickly asked, "May I call tomorrow afternoon and take you riding in Hyde Park, Miss Ravenwood?" he asked suavely.

"That would be nice," Jane answered before Roger could say, "No."

"Then I'll see you tomorrow," Wilford said silkily.

As Jane moved down the stairs, she felt better about herself. A polite man about town had taken an interest in her. A man who didn't appear to be in need of a fortune, or in search of a dalliance. Lord Wilford wasn't as dashing, or interesting as Lord Blackmoore, but at least he wasn't an aging country squire with a passel of motherless children.

The drive home with Roger was less than pleasant. "Why did you agree to go riding with Wilford?" he asked, his disapproval apparent in the tone of his voice.

Jane stared out the window and simply replied, "Lord Wilford is polite and a likable enough person. I don't see why I shouldn't go riding with him."

Roger frowned fiercely at her. "Jane, he isn't the best ton. I told you that."

Jane's temper began to rise. "Until you tell me why he isn't respectable, I don't see why I shouldn't associate with him. Aunt Lydia has said that I should try to meet new people, and Lord Wilford is an earl. He has much more status than a squire or a mere baronet, doesn't he?" she said, becoming defensive. Since Roger wouldn't tell her why she shouldn't see Wilford, she didn't see any reason to avoid him.

"Jane, you just have to trust me. You shouldn't be associating with Wilford," he said lamely, stubbornly refusing to give her any other explanation.

Jane lifted her chin defiantly. "Until you give me a good reason why I shouldn't ride with Lord Wilford, I refuse to cancel our outing tomorrow," she said, her eyes blazing.

"Fine, go riding with Wilford. You will have one our groomsmen go with you though," he said sternly, trying to discourage her.

"Of course, Roger," she said in a docile tone of voice, smiling to herself. *If Lord Wilford shows an interest in me, I may be able to avoid all the widowers and fortune hunters that will come after me,* she thought. *Then Aunt Lydia will stop her matchmaking and leave me alone,* she decided with a smile. Of course she liked the man well enough, but most certainly didn't intend to form a tendre for him. Yes, it would be profitable to be friends with Lord Wilford, as long as he understood that she was leaving London permanently after the Season.

CHAPTER FIVE

Lord Wilford is certainly different from Roger and Black-moore, Jane mused, as she rode next to the corpulent earl in Hyde Park. Wilford was the most amiable of companions, and complimented her incessantly on her very fashionable blue velvet riding dress, noticed how her eyes were sparkling, and even offered to buy her an ice at Gunther's. Jane politely declined, since Roger had been barely speaking to her since she accepted Lord Wilford's invitation.

As they promenaded through the somewhat busy Park, Jane kept a somewhat false smile pasted on her face, and decided to try to be the polite but empty-headed female that Aunt Lydia encouraged her to be. The warm spring sun beat down upon the pair, and Jane was daydreaming when Lord Wilford asked politely, "Are you enjoying your stay in Town, Miss Ravenwood?"

Jane glanced over at Lord Wilford who was atop an impressive gray gelding that appeared, despite his looks, to be rather docile. Wilford's dark plum riding jacket and buff breeches were far from being dandified, but he tended to be on the plump side and his clothes didn't fit him with the same finesse as Lord Blackmoore's. Lord Wilford seemed to be harmless enough, and introduced her to any number of people. Of course, the gentlemen she met were a bit rougher than Roger's friends, and the ladies wore a bit more paint than was fashionable, but nothing seemed amiss to Jane.

Smiling softly at him, Jane answered, "London is an

interesting enough place, Lord Wilford, but I do miss my papa and my brother."

Wilford smiled at a lady with flaming red hair and a very low cut gown that displayed quite a bit of her bosom, and asked, "Do you think you'll be staying after the Season?"

Jane focused on a group of military men about thirty feet away from them. They looked so impressive and dashing in their uniforms, and reminded her that they were only momentarily safe from Bonaparte. The sights and people around the Park were actually quite diverting and helped Jane in her quest to be Aunt Lydia's version of the proper London lady. All Jane did was concentrate on something other than the conversation, which made her appear to be rather simpering. She turned her large green eyes on him and smiled. "I'm sorry Lord Wilford, I wasn't attending. What did you say?"

Wilford returned her smile as they continued through the Park, walking along rather sedately. "I wondered if you were going to stay in Town past the Season?"

An imperceptible frown appeared on Jane's brow. Why was Wilford so curious about her time in Town? Something about his questions seemed odd, she mused, a strange feeling of paranoia overtaking her. Diablo sensed her change in mood, and began pulling on the reins, refocusing her attention. When she got him calmed down she mentally chided herself for being such a silly widgeon and replied, "This is just a brief holiday for me, Lord Wilford. I don't even know how long I'll be staying, but I doubt that I'll be here for the entire Season."

They began to head out of the Park, and Wilford was smiling once again. "I do hope that your aunt's carriage will be taking you home, the mail coach is so uncomfortable," he commented, nodding at an aging gentleman who looked to Jane to be bosky.

"No, I won't be in the family carriage, I'll be taking the mail coach. That's the way I came with my abigail," she answered simply, trying to shake off the feeling of impending doom that settled on her shoulders. *He's a perfectly nice gentleman,* she recited to herself, as they continued their ride. Perhaps Lord Wilford wasn't the most adept at polite conversation, and was simply trying to find something to fill the time, she reasoned.

They left the gates of the Park in a companionable silence and began the short walk back to the house on Grosvenor Street. London was so different from her home. The streets were filled with small children in tattered clothes, wizened old women selling oranges or bouquets of violets, and drunken men staggering about, looking for money to buy their next drink. It was all rather unsettling to her, after the rolling hills and the sweet air of peacefulness that she had grown to love in Wales.

They walked their horses back to Aunt Lydia's house, and, after gallantly helping her dismount, Lord Wilford asked in the most casual voice, "Can I take you riding again next week, or would you rather go driving in my phaeton?"

Jane was in a quandary. She knew Cousin Roger didn't really like her riding with Lord Wilford and driving with him in his phaeton would probably give Roger an apoplexy. "I really don't know what Aunt Lydia has planned for me next week. Why don't you send a note, and I'll let you know when I'm going to be available," she replied noncommittally. Hopefully she'd be able to sort out her mixed feelings for Lord Wilford before she made any more plans with him.

Wilford smiled at her, making him look almost handsome. The smile didn't reach his eyes, and Jane felt almost uncomfortable when he took her gloved hand and lightly kissed it. "Your wish is my command, Miss Ravenwood," he said lightly.

As Jane began the walk up the stairs to the door, she glanced down the street, and noticed her abigail Gwen there. She was a short way down the street, talking with some gentleman, or maybe he wasn't a gentleman, just another servant. Gwen was smiling radiantly and tossing her blond curls alluringly. Jane could even hear her rich laugh drift down the street.

The man whom Gwen was trying to impress was a stranger to Jane, which wasn't surprising, since Gwen enjoyed spending time with members of the opposite sex. He was of medium height, had sandy brown hair cut à la Brutus, and was dressed too well to be a servant, but not well enough to be a peer.

As Jeffries opened the door and Jane entered the house, a smile magically appeared on her face. Gwen was busy striking up a friendship with an impoverished young curate. The thought of her minx of a maid dallying with a curate caused Jane to giggle all the way up the stairs.

"This is so exciting, Miss Jane," Gwen bubbled as she tried to coax Jane's short, raven locks into some sort of suitable style. "Your first ball rout in London!" she exclaimed, as if this one ball was the highlight of Jane's life.

Jane sighed. She was tired of Gwen fussing with her hair and wanted the whole dreadful ball to be over and done with.

Gwen continued talking, completely unaware of Jane's mood. "I think it's devilishly unfair of Aunt Lydia to make you chaperon Charlotte," Gwen said in a soft voice. "You should be going as a guest, not as a servant. You were invited right proper," she added boldly.

Jane thought the same thing, but didn't want to cause trouble in the household, so she readily agreed to play chaperon. "I know Gwen, but Aunt Lydia isn't feeling up to snuff, and I am a bit more . . . mature than Charlotte. I don't mind acting as her chaperon," she finished in a voice that completely lacked conviction.

Gwen frowned. "But it's not fair! You should be going to the ball to dance, not to watch over Lady Charlotte."

Jane sighed. She agreed. Her papa didn't imagine her as a chaperon when he sent her to London. Yet, that's the role that Aunt Lydia forced her to play. At least for this rout. So, at five-and-twenty, she was destined, at least for this night, to sit with the dowagers and ape leaders, a fate that Jane really didn't anticipate when her father sent her to London.

"There! Your hair is done . . . à la mode," Gwen announced, horrifically fracturing the French phrase.

Jane giggled as she sat at her vanity, her maroon dressing robe wrapped around her. "I'm sure it looks fine, Gwen," she said with more conviction than she actually felt.

A knock on the door brought her out of her reverie, and Gwen immediately said, "I'll answer the door, Miss Jane."

Jane couldn't help grinning at her. It was Gwen's job to answer the door, something that she seemed to forget. Jane didn't overly mind, since Gwen was prodigiously loyal and good-hearted.

Molly, Charlotte's abigail, stood at the door expectantly. Although they were around the same age, Molly was the antithesis of Gwen. Gwen was friendly, especially with the males of the household; Molly barely spoke to anyone outside of Charlotte. Gwen had blond curls that even Charlotte envied; Molly had unfashionably short straight brown hair that tended to be limp and greasy. Gwen always smiled; Molly constantly wore a dour expression, as if she was in imminent danger of being thrown out onto the street without a reference. Needless to say, the two servants barely knew each other and had little in common.

"Lady Charlotte was wondering when Miss Ravenwood would be ready to go downstairs," Molly said in a meek voice, as if waiting for Gwen to berate her.

Gwen, being a simple country lass, took no notice of Molly's nervousness and looked over at Jane. "When will you be ready, Miss Jane?" she asked pertly.

Jane thought quickly. Her hair was supposedly done. All she really needed to do was have Gwen help her into her evening gown. "We should be ready in a quarter of an hour," Jane announced.

"You can tell Lady Charlotte we'll be ready in a quarter of an hour," Gwen said confidently to Molly before shutting the door in her face.

Gwen went over to the wardrobe, and pulled out Madame Mimette's creation for Jane. "This is such a lovely gown, Miss Jane, I bet you'll look like a princess," she said, placing the gown on the bed.

The cerulean blue silk in the Grecian style looked magnificent, and Jane even admitted that it was beautiful. When Madame Mimette said she would create a gown to suit Jane's very exotic, un-English looks, she was correct.

Madame Mimette was certain that every single young lady invited to the Blackmoore rout would be wearing frills, flounces, and yards and yards of decorative trim. This suited them, since most young ladies were tiny, fragile creatures. Jane wasn't tiny. Or even particularly fragile. Therefore, Madame Mimette decided that as long as she was in charge of Jane's wardrobe, all of her outfits would be bereft of all the annoying tiny little trimmings. Jane's gown was made of the finest silk, to emphasize her slim, suntanned figure. The gentlemen (as well as the ladies) could not help but notice the Goddess dressed in blue silk, who didn't need ruffles to proclaim that she was a desirable female.

As Gwen helped her into the dress, Jane stared down at herself. The décolletage was showing an alarming amount of her bosom, and she forced herself not to cover herself up with a shawl.

"As soon as I button you up, Miss Jane, you can see what you look like," Gwen said, her fingers flying over the buttons carefully concealed in the folds of the gown.

"I wish I was able to swoon, Gwen, then I wouldn't have to go to this dreadful rout that Lord Blackmoore's esteemed mother is holding," Jane commented, trying to stand.

"You'll have the grandest of times, Miss Jane," Gwen

assured her, finishing with the final button. "And your Lord Blackmoore is going to be there, isn't he? That should make the evening ever so much more fun," she said slyly, all but winking at Jane.

"He's not my Lord Blackmoore," Jane said in a harsh voice, staring at herself in the mahogany cheval glass mirror.

"Can I have my shawl, Gwen? It seems awfully chilly in here," she said as she stared at herself. Her bosom was on display, a look that she felt rather . . . uncomfortable with at the moment. Madame Mimette said it was all the crack, so she took a deep breath and tried not to think about the expanse of flesh that she was presenting to the world.

Gwen returned with a lacy blue shawl and her jewelry. "You know you can't leave without your pearls," Gwen complained, clasping the pearls around Jane's neck.

Jane covered herself as best she could and took a deep breath. "Do I look presentable, Gwen?" she asked in a shy voice.

"You look like a princess, Miss Jane," Gwen declared boisterously.

That made Jane smile. "Thank you, Gwen. I just hope I can get through this fête without doing anything disastrous," she admitted.

Gwen opened the door with a smile. "Please try to have a nice time, Miss Jane," she said, as she all but pushed Jane out of the room.

"I'll try, Gwen," she called, as she walked resolutely down the hall toward Charlotte's room. She hoped Gwen would be right and the evening would be something other than a complete failure.

Charlotte's door was open, and Jane let out a small gasp when she saw her cousin standing in front of the cheval mirror, examining herself. Charlotte was wearing a gown of cream satin with a golden gauze overdress that fell into a short train. Tiny gold beads were embroidered over the trim, and, to complete the effect, the most incredible gold and topaz necklace rested against her creamy white skin. Her golden blond hair was done up in ringlets, and flowed down onto her shoulders in a style of careful disarray. Yes, Charlotte was certainly a beauty.

"You look wonderful Charlotte," Jane said immediately, glad that Charlotte wasn't the type to purposely make one feel inferior.

Charlotte turned and faced Jane, and smiled a little. "Thank you. Madame Mimette was right about your evening gown. You look better in something that isn't so fussy," she commented, picking up her gold beaded reticule and cream shawl.

The two ladies continued down the hall and were met by the Earl of Stockmorton, who was looking very elegant himself in a pair of black pantaloons, shiny Hessian boots, white waistcoat, and a handsome blue superfine coat undoubtedly by Weston. A large ruby was placed prominently on his white silk cravat, which was tied in what he told Jane was the Oriental style.

"Are you both ready to leave?" Roger asked, momentarily forgetting to be polite and tell them both how lovely they looked.

"Of course," Charlotte replied, and soon the trio was on their way to the rout on Park Lane. This, of course, was one of the most fashionable areas of the city. As if the Marchioness of Blackmoore would live anywhere else.

The closer they came to their destination, the worse Jane began to feel. Her stomach began to churn, and she became even more nervous. At that single point in time, all she wanted was to be back home in Wales, tending her garden.

The crush of people was enormous, and Jane had never seen so many beautiful women in one place. Each and every lady, no matter what her age, was clad head to toe in the most expensive gown, adorned with the most enormous jewels Jane had ever seen. As the trio waited in line to greet their hostess, Jane's stomach began to churn even more. Everyone at the rout was elegant and sophisticated, and she was a simple rustic from Wales. In addition, she couldn't even talk about her home or Aunt Lydia would have her head.

Moments later, Jane, Charlotte, and Roger were being presented to the Dowager Marchioness of Blackmoore. The Dowager Marchioness was a lively woman with gray hair and a quick smile, and strangely enough, Jane liked her immediately.

Then she was face to face with Lord Blackmoore.

Once again, Blackmoore put the rest of the company to shame with his simple elegance. He was dressed all in black, except for a white shirt with ruffles at the wrists. His Hessians were polished so highly that they put Roger's valet to shame, and his only ornament was a family signet ring. As he stood greeting his mother's guests, he looked very much like a Lord of the Manor to Jane, who was becoming more nervous by the moment.

When Lord Blackmoore turned his golden gaze to her, the oddest expression came over his face. He stared at her for what seemed to Jane to be an eternity, before taking her hand and lightly kissing it. "I'm so glad you were able to attend, Miss Ravenwood," he said in a husky voice.

Jane began to feel quite strange. She most definitely didn't feel like that when Lord Wilford took hold of her gloved hand. Her eyes locked with Blackmoore's, and she heard herself saying in a breathless voice that didn't sound at all like her own, "Thank you for your kind invitation, my lord. Tonight I'm here as a chaperon."

That seemed to bring him out of the trance he had fallen into and he frowned at her. "Why? Didn't we send you a proper invitation?"

Jane smiled at him, her stomach still constricting nervously. "Aunt Lydia couldn't attend tonight, so I'm here to act as Charlotte's chaperon, since no one else was available," she explained, wondering why Blackmoore would care that she wasn't going to be participating in the festivities.

Before he could reply, another guest appeared before him, and Jane entered the most magnificent ballroom she had ever seen. Everywhere she looked were vases filled with the most exotic hothouse flowers, in every color of the rainbow. The most fashionable people in London wearing the most expensive of clothing filled the enormous room, much to Jane's amazement.

"Everyone that's anyone is here," Charlotte commented, as a group of young bucks approached her.

Jane studied the crowd, and recognized Lord Wilford with a beautiful young redhead. Which was surprising, since Roger said Wilford wasn't the best of ton. Obviously he was good enough to be invited to the rout. Overall, it was all quite impressive, Jane decided, watching Charlotte become engulfed by a plethora of young bucks of various sizes and shapes, handsome and not so handsome. Charlotte treated them all equally, much to Jane's surprise. Roger disappeared to a card room, leaving Jane to her own devices.

She smiled at Charlotte, and edged through the crowd of young men. "I'm going to sit down near the potted palm in the corner," Jane said, pointing towards an area filled with over-fed dowagers, desperate-looking spinsters, and bored chaperones.

"Of course," Charlotte said sweetly, turning to smile at one of her admirers.

Jane resolutely walked over to the seat near the palm tree, which was a trifle apart from the rest of the group. She glanced over at Charlotte, and tried to pretend she was enjoying herself.

She was not. Jane could feel the dowagers staring at her, but not one of them said a word. Jane simply sat next to the potted palm, tapping her foot to the music, glad that the ladies left her out of their conversation. She knew she couldn't say anything that could possibly interest them, and once she started talking, she risked the possibility of embarrassing herself. And Aunt Lydia. And the family, which wouldn't do. So she simply planned to blend unobtrusively into the wallpaper and would observe Charlotte. Not that Charlotte needed a chaperon, since she was well aware of the rules that a young lady about town must follow. Jane, on the other hand, was still hearing daily lessons from Aunt Lydia.

Her eyes scanned the room for her cousin, who was at that very moment playfully hitting a young blade in an ugly puce waistcoat with her fan. She could almost hear Charlotte's tinkling laugh, and was almost glad that no one paid any heed to her. In the crush, she also saw the handsome Lord Foxworth surrounded by a bevy of young beauties, and Lord Milnor was there as well. Lord Roarkston was engrossed in conversation with a group of men, and didn't appear to be dancing. Not one of them came over to pay their respects to Jane. It was as if sitting with the dowagers made her invisible.

Jane sat in the corner next to the palm for almost an hour, calmly watching the couples dance and listening to the music. She saw Lord Wilford glance her way, but she couldn't meet his eye, embarrassed. He wouldn't ask her to dance because she was a chaperon. It was all very galling. The dowagers and the spinsters were snubbing her as well, so she spent most of the evening watching Charlotte enjoy herself.

Unfortunately, a young gentleman wearing a striped green and yellow waistcoat was obviously unaware that she was a chaperon. "May I have this dance?" he asked in a drunken slur.

Jane stared at him in horror, realizing that every other

turban-wearing chaperon was now staring at them. And most especially at her. She turned crimson and quietly said, "I'm terribly sorry, I'm not dancing tonight."

The drunken fop in the horrible clothes stared at her in disbelief and then replied in a voice loud enough to cross the room, "Aren't we above ourselves, Miss High and Mighty," and staggered away, leaving Jane alone and completely embarrassed.

She could hear the other women whispering about her and pointing discreetly in her direction. That made her finally get out of her seat, to find refuge somewhere away from the gossiping dowagers. Jane glanced around the crowded ballroom and glided regally over to Charlotte, who was holding court for a dozen or so admirers.

"Excuse me, Charlotte, may I speak to you privately for a moment?" she asked, hoping no one would take much notice of her. Charlotte frowned, but moved to Jane's side. "Is something wrong?" she asked in a worried voice.

"I don't feel quite the thing. I'm going to find somewhere quiet to sit down by myself. Will you be all right by yourself?"

Charlotte smiled brilliantly. "Of course, Jane. The library is through those doors to your left, and down the hall," she said softly.

Jane gave her a weak smile. "Thank you so much, Charlotte," she replied and headed toward the library.

Blackmoore lounged against the wall, watching this damnable crush of his mother's proceed. He detested these gatherings, and if he didn't have to be in London for parliament, he would have rather been anywhere than in Town. He simply abhorred being polite to people he didn't like, dancing with simpering young women who didn't know Napoleon existed, and watching intelligent men, his friends, make complete fools out of themselves over some Diamond of the First Water who might favor them with a smile. He was the target of every matchmaking mama, and had been hit playfully with so many fans that night that he was considering banning fans at his mama's next rout. Then there were the fluttering eyes and the condescending remarks.

Blackmoore continued to watch the dancing, once again, completely bored. His eyes fell upon Wilford, who was dancing with Lady Wilkerson. She was one of Society's most notorious widows, and more than likely had brought Wilford as her escort.

Blackmoore found his gaze returning to the stunning Miss Ravenwood, but decided that he wouldn't seek her out. She was a chaperon tonight, and it wouldn't be quite proper for him to be socializing with her. He was convinced she was a liar, and that her motives were far from innocent. Under her respectable veneer, he had no doubt she had the heart of a scheming doxy.

When he saw her leave the room and head toward the library, he wondered what intrigue she was planning. He immediately suspected that she was meeting an errant lover in seclusion, but then reluctantly dismissed the idea. Roger said she hadn't become attached to anyone outside of Wilford, and that blackguard was still dancing with Lady Wilkerson.

Blackmoore frowned, and wondered why she would be going into his library. No one ever went into the library during a ball. Could she be looking for his estate books, to pry into his finances? That was a possibility, he thought, wondering if his desk was locked and if he had any money in the room. There was also the possibility that she was looking for something in the room to pawn—his mother collected priceless figurines, and there were some of those very figurines in the library. Roger had been very sketchy about Miss Ravenwood's finances and it was possible that she was looking for money.

The more Blackmoore thought about Miss Ravenwood

disappearing into his library, the more worried he became. The situation deserved an investigation, and, if he waited just long enough, he might be able to catch her in some nefarious plans.

Jane scanned the virtually endless catalog of books before her, more than impressed. One could say what one wanted about Lord Blackmoore, but he most certainly had a complete library. She finally picked up a copy of the complete works Sophocles, in Greek, and curled up in a large leather chair facing the fire. Soon she was oblivious to everything except the words on the page, the sounds of the orchestra in the next room and the warmth of the fire on her stocking feet.

The Blackmoore ball had suddenly become much more interesting to the admittedly bookish Jane Ravenwood.

Blackmoore glanced at his pocket watch, and decided now was the time to cross the ballroom and confront Miss Ravenwood in his library. He strode across the floor, his head held high, a glint of anger apparent in his gold-flecked eyes.

Each step seemed to take an eternity as he walked through the throng of guests. Occasionally, a drunken friend or casual acquaintance would try to stop him, to exchange pleasantries. Instead, he smiled and said, "I have some business to attend to."

The men usually accepted that and let him go on his way. The ladies that stopped him were a bit more persistent. They fluttered their eyelashes, brushed up against him and even offered to join him wherever he was going. At least that was the tactic of a few widows. Blackmoore wasn't amused.

It seemed to take an eternity to get to the library, and Blackmoore's mood was definitely less congenial than at the start of the ball. Miss Ravenwood was going to have a dreadful surprise when he caught her in the midst of her mischief.

The large wooden door of the library opened silently, as Blackmoore prepared to confront the sly Miss Ravenwood. As he quietly looked into the room, his eyes immediately focused on the large Chippendale desk. That's where she would be, reading his private papers or trying to open the locked drawers.

He stared in amazement at the desk, which looked exactly as he had left it. Stranger yet, Miss Ravenwood wasn't standing there. Blackmoore took a step into the room, ready to catch the tempting Miss Ravenwood in the middle of her crime.

CHAPTER SIX

The evening had improved considerably for Jane. The chair in the library was wonderfully comfortable, and the fire warmed the faint chill that had overtaken her. Jane was oblivious to all around her, immersed in Sophocles' tragedy, *Oedipus Rex*. It was a bit of a gruesome tale, but it was certain to get her mind off the rout and Lord Blackmoore.

Jane didn't hear the library door open, or Lord Blackmoore approaching her chair. Her back was toward the door, so in actuality, it wasn't too difficult to literally sneak up on her.

"May I ask what you're doing in my library, Miss Ravenwood?" a deep, male voice asked, and Jane almost jumped out of the chair in fright.

Jane looked up at Lord Blackmoore, a deep blush staining her cheeks. He looked so handsome in the firelight, the flames reflecting in his golden hazel eyes. "I'm so sorry, Lord Blackmoore," she began apologetically, certain that he had every right to be annoyed. She didn't have any right to invade the privacy of his library without permission. "I wasn't feeling all the thing so I decided to rest a bit in the library with a book. I'm terribly sorry," she concluded, in a soft voice, tucking her feet underneath her.

"Are you feeling unwell? Should I call a maid?" he asked immediately, looking a trifle worried. This completely surprised Jane, since she was expecting a thorough dressing-down.

"I've quite recovered, thank you," Jane replied softly, her eyes riveted to his. He had the look of a man of action, she thought dreamily, not the pale, dissipated features of most of the drunken wastrels found in the Upper Ten.

Blackmoore seated himself in the chair opposite hers, a relaxed smile on his face. The firelight created a golden halo around his long, dark wavy hair, and Jane all but forgot that Blackmoore didn't like her and accused her of snooping in Roger's ledgers.

"May I ask what you're reading?" he asked curiously, his eyes fixed on her blushing face.

Jane blushed and stared at the dark Turkish carpet. "I'm reading Sophocles' *Oedipus Rex,*" she said in a very soft voice, certain that Lord Blackmoore would be absolutely horrified by a woman reading Sophocles, in Greek no less.

Strangely enough, Blackmoore didn't flinch. "I didn't realize we had an English translation," he said lightly.

"You don't," she stated, waiting for his gasp of horror. And the look. The "you're a bluestocking" look.

Blackmoore's eyes never left her face, and he was silent for a very long while. Then, as if he were discussing something as commonplace as the weather he commented, "So you read Greek?"

Jane shifted her gaze into the fire, completely horrified. "Yes, my lord, I read Greek. My parents had very different ideas about education, and when they saw I had a penchant for languages, they encouraged me to make use of my abilities," she confessed, squirming a bit in the chair. She was disobeying one of Aunt Lydia's direct commandments for getting on in Society. She was admitting that she not only read Greek, but that her family actually encouraged her to be a bluestocking. Her social life in London, which she never really wanted in the first place, would undoubtedly be over when Blackmoore let the bucks and tabbies around Town know that Miss Jane Ravenwood could read Greek.

"May I ask what other languages you speak, Miss Ravenwood?" he asked nonchalantly.

Jane was afraid to look at his face, to see the revulsion he obviously felt for her. "I speak French as well as Greek," she admitted, and silently added Welsh to the list. There was no way that Lord Blackmoore could be told that she spoke Welsh; Aunt Lydia was most insistent about that.

If she had looked over, she would have seen him smiling. "My tutors were a bit more ambitious. I speak French, German, Greek, and Latin," he answered, his eyes taking in her lithe form.

A wave of relief passed over Jane, and she finally met his eyes, a sincere smile on her face. "Why that's quite impressive, Lord Blackmoore. Your family must be very proud of you," she said honestly, practically glowing in the firelight.

Blackmoore shrugged slightly. "Being the heir to the title, my family was more impressed by the fact that I didn't end up in debtors' prison or sire a passel of byblows," he commented sarcastically, then remembered his manners. "I'm sorry, Miss Ravenwood, that's not the sort of thing I should discuss in the company of a lady."

She smiled brightly at him. "It's quite all right, my lord. Even though I'm the granddaughter of the late Duke, I'm still not quite a proper lady, at least to Aunt Lydia," she said, surprised that she was enjoying their quiet coze.

"You're most certainly a proper lady," he began, then added, "Have you danced with anyone tonight?"

Jane frowned, wondering why he was asking about her dance card, or lack of it, as the case may be. "You know chaperones shouldn't dance," she replied simply.

A strange expression appeared on Blackmoore's face. If she didn't know that he disliked her, Jane would have sworn he was almost mooning over her.

The strains of a waltz drifted into the library, and a strange look appeared in Blackmoore's eyes. "Of course.

But that doesn't mean that you couldn't dance with me now," he said smoothly, holding out his hand to her.

Jane took his outstretched hand, a baffled expression across her face. She was convinced that Lord Blackmoore disliked her heartily, yet he was asking her to dance. He was the most curious and wholly unpredictable person, she decided.

He was also a graceful and accomplished dancer. As he led her around the narrow library, Jane could feel her heart beating wildly. She wanted nothing more than to dance with him all night, enveloped in his safe, strong arms. However, propriety and Aunt Lydia's endless lectures won out in the end. "This is most irregular, Lord Blackmoore," she commented in a voice that she didn't recognize as her own.

He didn't make a move to release her, but instead tightened his grip around her waist, bringing her even closer. "You've obviously waltzed before," he remarked inanely, his eyes dark and hooded with desire.

Jane was having a deuced hard time concentrating. She didn't remember feeling like this when she waltzed with her dancing master, or her brother, or any of the few other males in the area she had stood up with at their relatively small country routs. This was something else entirely, and her senses began to reel, responding to his nearness.

The music stopped, and she waited for Lord Blackmoore to release her. And thank her for the pleasure of the dance, which she was sure a proper partner was supposed to do.

Instead, much to her utter amazement, Blackmoore lowered his head and kissed her lightly on her full, quivering lips.

For that single moment in time, Jane could think of nothing, feel nothing but Blackmoore's large, capable hands pressing her body into his. As his lips moved over hers, Jane was lost in a mist of wanton emotions, forgetting that she was an ineligible spinster and he was a rich and handsome lord. All that mattered was the delicious sensation that careened wildly though her body when he held her.

"You smell like jasmine," Blackmoore murmured, in a voice husky with emotion. His hands lightly caressed her back while his lips gently fluttered over her neck. Jane was speechless. Blackmoore didn't even like her. She was convinced of that fact.

Jane's feeble attempt at logic was silenced as Blackmoore once again brought his lips down on hers, tempting and teasing her. She didn't even realize that she was pressing herself into his strong, masculine form, like a veritable wanton. All she knew was that he had awoken passions within her that she didn't even suspect existed. Jane knew somewhere in the recesses of her mind that it was most improper, probably even scandalous, for Lord Blackmoore to be kissing her in the library. But it didn't matter. The rational part of Jane's brain was obviously taking a break for tea, leaving only her emotions.

With a soft sigh, Jane unconsciously wound her arms around Blackmoore's broad shoulders even tighter, completely unaware that she was only encouraging his base and lurid desires.

"Perhaps we should repair upstairs. To one of the suites," he suggested softly.

Jane's brows knitted together in confusion. Once again, she was at a complete loss. What in the world did he mean? What was he talking about? Jane's heart was beating wildly in her breast, and she was having a hard time concentrating. All she could see were Blackmoore's golden eyes imploring her to join him upstairs.

Finally, after what seemed to be an eternity, Jane pushed him away gently and said, "Upstairs? Why?"

Blackmoore took her small, delicate hand in his and began to lead her toward the closed door of the library. "We won't have any interruptions there," he answered calmly, his eyes never leaving her face.

Jane stood rooted to her spot in the library. Then, the realization of what was happening dawned on her. *He thinks I'm a doxy,* she thought, her mouth dropping in abject horror. Her heart, which was beating so eagerly at his touch, suddenly lurched and lodged itself in her throat. *He doesn't care about me at all,* she thought dismally. *He just wants to dally with me as if I'm a common serving wench.* The delicious emotions that flooded her body a moment earlier gave way to a surge of white-hot anger. "I'm most certainly *not* accompanying you to a suite upstairs," Jane replied sternly, jerking her hand away from his.

Blackmoore stared at her, confusion marring his handsome features. "Don't worry, Jenny, I'll be generous to you," he said in a voice that was so sweet it almost dripped honey. Once more he took her hand in his and began to lead her toward the door. Jane had no idea what he was talking about, but was quite certain that she shouldn't even be thinking of accompanying him to his suite.

Jane froze in her tracks, rather like a recalcitrant mule. *He thinks I'm a . . . Cyprian,* Jane thought in horror. *He wants me to be his mistress. For the moment at least,* she realized in shock. "I beg your pardon," Jane said in her most regal voice. "I am most certainly not accompanying you upstairs," she announced, her anger finally surpassing her passion. And her momentary confusion.

Blackmoore frowned and tried a different tactic. "It's perfectly natural for you to be nervous, Jane," he explained simply, as if he were coaxing a frightened child onto a horse.

Jane wasn't a frightened child who needed reassurance before her first ride alone. She was a very angry woman, who was about to tell Lord Blackmoore exactly what she thought.

"I'm not nervous!" Jane almost shouted, stamping her foot in anger. "I am a lady, Lord Blackmoore, and I'm certainly not in the market for a dalliance with anyone," she announced, opening the library doors.

"Jenny," Blackmoore said in a soft voice, his confusion very apparent.

"You, Lord Blackmoore, you are a. . . a blackguard! How dare you assume that just because I don't possess a title that I'm open to a dalliance!" she said sternly, her cheeks flushed with anger.

"I . . . I . . ." Blackmoore stuttered, obviously shaken by the turn of events.

Before he could form a full sentence, Jane strode regally out of the library, her body consumed by anger. Aunt Lydia thought Lord Blackmoore was the most respectable of men; if only she knew that he was a seducer of innocent young women! Even women that weren't so young! Jane's outrage echoed in every step she took back to the ballroom.

Her rapid stride slowed considerably as she heard the music from the ballroom coming closer and closer. She knew she had to regain her composure or else face numerous rumors and Aunt Lydia's censure.

She took a few more steps and then leaned against the wall, a mixture of anger and disappointment. But mostly anger. She knew a confrontation like this would have never happened at home. She had a brother, and a father who would protect her from that sort of man. Unfortunately, Jane was alone in London. In addition, she was the daughter of a Welsh tradesman who had no real protection. Especially from the wildly unpredictable Lord Blackmoore, a man who was apparently respected and doted on by Society.

Jane marshaled her courage and headed into the ballroom, still shaken. She could see Charlotte over in a corner, surrounded by a veritable herd of young bucks vying for her attention. As Jane turned to her left, she saw the balcony. In that instant, Jane wanted nothing more than to be alone with the cool breeze on her cheeks.

As she stepped out into the main ballroom, Jane glanced around guiltily. No one noticed her absence, which was a good sign. She headed toward the wonderfully isolated terrace, her face still very becomingly flushed.

Jane crossed the room and went out onto the terrace, alone. Almost out of nowhere, Lord Wilford appeared, drink in hand.

"Good evening, Miss Ravenwood," Wilford casually said, glancing around the small terrace. They were alone.

"Good evening, Lord Wilford," Jane replied, her face still flushed with anger.

"Are you enjoying your evening?" he asked cordially, ever the polite gentleman.

Jane shrugged ever so slightly and continued to stare out into the darkness. "I expected my first large rout in London would be different," she stated simply.

Wilford nodded sympathetically. "Of course, it's a dashed shame that you're not dancing tonight."

Jane shrugged.

"Then of course, you have other problems to deal with as well," he added cryptically.

Jane frowned. "Other problems?"

"Well, you'll undoubtedly be beset by suitors in the next few weeks, and you don't have a father or a brother in Town to discourage men of certain morals," Wilford finished enigmatically.

It was as if he knew what happened with Lord Blackmoore. Jane was stunned. "Is there anyone in particular I should avoid?" she asked in a worried little tone.

Wilford stared off into the distance, a slight frown on his face. "It's not surprising that your relations wouldn't tell you, since they're anticipating a wedding announcement. In the past, it has been rumored that Blackmoore isn't adverse to taking respectable women into his bed," Wilford commented, his eyes never meeting Jane's.

Jane stared at him, her eyes wide in amazement. "Lord Blackmoore seduces young women?" she asked, completely shocked.

"There are dozens of rumors circulating about Lord Blackmoore. He's not a trustworthy person and has been known to use females to his own advantage," he said, sipping his champagne. "But of course he would deny all of the facts, as would your relatives, since they're so close to him," he added for good measure.

Jane frowned and said, "Thank you for your advice, Lord Wilford. I will certainly keep it in mind."

Before Wilford could utter another word, Jane glided from the terrace into the main ballroom. A slight sneer came over the face of Lord Wilford, a sneer that Jane unfortunately didn't see.

Jane found a perfect place to sit, next to a different potted palm, almost hidden from the rest of the guests. Actually, Jane was hiding, but realized she had to be discreet about it. The chair next to the potted palm wasn't too terribly obvious, and she did catch Charlotte's eye. Jane was doing her duty as a chaperon.

Actually, Jane was still in high dudgeon over the incident with Lord Blackmoore and disgusted with herself. She knew that she shouldn't have let him kiss her. And that a proper lady would have never responded so wantonly, she recalled with horror. Wilford's words also confused her, since she thought she could trust Aunt Lydia's and Cousin Roger's judgment. Could they be so wrong about Blackmoore?

"Jane?" a soft voice said, startling her out of her reverie. Charlotte was standing in front of her, frowning.

Jane looked up guiltily. "Yes?" she replied in a small, almost squeaky voice.

"The Dowager Marchioness of Blackmoore would like to speak with you."

Jane paled, a fact that wasn't lost on Charlotte. "Why?"

Jane questioned in a hesitant voice, hoping the mother wasn't as unpredictable as the son.

Charlotte dramatically shrugged her shoulders and replied, "I have no idea, Jane. The few times I've spoken to her, I've found her to be extremely cordial," Charlotte added, leading Jane reluctantly through the ballroom.

Scarce moments later, Jane was having an intimate coze with the Dowager Marchioness, who appeared to be brimming with curiosity about Jane. "Are you enjoying the ball, Miss Ravenwood?" she asked, hoping to draw Jane out a bit.

Jane smiled a bit shyly, a little intimidated by the Marchioness. "Charlotte tells me this is a very exclusive rout. Thank you so much for including me in your invitation," she said in her most proper tone of voice.

"I noticed you haven't been dancing tonight."

Jane fidgeted in her chair. "Aunt Lydia asked me to chaperon Charlotte tonight, so I'm not dancing," Jane explained.

"That's too bad. I'm sure you would have enjoyed yourself as much as some of the girls who are just coming out," the Dowager Marchioness replied, a slight frown settling on her face.

Jane stared at the floor, and, feeling a bit more daring raised her eyes to the ornamental cane the Dowager Marchioness was using. It had a wonderful ivory eagle carved at the top, and was actually more decorative than useful. Jane noticed her gnarled knuckles, and, before she realized what she was saying, asked, "My papa has the same problem with his hands. Do your fingers hurt you very much when the weather is changing?"

The Dowager was obviously startled. "Yes, they bother me occasionally, but my physician says there's nothing he can do," she answered reluctantly.

Jane looked up at the Dowager, her eyes brimming with concern. "That's what my papa's physician said. It took some experimenting, but I've concocted a herb poultice that sometimes helps relieve the pain. If you'd like, I'll send my abigail over with the recipe. I don't think you'll have any trouble in locating the ingredients," Jane finished in a rush, hoping her herbs would help the Dowager.

"It's rather unusual for a gently bred young woman to work with herbal medicines," the Dowager Marchioness commented, leaning forward with interest.

Jane felt comfortable with the Dowager Marchioness, and forgot all the rules of polite Society that Aunt Lydia drilled into her brain.

"My Papa likes to try to keep all of our tenants in good health. I've been working on mixtures for them for years, and happened upon something that helped his hands," she explained simply, her eyes practically glowing.

"How amazing!" the Dowager Marchioness exclaimed. "Do you know all of your tenants?"

Jane smiled broadly at the elderly Dowager Marchioness. "I know them all, even if my papa and my brother Jon don't. They have responsibilities outside of the estate, so, since my mama died, the running of the household is my domain."

"That's quite impressive, my dear," the Dowager Marchioness said, glancing towards her son.

Lord Blackmoore sulked in a corner, still angry with Jane. He knew her respectability was just an act, and couldn't explain why she wouldn't retire to his chambers with him. Miss Ravenwood was not what she seemed, and he was determined to find out what she was hiding from polite Society.

He scanned the room for Jane, expecting her to be sitting with the other chaperones. He was shocked to find her sitting with, of all people, his mother, having a private coze. His curiosity got the better of him, and he marched over to the pair to see what lies Jane was telling his trusting mother.

The Dowager Marchioness smiled ever so slightly when her son suddenly appeared at her side.

Blackmoore gave his mother a strained smile, and asked, "I was wondering if there was anything I could do for you, Mother."

There was a twinkle in her eyes when she replied, "It's been brought to my attention that Miss Ravenwood has been denied the chance to dance tonight. They're striking up a waltz. Would *you* stand up with her?"

Jane flushed a deep shade of crimson. Blackmoore could tell that she definitely didn't want to dance with him. "I couldn't," Jane said weakly.

"Nonsense. Lead her out Richard," his mother demanded, waving her hand towards the dance floor.

Blackmoore knew better than to argue the point in company. He reluctantly took Jane's hand and silently led her out to the floor.

As they danced, a trickle of a doubt began to form in his mind. Maybe she was a perfectly respectable young woman. There was also the possibility that he was overreacting after the awful incident with Yvette. Possibly he was simply too suspicious of her.

Blackmoore gazed down at Jane, and fought the urge to bring her lithe form closer to him. He shouldn't have kissed Roger's cousin, and if she told him about the incident, it would put a strain on his relationship with the Wyndmere family. So he reluctantly said, "I'm sorry if I offended you in the library," not sounding sorry at all.

Jane stared at the other couples dancing, refusing to meet his eyes. After an interminable silence she said, "It's of no consequence. I'm only going to be in Town for a short while, and I'm sure that all of this will only be a vague memory when I'm back home."

Blackmoore frowned again. She was vastly impertinent.

However, he did enjoy dancing with her, and relished the feeling of her warm body moving in concert with his. He was deuced tired of dancing with devilishly short women, and on that front, Jane was a welcome relief. In fact, she was the tallest woman in the room, except for his mother. And the loveliest, he realized in shock.

Their dance ended much too soon, and Blackmoore was in a quandary. He wasn't in the habit of seducing respectable females, and he felt somewhat guilty about what happened in the library. Unfortunately, he had no idea what to say or do, and was still suspicious of her motives. So he silently escorted her back to Charlotte, lost in his own thoughts. Before she could make any comment he quickly said, "If you both will excuse me," and sauntered off towards the terrace.

That night, as Gwen helped her out of her exquisite gown, Jane came close to disciplining her. Gwen was extremely excited about the ball, and demanded to know every detail. Jane was tired, homesick, and in a rather disagreeable mood, so she answered her abigail with short, curt remarks.

Finally, after Gwen had settled her in her nightdress, she commented, "I know you're not finding London to your liking, Miss Jane, but I think the men here are ever so nice. I've found myself a swell in London and I think you should too, Miss Jane." Before Jane could answer, Gwen left the room, humming softly.

Once again Jane listened to the sounds of the English night, and wondered if she would ever return home. Things were not going well, and the episode with Lord Blackmoore was certainly proof of that.

She had been to her fair share of routs back home. Nothing as elaborate as the Blackmoore ball, but close enough. She had stood up with any number of her brother's friends, who were always very cordial to her. She even had the odd and occasional suitor, but no one captured her heart.

And they never treated me like a doxy, she thought miserably. When Blackmoore took her in his arms, all thoughts of resistance fled, and she knew she acted like a green girl. A green girl who had never been singled out by a dashing, handsome lord.

The tears began to slowly run down her cheeks, but she didn't know why. Maybe it was because London was such a strange foreign place, so different from the green rolling hills and the solitude of home.

Or maybe it was because she was falling in love.

"I do believe that you have more admirers now than you have ever had, my dear," Lydia announced, strolling through the sitting room examining the flowers sent by Charlotte's adoring swains.

Charlotte sat in a rather uncomfortable, straight-backed chair and gazed out the window, as if she were pining for someone. "Do you think so, Mama?" she asked in a dispirited voice, wondering when she could see James again.

"I don't see any flowers from Lord Blackmoore," Lydia commented in a humorously scolding voice.

"Lord Blackmoore is a friend of mine, Mama. You know he doesn't have any serious intentions," Charlotte said, still staring out of the window.

"Charlotte, you're too modest by far. All of Society knows that Lord Blackmoore is besotted with you; we are all waiting for him to make you an offer."

"Mama, Lord Blackmoore is a friend of the family. He is not going to offer for me," she insisted, wishing her mama wasn't so set in her ideas. She wouldn't marry Richard. She wanted to marry James Clayton, her talented and charming artist. Richard was much too ill-tempered and could be rather intimidating at times. She knew that he would not make a comfortable husband for her, and she wouldn't be interested in him even if she wasn't already attached to James.

Aunt Lydia looked up from the flowers she was studying, only to see Jane stroll into the room wearing one of her new muslin dresses.

"Good morning," Jane said, sitting on another straight, wooden chair.

"There are some flowers from Lord Wilford and a note," Aunt Lydia said, bringing the note over to Jane, and waiting expectantly while Jane read the brief missive.

"Lord Wilford has asked me to go riding with him in a few days. May I accept, Aunt Lydia?" she asked, knowing that she would accept regardless of Aunt Lydia's response.

"Wilford . . . He is an earl; why yes, I suppose you can go riding with him. His father was one of your mama's conquests," she added.

"Thank you, Aunt Lydia," Jane responded obediently, and penned a note back to Lord Wilford accepting his invitation while Charlotte and Aunt Lydia entertained a passel of young bucks who came to call on Charlotte.

"Gunther's is marvelous," Jane announced, grinning like a mischievous child.

Charlotte delicately ate her ice and smiled. "It's one of my favorite places in Town. We can sit and have an ice and watch all of London pass us by. It's a nice way to spend the afternoon," she declared, looking young and innocent in her jonquil sarconet walking dress.

Jane smiled back at her cousin. "I'm certainly glad you suggested an outing this afternoon. And we can tell Aunt Lydia that we were here all afternoon rather than telling her we went to see James," she said, looking almost as young as Charlotte in her Bishop's blue walking dress.

Jane devoured her lemon ice. Gunther's obviously had the best food in all of London, she decided.

As usual, the streets were rife with activity. There were footmen, carriages, and children everywhere. There was even a rather handsome chap across the road, almost in the shadows, watching the ladies. Charlotte didn't notice him, but she did notice Lord Blackmoore.

"How odd!" Charlotte exclaimed. "Richard is out driving with Lady Wilkerson." Jane followed her gaze, only to see Lord Blackmoore in his phaeton with the crimson-haired lady who was with Lord Wilford at the Blackmoore rout. Lady Wilkerson looked very young. She was wearing a bright Pamona green dress with a very revealing décolletage and was laughing and sitting much too close to Lord Blackmoore. "Lady Wilkerson is a widow," Charlotte explained, and added, "It's rumored that she has quite a number of cicisbei. I wonder why Richard is with her?"

Jane could tell her exactly why Lord Blackmoore was out driving with the luscious widow. He obviously got tired of trying to seduce spinsters from the country, and was moving on to easier prey.

CHAPTER SEVEN

Blackmoore could hardly contain his boredom. Lady Anne was a veritable Cyprian. "You must call me Anne," the dashing young widow whispered in her most seductive voice, placing her hand on his very muscular thigh. Blackmoore removed it from his leg as nonchalantly as possible, and decided that Lady Wilkerson was simply the most hen-witted creature he had ever met. Not only was she monumentally boring, she was actually trying to lure him into her bedroom, which was rumored to be quite busy.

He stared at the road ahead, looking at anything but the very forward widow at his side, cursing his curiosity. The only reason he asked her to go driving in the first place was to find out why she let the detestable Wilford escort her to his mother's rout. As luck would have it, Lady Wilkerson told him nothing useful, and he couldn't wait until their drive was over and this strumpet of Polite Society was out of his company.

Nevertheless, he was still on a mission of sorts, so he was obliged to carry on a conversation with her. He was trying to be attentive to Lady Wilkerson's babbling when he saw her, across the road.

Jenny, Jane, Miss Ravenwood. She was at Gunther's, having an ice with Charlotte. Jane was saying something to Charlotte, and she looked quite fetching in a simple blue dress that didn't have all of those horrible ribbons and bows

that ladies these days insisted on wearing. Jane actually
looked younger than her cousin, and much more exotic.

"Richard dearest, is anything wrong?" Lady Wilkerson
asked in a low voice, turning to follow his eyes.

Blackmoore actually blushed like a callow youth and
hastily tore his eyes away from Jane. "Sorry, what?" he muttered, tugging at his neck cloth a bit.

"You must be anxious to get back into the arms of your
intended," Lady Wilkerson commented, staring at Charlotte.

"My intended? Who? You mean Jane?" Blackmoore
blurted, completely confused.

The redheaded beauty stared at him as if he had run
mad. "Silly, I mean Charlotte Wyndmere!" she exclaimed
merrily, daintily hitting him with her fan.

He turned a deeper shade of red. Why did he think Lady
Wilkerson had meant Jane? *She doesn't even know Jane,*
he mused, thoroughly and completely embarrassed.

As they continued their drive back to Lady Wilkerson's
lair, all Blackmoore could think about was the spirited
beauty he saw at Gunther's.

Jane sat in a minuscule chair in a dreadfully cramped office, studying the man behind the desk. James Clayton,
artist and accountant at the gallery, was hardly the man she
would have thought would claim the heart of the Incom-
parable Charlotte Wyndmere. He wasn't magnificently
handsome, and actually seemed to be a bit retiring. As she
watched the pair converse quietly, one could easily see that
they were both taken with each other.

James turned to Jane, a slight blush staining his cheeks.
"I'm so sorry that you have to be involved in our hoax,
Miss Ravenwood," he said apologetically.

Jane smiled a bit, and replied, "I do understand, Mr.
Clayton. We don't always choose the most convenient per-

son to fall in love with, but, if you're supposed to be together, it will all work out in the end."

Charlotte gazed imploringly at Jane with troubled blue eyes. "Jane, we want to marry, but James won't consider it without approval from my family. What am I going to do?" she asked in a quivering voice, reaching for James's hand. James looked down at her, his eyes wide with concern.

"Charlotte, things will come about. We'll just have to wait a bit. You'll see," he said in a soft voice that really didn't convince anyone in the small office.

Jane sat quietly in the corner, and thought of all the paintings that Charlotte and James had shown her with pride. James was a talented painter who, with the right patronage, would more than likely end up with a successful show in the Royal Academy. The thing was to bring James to her family.

While James and Charlotte were wrapped up in their private conversation, Jane continued to think about all of the wonderful paintings that James had created. They were all landscapes, but it would be interesting to see if he did portraits. Every family had dozens of portraits of all of their ancestors, no matter how unattractive. Someone like Charlotte would be a tribute to her family, and no one would turn down the suggestion of having her stunning beauty grace a wall.

"Excuse me, Mr. Clayton?" Jane asked in a hesitant voice, not really wanting to interrupt the pair.

"Yes, Miss Ravenwood?" he asked expectantly, holding Charlotte's small, white hand in his.

"Can you do portraits?"

"I primarily do landscapes, but yes, I can paint a tolerable portrait. Why?"

"Well, if you painted Charlotte, you could spend more time with her and get to know the family," Jane suggested.

"That's a grand idea, Jane!" Charlotte exclaimed enthusiastically. "But how will we get Mama to choose James to do my portrait?"

"You'll simply have to convince her that you've seen his work and no one else will do, not even Turner himself," Jane replied, thinking the idea might actually work.

Charlotte was practically glowing. "The idea is wonderful, Jane! If Mama and Roger get to know James, they couldn't object to a match, I know they couldn't," she said, gazing at her beloved.

Jane studied the pair with envy, and wondered if anyone would ever gaze rapturously at her. It was doubtful she decided, since she was five-and-twenty and practically an ape leader.

Life in London was not the continuous party that her Papa had told her to expect.

That night, as Charlotte and Jane played piquet to pass the time, Charlotte commented, "So you're going riding with Lord Wilford again. Do you like him?" she asked, playing her card.

Jane stared at the worn cards in her hand and thought about the question. "Lord Wilford is polite enough," she finally answered, hoping Charlotte didn't press on with her line of questions.

"But do you like him? Do you hope he makes you an offer?" Charlotte asked, worry lines etched in her fashionably pale brow.

Jane played her card, and tried to honestly answer the question. "I don't want Lord Wilford to offer for me. But if I'm seen in public with him, your mama will quit plaguing me about attracting eligible men," she finally answered, hoping Charlotte would let the subject drop.

Strangely enough, Charlotte smiled at her. "I'm glad you haven't formed an attachment for Lord Wilford. I don't know what it is about him, but he makes me nervous. Roger doesn't like him, and I wish Richard could help you

like he was helping me, so you didn't have to continue to
socialize with Lord Wilford," she finished frankly.

Jane cringed at the thought of Lord Blackmoore feign-
ing interest in her. That would certainly not do. "I think
not," Jane replied tersely, immediately dismissing the topic
of Blackmoore.

Diablo was restless today, Jane decided, as she tried to
control the massive stallion. Low, gray clouds filled the
sky, and a spring shower wasn't out of the question. Hyde
Park was becoming the most familiar sight in London to
Jane, who was becoming quite adept at these rides with
Lord Wilford.

Their outings were beginning to follow a pattern: Lord
Wilford would arrive at the Stockmorton residence, and
compliment her on any one of a million attributes he
claimed were hers alone. Jane's favorite compliment to
date came when Lord Wilford gazed into her eyes and
claimed that he could "See the thoughts racing through
your mind by looking into your magnificent green eyes."
Jane was hard pressed not to burst out into peals of laughter when he fabricated such ridiculous praise.

After what she started to term "compliments in the
house," they rode out to Hyde Park in companionable silence, moving their mounts through the traffic on the
street. Lord Wilford would routinely ask if Jane would like
oranges or flowers from one of the children on the street
selling them; Jane would always refuse.

Once they arrived in the Park, Lord Wilford would gossip incessantly about whomever they ran across, and Jane
would pretend to be fascinated by his babbling. Then, as
they walked back home, he would inquire after her social
plans for the future. In fact, any observer would be convinced that Lord Wilford was besotted with Jane.

Jane didn't believe that for an instant. Lord Wilford was

pleasant enough, but his smiles didn't reach his eyes, and he seemed to be concealing something or another. However, he was an Aunt Lydia–approved companion, so Jane would continue to put up with his excessive flummery.

On this journey through the Park, Diablo was restless and taking all of her considerable skills as an equestrian to handle him. Wilford was oblivious to her distress, finding the other riders on Rotten Row much more interesting.

In the distance, atop a magnificent stallion, was Blackmoore. He obviously spotted Jane and Wilford, and was glaring at them across the Park.

"Miss Ravenwood, have you done something to bring up Lord Blackmoore's dander? He seems to be staring quite markedly at you from near the hedgerow," Wilford remarked, a look of abject innocence on his face.

Jane looked quickly over to where Lord Blackmoore sat on his utterly magnificent chestnut stallion and blushed furiously. "I don't think Lord Blackmoore cares for me."

Wilford's lips tried to form a smile, but instead, turned into a slight sneer that wasn't very attractive. Unfortunately, Jane was looking everywhere but at Wilford or Blackmoore. "It must be hard for you, since Blackmoore is your cousin's favorite suitor. He must be constantly underfoot."

Jane looked straight ahead, avoiding the eyes of both men. "Lord Blackmoore is just a friend of Charlotte's. He's not courting her," she declared, wishing she were home.

Wilford was genuinely surprised by that fact, and was silent for a moment. "I'm certainly glad to hear it's not true. Your dear Cousin Charlotte deserves someone better than a hardened rake," he said smoothly.

"I know," Jane said softly. *Blackmoore doesn't seem to be a hardened rake,* Jane thought, staring at the other riders. *But Lord Wilford has been in Town much longer than I have, so perhaps he is right after all,* Jane concluded.

They rode on in a companionable silence until Wilford

asked, "When will we see you around Town?" This was actually a proper question for a suitor.

"I'll be at Almack's in a sennight," she said unenthusiastically. Going out riding with Lord Wilford was a perfect way for Jane to avoid Aunt Lydia and her matchmaking. While Wilford was always cordial to her, he never slipped into the almost romantic haze that seemed to envelop Lord Blackmoore, so Jane was certain he wasn't forming an attachment to her.

Wilford gave her another false smile. "Then you must be sure to save me a dance."

Jane glanced over at him, and a shiver ran down her spine. But she didn't know why.

The next few days passed in a flurry of activity for Charlotte and Aunt Lydia. Each day they made a number of morning calls, visiting Lady So-and-So and Dowager Countess What's-Her-Name.

Thankfully, Jane was able to avoid all of the morning calls by claiming that cook's congealed breakfast meat, whatever it actually was, didn't quite agree with her. Consequently, she spent most of the time in her room, feeling not quite the thing. In actuality, Jane didn't feel nearly as terrible as she let on, and used the time to read some of the gothic romances she found in the library. They got her mind off the fact that she was on the verge of becoming besotted with Lord Blackmoore. Even though he insulted her. Even though he treated her like a jaded strumpet who had questionable morals. It didn't matter. In those moments when he forgot who he thought she was, he was the most charming, desirable companion a woman could want.

Aunt Lydia was in alt, since Blackmoore's attentions caused Charlotte to be even more popular than in her first Season. Charlotte's dauntless suitors filled their salon, and the house was beginning to resemble a greenhouse.

It was harder for Jane to avoid the gentlemen in the salon. Charlotte would sit on a chair, and the gentlemen would gather around her, competing for her attention. "Lady Charlotte, I've composed a sonnet to your eyes," declared Lord Prosy. "Lady Charlotte, you're the most accomplished dancer in all of London," declared Lord Twinkletoes. "Lady Charlotte, I stay up nights dreaming of your beauty," proclaimed Lord Sleeplessnights.

Of course, the fashionably dressed dandies didn't completely ignore Jane. They would occasionally look over at Jane and favor her with a comment. She was often assailed with questions like "What kind of flowers does Lady Charlotte favor?" Or perhaps "Does Lady Charlotte prefer wine or champagne?" Then there was Jane's favorite comment of all. "Can you get our glasses refilled?" The life of a spinster cousin was so lowering at times.

Jane sighed heavily. She was obviously blue deviled. She missed her home, and the blessedly normal food she ate instead of the grayish poached fish and turtle soup that Aunt Lydia served. She missed her garden, the walks in the forest, and the long rides to the sea she would take on sunny summer days. London definitely wasn't home, but she couldn't bring herself to tell Papa that she was having a less than perfect time. Each time she tried to write him a letter, she ended up throwing it away. In the end, she wrote him a short missive that said all was well, and that she looked forward to being back home.

The next evening, while Jane and Charlotte played piquet and Aunt Lydia worked on some needlework Charlotte decided to throw caution to the wind and bring up the portrait.

"You know, Mama, Jane was telling me about all the friends she has back in Wales who have had their portrait done. In fact, she says it's all the crack. Could I sit for a portrait?" she asked innocently, as if the idea had just struck her out of the blue.

Aunt Lydia didn't even bother to look up, concentrating on her stitching. "I suppose we could look into it, my dear. But who would we commission?" she asked distractedly, wondering if this was one of Charlotte's willy nilly schemes.

"You know Aunt Lydia, I visited a gallery a few days ago with Charlotte and some of the most wonderful pictures were done by a Mr. Clayton. I heard some of the ladies talking about him at the Dowager Marchioness' rout, and they say he's going to be all the thing in a very short time," Jane remarked innocently, coloring the facts very prettily.

Aunt Lydia appeared to consider the idea. "We'll go to see this Mr. Clayton tomorrow morning. If I find his work acceptable, we'll commission him. If not, we'll find someone else," she proclaimed.

Jane and Charlotte exchanged a telling look over the card table. Moments later, when Aunt Lydia left the room, Charlotte began to pen a note to James, alerting him of their upcoming visit.

"Thank you very much for taking the time to examine my work," James said, in his most formal tone.

Aunt Lydia didn't reply. Instead, she walked from painting to painting, studying them intently.

"Has anyone else been by to inspect your work?" Jane asked, moving the conversation along.

James gave her a winning smile. "Why yes, Miss Ravenwood. Lady Bloomberg was by last week, as well as Lord Langely," he said calmly.

"Don't see many portraits here," Aunt Lydia practically grunted.

"Of course, Mama," Charlotte said, logically. "Mr. Clayton has been working on landscapes, because those are the ones that his customers purchase. But his real talent is in portraits," she explained.

Aunt Lydia strolled over to a portrait of a rather corpulent older woman, which was actually very flattering and studied it in silence for a very long while.

"Charlotte, didn't Lord Blackmoore mention that he was planning on commissioning Mr. Clayton to do a portrait of the Dowager Marchioness?" Jane asked, deliberately dropping Blackmoore's name.

"Oh yes, Jane, he's quite keen on Mr. Clayton's work," Charlotte answered with a smile.

Aunt Lydia sighed and turned to Charlotte. "Sitting for a portrait will be dashed tedious, you know."

"Oh I know, Mama, but I do so want to have my picture in the family gallery," Charlotte said imploringly.

"And Charlotte is the beauty of the family," Jane added for good measure.

Aunt Lydia sighed. "Your father would have wanted it," she said, then turned to James. "I suppose we're going to hire you, Mr. Clayton."

On that instant, Charlotte was the happiest woman in England.

After their triumph at the gallery, Jane expected a pleasant ride home. She was wrong. As Jane calmly stared out the window, Aunt Lydia remarked, "You know, Jane, I think I've found a few possible matches for you."

Jane cringed in abject horror. "May I ask who you have in mind, Aunt Lydia?" she said in a quiet voice.

"Well, Squire Malvern is looking for a wife for his three, or is it four children? His wife died in childbirth. Then there is Baron Deverell. He's still a prime catch, even though he has lost his leg in the war," she commented, completely serious. Jane cringed. A man who needed a mother and a one-legged former soldier. Any minute now Aunt Lydia would mention a member of the clergy.

"And of course, there is Vicar St. John. He's a very pious young man and your fortune would be an immense help to his flock," Aunt Lydia said on cue, making Jane shrink into the squabs of the coach.

Charlotte tried in vain to come to the rescue. "Mama, you know Jane isn't here to make a match," Charlotte chirped, patting Jane's hand reassuringly.

"Nonsense. All girls need husbands. A respectable member of the peerage with a good income is the dream of every mother. I'll help Jane make a good match, as I've helped you along with Lord Blackmoore. Now he is a catch, my dear, not like some artist or a clerk. A marquess is no less than what you deserve Charlotte, with your beauty and polite manners," her mother remarked, unaware that both girls were now staring determinedly out the window.

Before Aunt Lydia could throw another wonderful man in the arena for her, Jane remarked, "I had a pleasant ride with Lord Wilford today."

"I suppose that's promising. However, you shouldn't get your hopes up on that front, Jane; he's quite above your touch. Being seen with him in public can only heighten your consequence, since you're only a miss and you're at that certain age where your eligibility is highly questionable," Aunt Lydia concluded in a sage voice.

Jane and Charlotte gazed out the window. Neither one of them noticed the black carriage that all but followed them to their door.

"Do we have to do more shopping, Charlotte?" Jane complained, already heartily tired of visiting shop after shop for the seemingly endless items a young lady of quality needed.

"Jane, you need something special for Almack's," Charlotte explained in her "Jane, don't be such a quiz" voice.

Jane wasn't convinced. She had dresses for every moment of the day. In fact, Aunt Lydia even made her purchase several dresses to wear that would flatter her coloring if she didn't feel well. She had walking dresses, ball dresses, riding outfits, more outfits than she had ever had in her life. It appeared that fashionable ladies did nothing but gossip and continually change clothes throughout the day.

"If you say so, Charlotte," Jane replied, trailing after her cousin.

They finally reached Madame Mimette's, and, after what Jane thought was hours of looking over fashion plates, they all eventually agreed on a dress of green- and gold-shot Indian gauze with a startlingly low décolletage. It was a bit more revealing than Jane liked, but since Madam Mimette had not been wrong yet, Jane submitted to her bullying and went through with the tedious fittings. Of course, she would be spending most of her time there with all of the other not-so-young women who were firmly on the shelf, watching the young, beautiful Diamonds of the First Water like Charlotte have a wonderful time. Her father wanted her to have some Town bronze, and Jane would dutifully submit until August twelfth, the official end of the Season. That is, if she didn't flee home before that day.

The shopping didn't stop at Madame Mimette's. The ladies then moved on to find Jane a perfect reticule to match her new gown, as well as a matching golden fan. Jane, in her ignorance, did not have the proper number of fans in her wardrobe, which absolutely appalled the fashion-conscious Charlotte.

By the end of the day, when Gwen was helping her into her simple white cotton nightdress, Jane was truly exhausted. Shopping was a very time consuming activity, and she would be glad when she was back in the country.

There she could wear the same drab muslin dress every day and Jon's friends would still compliment her.

Jane snapped out of her reverie when she noticed that Gwen was not only bouncier than usual, she was singing to herself. "And why are you in such a sunny mood tonight, Gwen?"

"I'm seeing a new man and he treats me ever so nicely. We're going to go to the market on the next day I have off," Gwen stated, fussing with Jane's nightgown.

Some things never change, Jane decided, smiling at her maid. Gwen collected men like other women collected fans. "May I ask your man's name?" Jane asked politely, wondering how Gwen had enough energy for both a man and a job.

"His name is Charley and he is the most handsome cove I've seen in London. He has one of those Brutus haircuts and has the most proper manners I've ever seen. And he's ever so charming and fun to be with."

Jane smiled at her as she got into bed. "I'm glad you've found someone to spend your time with, Gwen," she said honestly, certain that she herself was always going to be alone.

Gwen had the temerity to actually wink at her. "You'll see, Miss Jane; your Lord Blackmoore will come up to scratch soon, you mark my words," and bounced out of the room merrily. As Jane lay on the lumpy bed and listened to the sounds of the horses' hooves on the cobblestones, she wondered if she should tell someone what happened with Blackmoore. Of course, she shouldn't have been there alone with him in the first place, and she would probably end up getting a dressing-down from Aunt Lydia on propriety, even though she was completely innocent. No, she would simply avoid Lord Blackmoore in the future, and hope he decided on the same tactic.

CHAPTER EIGHT

"I told you we had remarkably attractive females in our family, Richard," Roger commented, standing with Blackmoore at the bottom of the stairs as Charlotte and Jane descended.

Charlotte, as usual, was a vision in a pink satin gown trimmed with yards of white lace, and a neckline that was just a little more modest than the one Jane was sporting. She carried a delicate, oriental-looking fan and her hair was done up with a pair of jeweled combs. Yes, all of the gentlemen in the room would be envious of Lord Blackmoore for escorting the ever-beautiful Lady Charlotte. The Wyndmere rubies graced her lovely swan-like neck, and she couldn't have looked lovelier.

Jane presented an entirely different picture as she trailed after her younger cousin down the stairs. Her gown clung to her in the most provocative manner; in fact, she couldn't have been more seductive if she had dampened her petticoats. The golden green material enhanced her incredible eyes, and she looked like an exotic flower in a garden of common daisies. She walked down the stairs with an innate grace that she didn't realize she possessed, carrying her shawl and her delicately beaded gold reticule on her arms. She didn't know until moments before that Lord Blackmoore was escorting Charlotte, and she didn't look forward to the carriage ride over with them.

"Jane, you look magnificent," Roger stated, looking

quite the man about town with his buff breeches, golden brocaded waistcoat, and his satin cravat tied in a mathematical. His maroon coat, designed by Weston, would make many of the young ladies take notice of the very handsome and cordial Earl of Stockmorton.

Blackmoore, as usual, was wearing black from head to toe, save his white shirt. He wore his family signet ring and a rather impressive diamond on his cravat. He gave a picture of unstudied elegance that many of the gentlemen wished they could portray, but didn't have the panache to achieve.

Aunt Lydia, clad in a voluminous magenta gown, complete with matching turban, bustled in from the salon.

"Are we all ready to go?" Aunt Lydia said cheerfully, acknowledging Blackmoore with a regal nod.

Jane all but mesmerized Blackmoore. His eyes swept over her figure, as if he was memorizing every detail. He could even smell the soft scent of jasmine when she was near him. He was nearly entranced.

A cough from Roger brought Blackmoore back to earth. "Yes, of course we're ready to go," he said gruffly, as they headed for Almack's, the official Marriage Mart of Polite Society.

Jane found her first outing into polite society was a bit less exciting than what she had imagined. Rather than having a spirited discussion about politics, or even having someone even slightly eligible fetch her a drink, Jane simply sat with the other ineligible females. Not the chaperones, but the other spinsters who "didn't take." It was rather like being a chaperon, but more lowering, since one was actively ignored as a spinster.

"Is this your first time at Almack's?" asked Miss Spindleworth, who was sitting next to Jane.

"Yes. Is it always like this?" Jane asked innocently.

"What exactly do you mean, Miss Ravenwood?" Miss Spindleworth asked, her birdlike features forming a frown.

"Well, will we dance at all? Will we socialize? Or do we just spend the entire evening sitting here?" Jane asked bluntly.

Miss Spindleworth looked Jane up and down. "Pardon me for saying so, Miss Ravenwood, but you are of an age. Almack's is for girls out of the schoolroom, surely you know that?"

Jane sighed. *So I am going to sit here all evening,* she mused.

On the other side of the room, Blackmoore casually studied Jane. She looked every inch the proper lady, casually conversing with the other spinsters. Strangely enough, she looked like she was having a dashed dreadful time. Wilford was on the other side of the room, chatting up some rich young heiress. He was ignoring Jane, which Blackmoore found odd, since Wilford seemed to be courting her.

Blackmoore was staring so intently at Jane from his vantage point that he didn't notice the lady that appeared in front of him.

"You seem to be quite interested in Miss Ravenwood," Lady Sefton remarked with a smile.

Blackmoore's eyes shifted to the patroness of Almack's that was standing by his side. "Good evening, Lady Sefton," he said with a smile. Lady Sefton was undoubtedly the most popular patroness of Almack's, and she was a bosom bow of his Mother's as well.

"She looks lovely tonight, doesn't she?" Lady Sefton asked casually, her eyes never leaving his face.

Blackmoore shrugged slightly. "Miss Ravenwood is attractive enough, but I've found her to be a slightly questionable person."

Lady Sefton let out a merry laugh. "Richard, you are the

veriest sapskull! Miss Ravenwood? She isn't questionable in the least!"

Blackmoore raised an eyebrow at Lady Sefton's proclamation. "Begging your pardon, Lady Sefton, but I have had a greater opportunity to observe Miss Ravenwood than you have," he said stiffly.

Lady Sefton was nonplussed. "That may very well be, Richard, but I'm certain nonetheless. I was great friends with Miss Ravenwood's mama, and she is everything that is respectable."

Blackmoore's mind was reeling. Perhaps Lady Sefton had the answer to the mystery of Jane's home. "So you knew Miss Ravenwood's mama. Have you ever visited her family at their country home?" he asked a bit too casually.

Lady Sefton smiled benignly. "No, I can't say that I have," she replied in the casual tone.

Before Blackmoore could inquire any further about Jane, Lady Sefton said, "Excuse me," and slipped back to her official duties.

A distinct flush crept over Jane. The room was dreadfully warm, and the lemonade, combined with the awful mock turtle soup she had for supper made her feel quite ill. She made her apologies to Colonel Kinver, the military gentleman with a broken leg who befriended her, and headed out for the terrace.

The night air felt good on her damp forehead, and she wished that she could only sit down. She wasn't really feeling the thing at all, and wished that Roger could whisk her home in the carriage before she disgraced herself by being indisposed at Almack's. Unfortunately, no one noticed her absence, so she was alone on the terrace, feeling miserable.

Leaving the ballroom proper didn't help. Jane wasn't feeling any better. The slight breeze had stopped, and the air was still and stifling. Her head was beginning to spin, and she thought she was going to be seriously sick. Out of nowhere, Lord Wilford appeared and said, "I say, Miss Ravenwood, are you felling well?" she could only shake "No" before swooning into his arms.

Wilford had Jane in his arms, rather like a sack of potatoes, when Blackmoore strolled out the terrace. Wilford was still muttering, "Do wake up," and shaking Jane gently.

Blackmoore was shocked. Miss Ravenwood, the jade, was carrying on with the detestable Lord Wilford. Who was a suspected spy, as well as a drunken wastrel. Well, they were going to get a shock when he walked in on their little coze on the terrace.

Wilford was unaware that they were no longer alone. In fact, he was still trying to wake Jane up when Blackmoore commanded, "Let her go, you blackguard."

Wilford stared at him blankly. "The chit fainted," he explained, and thrust her limp form in Blackmoore's arms. As Blackmoore tried to get a grip on Jane, Wilford quickly escaped into the main ballroom.

Jane finally began to come out of the awful fog that engulfed her when she felt the cool breeze on her forehead. She wondered where she was, and groggily opened her eyes, only to find Lord Blackmoore staring down at her in concern.

"Are you feeling any better, Miss Ravenwood?" he asked in a voice that seemed to be full of concern. Which made no sense at all to Jane's befuddled mind, since Lord Blackmoore detested her. It was all so confusing.

Jane looked at him a trifle out of focus and muttered, "What happened?"

"Apparently, you swooned," he said simply, still holding

her firmly in his arms. Jane was utterly confused. She was convinced that Lord Blackmoore held her in disgust, but here he was, being ever so cordial to her. Then, with a start, she realized that she once again was in his arms. Like a common doxy. She stood up straight, disengaged herself, went over the stone railing, and leaned against it. "Thank you for your help, Lord Blackmoore," she said, staring at her feet.

Lord Blackmoore studied her, then quietly said, "It's not the thing to be alone out here with someone like Wilford. He is a rake of the worst sort and will only try to use you," he concluded, wondering why he was giving her this information.

Jane stared at him in astonishment. He tried to seduce her and now he was warning her that Lord Wilford, who had always acted properly with her, was a womanizing rake. *What a cock-and-bull story,* she thought. She finally said, "I find that quite amusing, Lord Blackmoore. Lord Wilford said almost the same thing about you. But then he has always behaved properly in my company," she concluded, waiting for his short temper to erupt.

There was a long, uncomfortable silence before Blackmoore remarked oddly, "Be assured you're not fooling me with your little deception."

Jane paled at his remark. Did he know she was an heiress from Wales? She knew Aunt Lydia made sure that no one knew she was tainted with trade, let alone Welsh, and there hadn't been any other rumors. So Blackmoore must be thinking of something else entirely, she decided. "I don't know what you're referring to, Lord Blackmoore, but let me make my position clear to you. My father has sent me to London to have a Season and perhaps find a husband. Aunt Lydia is trying to help me get on in Society by shaping me into a perfect young lady like Charlotte. I'm sorry if you don't approve of my behavior. I don't want to be in London, I don't want to be at Almack's, and I'm counting the days until I can go home," she concluded passionately.

Blackmoore stared at her, absolutely astonished. "You don't want to be in London or find a husband?" he asked in disbelief.

Jane walked to the end of the terrace and looked out into the darkness, the moonlight making her skin glow. "I didn't even want to come to London. Nevertheless, I promised my papa I would have a Season in London to please him, and so I shall. I won't make any more scandal for the family, but I won't return home married," she finished, the tear falling dramatically down her silken cheek.

Blackmoore stared at her back, completely at a loss. Instead of saying anything, he moved next to her and slid his arms around her slender waist. "I'm so sorry, Jenny," and began to involuntarily drop light kisses on her neck.

Jane was completely paralyzed. The whole situation was like something out of a very badly written Minerva Press novel. One minute the hero thought that the heroine was a strumpet, the next minute he was declaring his love for her. It was all very confusing, and Jane knew she should really stop Lord Blackmoore from kissing her neck, but it felt remarkably nice and, in all honesty, she didn't want him to stop. In fact, she wanted to kiss him again, which would probably only convince him she was a strumpet.

A very discreet cough interrupted their intimacy. Blackmoore and Jane both turned their heads and found Charlotte staring at them.

Blackmoore released Jane immediately, and tried to maintain some composure. "Charlotte, it's good that you're here. Jenny, Jane, Miss Ravenwood wasn't feeling well. She swooned in fact. You might want to stay with her for a moment," he said nervously.

"Is that so, Jane?" Charlotte asked.

"I'm fine now. I just needed some fresh air," Jane finished, blushing furiously in the darkness.

"If you'll excuse me, ladies," Lord Blackmoore said suavely, striding rapidly back into the ballroom.

Charlotte looked after him and giggled, "I cannot believe it! Richard is acting like an unlicked cub!"

When Jane didn't answer, or find Blackmoore's behavior amusing, Charlotte frowned. "I'm sorry, Jane, I didn't mean to make light of the situation. What happened?"

Jane faced her cousin and didn't know where to start. "I don't know. I fainted when Lord Wilford was here. The next thing I knew Lord Blackmoore was holding me in his arms, trying to wake me up," she said in a small voice, completely embarrassed.

"Richard followed you out here?"

Jane shrugged. "I suppose."

"Jane, I know you're not really acquainted with Richard, so let me assure you, he doesn't usually act this way," Charlotte reassured her.

Jane threw caution to the wind. "You mean that he doesn't accost ladies on balconies? Or kiss them in libraries?"

Charlotte's mouth dropped open in shock. "He's kissed you before?"

Jane stared at the ground and said, "Yes. Lord Blackmoore kissed me in the library at his mother's rout and asked me to his suite."

Charlotte gasped audibly. "Richard?"

"Yes. Lord Blackmoore. I refused him at his mother's rout, but I think he believes me to be of questionable morals," she concluded, feeling a bit better. It was good to tell someone about the whole lurid mess.

Charlotte's eyes widened in shock. "Jane, I've known Richard for years, and I've never known him to act like a . . . blackguard. It's true that he's been acting dashed strange since he returned from the Continent, but I never realized he was accosting you. Do you want Roger to speak to him?" she asked worriedly.

Jane smiled weakly at her. "Goodness no, Roger doesn't have to speak to Lord Blackmoore. I'd just rather forget the whole episode ever happened," she admitted.

There was a long silence as Charlotte pondered Jane's words. Finally she shrugged slightly and said, "If you don't want to tell Roger, we won't tell him. Do you feel well enough to stay at Almack's?" she asked, obviously still concerned about Jane's health.

Jane smiled weakly at her. "Of course, Charlotte. You won't tell anyone about this mess with Lord Blackmoore, will you?" she asked, hoping Charlotte wouldn't let her mother know this bit of gossip.

"No. Mother certainly doesn't need to know anything about this. It would serve her right though if you got leg-shackled to Lord Blackmoore instead of a one-legged vicar with fourteen children!" Charlotte exclaimed with a laugh.

Strangely enough, the rest of the evening at Almack's was without incident. Lord Wilford apparently left Almack's after Jane fainted, and Blackmoore kept himself busy dancing with beautiful, simpering proper young ladies.

After a short time, Charlotte broke away from her herd of suitors to ask her mama if they could leave early. Without Roger and Lord Blackmoore.

Roger was paying the most particular attentions to Lord Huffman's daughter, a match that Aunt Lydia more than favored. So she didn't mind leaving her son, as well as Blackmoore, alone as she escorted Charlotte and Jane back home.

Blackmoore sat in his study, staring at the fire. There was an empty bottle of port next to his chair, and he was making progress on a second. He was also fairly certain he couldn't walk. This was the first time he had been so completely in his cups since before the incident in France.

He stared into the flames, thinking about the lovely and accommodating Yvette, and how she was so very much like Miss Ravenwood. So beautiful, so charming, and so very passionate. Miss Ravenwood was passionate, even though she was an aging spinster. As he held her in his arms, he admitted that it was dashed hard to remember that Jenny was on the shelf.

Of course, Yvette was probably still somewhere in France, working for Boney. At least that's where he expected her to be. She undoubtedly thought he was dead, and he wasted more than one night plotting his revenge on the jade. Now the episode with Yvette felt like it happened years ago, in another lifetime.

He poured himself the last of the bottle and raised his glass to Yvette: the woman who taught him never to trust anyone again. The seductress that taught him that ladies could be as faithless as a Cyprian. The only woman he thought he had loved had convinced him that he would never love again. That didn't leave very much in the life of a man who was expected to start up his nursery.

As he drained his glass, he smiled wryly in the firelight. His long wavy black hair made him look like a gypsy rather than a peer, and he chuckled to himself, contemplating his future. His short-term plan was to find some biddable bird-witted chit in her first Season to provide him with an heir, while he took his pleasures elsewhere. Now all he did was follow Miss Ravenwood around like a green youth, waiting for her to favor him with a smile.

Jenny. He actually called her Jenny on the terrace. If she was lying, she made Yvette look the veriest amateur. What was her relationship with Wilford? he mused. His instincts told him that she was lying about something, but her words seemed so passionate and sincere. Wilford was known to be a traitor to England, and it seemed suspect that he was the only man that seemed to interest her.

Blackmoore sighed. The whole situation was becoming more complex every day, and he hadn't a clue what to do.

Jane sat in the parlor with Charlotte, mentally congratulating herself. It had been four days since the fête at Almack's, and she was doing a remarkable job pretending not to care about Lord Blackmoore. To the world, she appeared to be not the least bit interested in the peer, or even notice the fact that he didn't send Charlotte any flowers. Charlotte gazed out the window, and was doing a sketch in charcoal; Jane was reading, or at least attempting to read.

Aunt Lydia broke their silence. She bustled into parlor dramatically, wearing a turban that was even more enormous than the last one Jane saw her in. This time she was in an ornate puce dress, with a puce turban decorated with several ostrich feathers that naturally moved when she spoke. The bobbing feathers all but mesmerized Jane, who was so transfixed by the feathers that she was inadvertently ignoring her Aunt.

"And do I make myself clear, Jane?" Aunt Lydia asked expectantly.

Jane, who had no notion of what Aunt Lydia had been saying, decided it was best to just nod and reply, "Of course, Aunt Lydia," in her most placating voice.

"Why Charlotte wants you to chaperon while she's having her portrait done is beyond me, but I can see no harm in it. You will remember the rules I've told you?" she said, her turban feathers starting to bob again.

Jane commanded herself not to look at the turban feathers, and instead concentrated of her Aunt's gray-blue eyes. "Oh yes, Aunt Lydia," she replied, wondering what her Aunt was talking about. From the far corner of the room Charlotte looked up from her embroidery and smiled at her. Jane shrugged slightly, since she actually had no idea what was going on. She was simply too distracted by Aunt Lydia's turban to focus on anything else.

Aunt Lydia favored her with a magnificent smile. "You know, Jane, I'm glad you came to London to visit. You've been a wonderful companion to Charlotte, and don't think that I don't appreciate it," she said.

Since Jane wasn't paying any attention at all, she was completely confused. What was Aunt Lydia talking about?

Jane found out her answer soon enough. She had changed from simple spinster relation with no real expectations to handy respectable chaperon. Aunt Lydia went over her rules several more times, so she was prepared when James appeared at their front door.

After James had a brief interview with Aunt Lydia, which Jane assumed was to discuss the cost of immortalizing Charlotte for the walls, the trio headed upstairs to what Charlotte now called "the studio."

The studio was nothing more than a bedroom on the south side of the house that was cleared of most of the furniture.

James now had room to paint, Jane had an escritoire for writing, and Charlotte had a view from the window. It was a perfect arrangement for all three of the participants.

As the portrait began, Jane realized that this was going to be a long-term project. James started making dozens of thumbnail sketches of Charlotte, and they laughed and joked as if they had known each other for ages. Charlotte blossomed when James was near, transforming from a slightly spoiled beauty to a warm and caring young woman. James also became more outgoing and a bit less serious. Chaperoning the pair was actually highly entertaining and no chore at all.

The morning passed quickly, and when Aunt Lydia stopped in to see the progress James was making on his sketches, she was suitably impressed. This surprised everyone, including James himself. When Aunt Lydia announced that her Charlotte would sit for him every Tuesday morning until the portrait capturing her glory was completed, Jane thought Charlotte would jump with joy. Unless something unexpected arose, Jane would continue to act as a chaperon. Aunt Lydia was actually tactful enough to turn to Jane and ask, "You won't mind, will you?" Jane readily agreed to the responsibility—for the sake of young love.

Life had settled into an unchanging pattern for Jane. In the mornings, she accompanied Aunt Lydia and Charlotte for endless social calls to gossip, discuss the latest fashions, and drink lukewarm tea. Jane was becoming an expert at sitting and looking ever-so-proper. She had finally realized how to be the perfect spinster in Society: say absolutely nothing and smile weakly. It was rather like being a small child forced to sit in a room with relations that, he didn't know. Her answers to all questions were limited to "Yes," "No," and the ever dramatic "Perhaps." This discouraged further conversation, which was Jane's intention, since she wasn't interested in gossiping about people she didn't know, or worse yet, chatting about fashion. Days were spent talking about ruffles, or shoes, or beaded reticules.

Thankfully, all Jane had to do was sit in the salons and look demure, leaving her free to observe some of the most hideous interior decoration in all of England. If she saw one more Oriental vase or hideous statue she thought she would scream. Each day in Town convinced her that life in Wales was vastly superior and much more . . . normal.

Gwen had a completely different opinion. She went about her meager chores with a smile on her face and a song in her heart. When Jane's curiosity had the better of her, she asked her one morning, "Why are you so dashed happy, Gwen?" in mock irritation.

Gwen bestowed on her a smile that would have put even a beauty like Charlotte to shame. "I've been seeing Charley almost every night. We're even going to meet at the market on my day off," she replied, combing Jane's hair.

Jane smiled at her. At least one of them was having a good time. She was bored to tears most of the time. Except when Lord Blackmoore was around. However, since Charlotte was having her portrait done, Blackmoore was an infrequent visitor to the house. *In fact, I may be able to avoid Lord Blackmoore for the rest of my stay in London,* Jane decided.

Jane was wrong. Aunt Lydia had plans.

Jane and Charlotte presented a lovely picture, alone in the library. Charlotte was gazing out the window, working with her watercolors, while Jane read a novel by Mrs. Radcliffe. Both were lost to the world.

Until Aunt Lydia swept grandly into the room, a magnificent jeweled blue turban perched atop her head. "I have a special outing planned for you both," she announced, sitting on one of the straight-backed chairs.

Charlotte looked up and smiled one of her "I'm an obedient daughter" smiles, while Jane simultaneously thought, *Oh, no.*

"I'm inviting Lord Blackmoore for a picnic. Roger will escort Jane, and I'll chaperon all of you. I know a wonderful place outside of Town that will be perfect," she announced, pleased with herself. If all went right, Blackmoore might even propose to Charlotte that day.

Charlotte looked at her mother calmly and replied, "Please don't be upset if Lord Blackmoore can't attend. You know how horribly busy he is when Parliament is in session."

"Gammon. Blackmoore will jump at the chance to escort you to a picnic. You'll see," she said confidently, smiling at the girls.

"Have you sent a note round to Lord Blackmoore yet?" Jane asked, hoping the unpredictable lord would refuse.

"I'm sending it directly. I thought I'd let both of you know first," she concluded, sweeping out of the room dramatically, leaving a turban feather behind.

CHAPTER NINE

"You know, Richard, if you had any sense, you would offer for Miss Ravenwood before someone else comes up to scratch," the Dowager Marchioness stated calmly.

Blackmoore began to cough violently. "Mother! I am old enough to choose my own bride," he finally managed to choke out, gulping down some sherry.

"Well, you are getting on in years, and the only chit that you've shown any interest in is Charlotte Wyndmere, and she's undoubtedly the most hen-witted chit in Town, so it's obvious you need some direction," the Dowager Marchioness concluded firmly.

Blackmoore stared at her, stunned. His own Mother doubted his ability to find a proper bride. He took another sip of sherry and tried to reason with her. "I'm not going to offer for Charlotte Wyndmere, if that's what you mean. I'm not going to offer for anyone any time soon," he added for good measure.

The Dowager Marchioness folded her hands on her lap, and regarded him calmly. "That's too bad, Richard. Miss Ravenwood is one of the most charming ladies that has come through Town in a long while. Did I tell you that her poultice all but cured the aching in my hands?"

Blackmoore sighed. "Yes, Mother, I believe you have mentioned it several times."

The Dowager Marchioness leaned forward expectantly.

"Is it because she doesn't hold a title? Is that why you're not interested in her?" she pressed.

Blackmoore finally lost his temper. "Mama," he began firmly, "for your information, I don't care if Miss Ravenwood has a title or not. I don't care if she has a fortune, which she doesn't. If you must know, I actually find Miss Ravenwood to be an amiable companion. Now will you quit plaguing me about her!" he demanded, his voice a bit louder than polite company dictated.

The Dowager Marchioness leaned back in her chair calmly. "Why, Richard, there's no need to get upset," she said with a slight smile.

Blackmoore sat in his library and stared blankly at the regal sounding summons for a picnic from Lydia Wyndmere. His black hair was rather unruly looking, undoubtedly caused by continually running his hands through it in frustration. His day was definitely not going well. First the interview with Mother, who obviously adored Jane. Now this: a summons.

As he leaned his large, muscular frame back in the mahogany chair, he knew that he had to attend this picnic. Of course, if he was going to be joined by just Charlotte, Roger, and their mother, that would be fine. Unless he missed the mark, Miss Ravenwood would also be attending.

There was the problem. He never properly apologized to Jane for the episode on the terrace. Or for trying to seduce her. What was there to say? He was four-and-thirty. He should know better. He was a man of the world. He couldn't say that he was overcome by her nearness, or whatever foolish jackanapes said when they were in the throes of calf love. The whole situation was taking on the flavor of a bad novel.

He could still remember the smell of jasmine wafting around her as he held her in his arms on the terrace. The way her tall, lithe form clung to his. The feeling of her soft skin against his lips. Blackmoore sighed.

He got up, strode across the room, and poured himself a glass of claret. He promised Charlotte he'd help her, so he was honor-bound to attend the upcoming picnic, even though that was the last thing that he wanted to do. Because he didn't want another opportunity to insult or molest Miss Ravenwood.

He sipped the claret and stared out the window. He hoped the picnic would be uneventful and he would be able to behave like a gentleman. This was never a problem in the past.

"Charlotte, your wedding is going to be the high point of the Season," Aunt Lydia declared triumphantly.

Charlotte and Jane both stared at her from across the closed carriage. "Mama, Richard hasn't proposed yet."

"Oh, he will, my dear, he will," Aunt Lydia intoned like a sage. "You're a vision of loveliness. Why wouldn't he propose?" she added with a smile.

Jane sighed slightly. Of course, Charlotte did look like a vision in her baby blue morning dress. Her hair was once again done up in perfect ringlets and her skin gleamed like porcelain.

"Mama, did it ever occur to you that I don't want to marry Lord Blackmoore?" Charlotte said recklessly.

Aunt Lydia's mouth dropped open in a rather fish-like manner. "Not marry Blackmoore? Don't be a simpleton. Of course you'll marry Blackmoore," she proclaimed.

The carriage rolled on, and Charlotte tried another tactic. "Mama, I rather think Richard has taken a liking to Jane," she said calmly.

"Of course not," Aunt Lydia replied with a wave of her hand. "He's just trying to be polite."

Jane could recall several instances where Lord Blackmoore was far from polite. But Aunt Lydia would never know.

While Jane was finding London less than enjoyable, Gwen enjoyed the city to its fullest. She had a man in her life and was the picture of contentment.

Each time Gwen had a day off, Charley was there, courting her like a proper gentleman. Well, almost like a proper gentleman.

Their trips to the pub were fairly frequent, since Gwen liked her ale, and blunt didn't seem to be a problem for Charley. Gwen regularly consumed a significant quantity of the frothy beverage, which actually loosened her tongue. Not that she was good at keeping secrets in the first place.

"So how is your miss and her gentleman—what was his name—getting on?" Charley asked ever so casually one night, his eyes riveted on her face.

Charley was a handsome devil, and the more ale Gwen consumed, the more handsome he became. Of course, she wasn't really a proper abigail, so she didn't think twice before replying, "Her gentleman is Lord Blackmoore and they're going on a picnic in a few days. Friday, I think."

"Do you know where they're going?" he asked, then noticing that she frowned, added, "If it's a nice place, I might take you there for a picnic, my girl."

Gwen gulped down her ale. "Don't really know. All of the family is attending, and Lady Stockmorton is chaperoning. It sounds like a grand idea."

"What time are they leaving?"

"At noon I think. I heard one of Lady Charlotte's maids complaining about the time, since Lady Charlotte never gets out of bed until half past twelve. But they're getting up early for the trip," Gwen added, arranging her skirt so Charley could glimpse her shapely ankle.

"So the picnic is nearby?" Charley asked curiously.

Gwen shrugged. "I don't know. But they're returning before supper, so I guess so. They never tell me any details unless I ask, then Miss Jane will let me know whatever I want," she concluded, feeling a bit frisky.

Charley smiled, showing off his remarkably straight teeth. "Then you've got to be askin', Gwennie. How can I take you there if I don't know where it is?" he remarked.

As Charley continued to beam his incredible smile at her, Gwen melted and replied, "Sure, Charley. I'll find out what you want to know," and showed him a bit more of her ankle.

Blackmoore sat rigidly in the office of the Foreign Secretary, waiting for Lord Castlereagh to finish his paperwork before their monthly discussion.

He had been working for the Foreign Office for almost two years now. Drinking, gambling, and whoring bored Blackmoore, so instead of just taking his seat in Parliament, he spoke with Castlereagh. There were a number of nobles who did clandestine work for him, and Blackmoore welcomed the opportunity to serve his country.

The work had been his salvation. His life once again had a purpose, outside of the immediate gratification of the pleasures of the flesh. He completed several very successful missions involving French smugglers in Dover and, when one of the operatives in Paris returned home, Blackmoore all but begged for the post.

The mission was simplicity itself. Generally, he did little more than attend parties, visit cafés, and keep his ears open to what news might come his way. Blackmoore looked more French than English, and blended into society there flawlessly. For about seven months, the project went smoothly.

He had worked with a member of the French aristocracy, Yvette, a stunning widow who disliked Napoleon and all he stood for. They worked as a team, ferreting out information and, when the situation arose, planting selected incorrect documents. Then they became more than a team, and he fell deeply in love with her.

Everything was going smoothly until the day that Yvette told him of a clandestine meeting in a remote part of the country that involved an exchange of documents. All he had to do was intercept the gentleman before his rendezvous, take his place and deliver a false set of papers. He had played the messenger role numerous times before, and never had a hint of trouble. In fact, some of the other operatives claimed that Blackmoore lived under a lucky star.

His luck ran out that night. He delivered the false documents to a group of three Frenchmen, who, to put it candidly, physically beat him to an inch of his life.

As he lay in the cold, damp grass, bleeding from a gunshot wound in his arm and several broken ribs, Yvette appeared from the shadows, laughing at him. She had changed her allegiance.

He could still hear her words ringing in his ears. "Stupid Englishman! You thought I loved you. Ha!" she claimed with a passionate ferocity. "I despise everything you stand for, and I will celebrate your death, English dog!" she laughed viciously, kicking his ribcage. Then, as she left, he was pistol whipped by her cohorts and left to die in the night.

He didn't die. He lived to see another day, and recognize deception in a woman.

Blackmoore was drawn out of his reverie by the sound of the door opening. Castlereagh appeared, holding a sheaf of papers.

"Sorry to keep you waiting. State business and all of that," Castlereagh said simply, as he walked over to his desk and laid down the papers.

"Brandy?" Castlereagh asked cordially.

"Of course," Blackmoore replied.

Castlereagh walked over to a zebrawood table near the window, where he kept his brandy. He poured the amber liquid into two crystal glasses, and handed one to Blackmoore.

Blackmoore smiled and took a sip of the brandy. "Thank you," he said cordially, enjoying the company of the Foreign Secretary. Castlereagh was a brilliant foreign policy man, as well as an understanding friend.

"How have you been adjusting to the civilian life?" Castlereagh asked, relaxing behind his elaborately carved mahogany desk.

"I'm still at loose ends. Being a wastrel is fine when you're young, but I need something more solid to do with my life."

"I might have an assignment for you in the near future. Will that suffice to keep you out of Bedlam?" Castlereagh asked, a smile appearing on his classically handsome face.

"I suppose it will have to do," Blackmoore answered, wishing he could leave London immediately to sort out his thoughts.

Castlereagh leaned forward, folded his hands atop his desk and asked, "Have you been keeping watch on Wilford?" in a grave voice.

"Of course. I don't have any proof against him, but I have been seeing him out in Society more."

"With whom?"

"I saw him one evening talking with an unknown cove outside of White's. It was all very covert looking. Wilford has also been sniffing around a Miss Ravenwood, who is new in Town, and even had the audacity to show up at my Mother's rout," he answered, wondering if Castlereagh knew anything about Jane. "Wilford is still involved with Lady Wilkerson, but I've spoken to her and I can't believe that she has any nefarious motives. The woman in too birdwitted," he concluded.

"Who is this Miss Ravenwood?" Castlereagh asked curiously, jotting down some notes as he chatted with Black-moore.

"She is the cousin of Roger Wyndmere, the Earl of Stockmorton. On his mother's side. Granddaughter of the late Duke of Palmerston. The story is that she's been hidden away in the country. She's a spinster and a bluestocking," he finished, not really pleased with his description of Jane.

"Is she attractive?" he asked, scratching his head.

Blackmoore squirmed in his seat a moment before replying, "She reminds me of Yvette."

Castlereagh stared at him in shock. "In what way?" he asked with a frown.

Blackmoore had an immediate answer to that question. "Something about her doesn't ring true. She's involved in some sort of deception, I just can't put my finger on it."

Castlereagh looked off into the distance, deep in thought. "Is Miss Ravenwood encouraging Wilford?"

"Not particularly. She says she doesn't like Town and wants to return home. Wherever that is. She doesn't speak of her life, but has said she plans to leave here a spinster," he said, knowing that he made Jane sound dreadfully eccentric.

"Why is Wilford pursuing her?" Castlereagh asked.

"I have no idea. Miss Ravenwood certainly doesn't appear to be his usual type of female, and he is most certainly courting her," Blackmoore said.

Castlereagh relaxed in his chair and stared out the window. Blackmoore was silent, since he knew there were moments when Castlereagh needed to sort his thoughts. He simply sipped his brandy and waited.

Castlereagh finally said, "Wilford is rumored to be strapped for funds, although I personally can't find any evidence of that. Perhaps he is hanging out for Miss Ravenwood's blunt."

Blackmoore ran his hand through his hair, making it more disheveled. He frowned and replied, "Miss Ravenwood doesn't have any particular expectations as far as I'm aware."

"Then obviously you don't know very much about Miss Ravenwood. Her father is as rich as Croesus, and has an income of thirty thousand per year. She is quite the heiress, but the family is more than likely keeping it mum to ward off fortune hunters," Castlereagh replied, watching the emotions flicker over Blackmoore's face.

Blackmoore let out a low whistle. Thirty thousand per year made his income seem almost paltry. "Are you certain? I've felt that she's been lying to me since I've met her, but I hardly expected this," his utter astonishment apparent on his face.

Castlereagh frowned and proceeded cautiously. "There are certain aspects of Miss Ravenwood's life that I'm aware of that shouldn't really be public knowledge. They don't have anything to do with her behavior at all, but these issues could have a negative effect on her stay in London."

Curiosity consumed Blackmoore. What was Castlereagh talking about? Why was he being so evasive? "Is she personally involved in any illegal activities?" he finally asked, wondering if Jane was, in fact, a spy.

A merry laugh escaped Castlereagh. "No, I would bet against that my friend. As far as I know she is completely respectable and if she wants to tell you about her life, then that is her choice. I probably shouldn't have told you her financial status."

Blackmoore sighed. "I suppose I'll stop interrogating you then. What should I do about Wilford?" he asked, still amazed that Jane was an heiress.

"Watch him. If he is interested in Miss Ravenwood, then you should be. There is some reason he is after her, and I don't have a good feeling about it," Castlereagh replied, draining his glass of brandy.

Blackmoore slumped a bit in his seat. The entire world

was conspiring to throw him together with Jane, a blue-stocking spinster who continually infuriated him.

"Charlotte, you are simply the most taking creature I've ever seen," Aunt Lydia exclaimed, examining her daughter from head to toe.

To be truthful, Charlotte did look particularly enchanting, her long, golden tresses caught up in elaborate combs that reflected the sunlight. Her blue eyes sparkled against the white walking dress she was wearing, which was enhanced with small, delicate pink rosettes. The entire outfit made her look rather like a bride. It was the exact impression Aunt Lydia wanted to convey to Lord Blackmoore.

Jane sat up in her room, delaying her entrance downstairs. She didn't want to go to this picnic, and would have begged off if Charlotte hadn't pleaded with her to attend. So she lounged on her bed, trying to read, until the very last moment when Aunt Lydia would send one of the servants up to fetch her.

A few short moments later, Jane heard a knock on her door and her stomach did a somersault. It was time for the picnic. "Come in," she called. Aunt Lydia's Friday-faced abigail appeared.

"Lady Stockmorton requests your presence downstairs immediately," the woman said meekly and all but rushed out of the room before Jane could even answer her.

Jane sighed. Fate was not kind to her today. She took a deep breath and slowly made her way down the long, imposing hallway and eventually to the steps, where the rest of the party was waiting for her.

Aunt Lydia, a magenta turban perched on top of her graying hair, had cornered Lord Blackmoore, and was lecturing him intently. Roger was talking to Charlotte, who looked rather blue-deviled. Every now and again, Lydia would look toward Charlotte and frown, obviously unhappy with her daughter's dour mood.

Jane descended the stairs unnoticed, once again feeling like an impoverished relative visiting on sufferance.

"Good, you're here, Jane!" Roger exclaimed, and smiling his boyish smile, bustled her into the Stockmorton carriage where they were joined by Aunt Lydia moments later.

"Charlotte's going to be riding with Lord Blackmoore," Aunt Lydia proclaimed with a wink. "They need some time alone to discuss . . . private matters," she concluded vaguely. Jane could feel the knots in her stomach tighten.

The trip into the country took forever, and Jane gazed out the window, as blue-deviled as Charlotte. As they turned a corner, Jane spotted a hack that was trailing behind them at a discreet distance. Obviously someone else was going into the country for a god-awful picnic, Jane mused.

Aunt Lydia was having a case of the high fidgets. She craned her neck out of the carriage and noticed that Charlotte and Blackmoore were barely talking.

"Roger, why isn't Blackmoore talking to Charlotte?" Aunt Lydia asked in frustration.

"I don't know, Mama, you'll have to ask Richard," Roger answered vaguely.

"What do you mean you don't know, Roger? You're Blackmoore's bosom bow. What's wrong with him?"

Roger sighed. "I don't know, Mama."

Jane continued to stare out the window. This line of questioning went on for the entire trip. Aunt Lydia found out that Roger didn't know why Blackmoore wasn't talking to Charlotte. Jane found out that answer wasn't acceptable to Aunt Lydia, who continued to quiz him fervently.

The small party finally arrived at the picnic site, which was near a modest river that rented small boats. The grass was a lush green, the sun was shining overhead, and the only member of the party who was in a good mood was Roger, who obviously was immune to his mother's interrogations.

Aunt Lydia arranged them on blankets in a small grove of trees near the water, the most romantic spot in the entire area. She directed Roger and Blackmoore to set everything in place with more authority than Wellington himself, and purposely put Blackmoore and Charlotte off by themselves a bit.

They began their meal almost immediately, and Aunt Lydia did most of the talking. This wasn't unusual. Jane decided to try a piece of the chicken, and was astonished to find that it was actually somewhat familiar tasting. Obviously, she had spent her entire life eating London picnic food.

The picnic was something of a disaster. Charlotte was sulking, Blackmoore was distant, and Roger answered Jane in monosyllables.

Aunt Lydia walked over to Charlotte, who was delicately eating a chicken drumstick, and smiled down at her indulgently. "Charlotte, I'd like to have a word with you."

Jane shot Charlotte a look of pity as Charlotte stood up, a horrified look on her face. "Now behave yourselves," she chided, smiling at Roger and Blackmoore.

While Aunt Lydia strode off with Charlotte for a coze, Roger decided it was time to look to the horses, leaving Jane alone with her strawberry tart. She nibbled at the tart and stared at the blanket, hoping to be as unobtrusive as possible.

She was quite startled when Lord Blackmoore dropped down beside her and amiably asked, "Are the tarts edible?"

A small smile crept up on Jane's face as she noticed how handsome he looked in his more casual clothes. Lord Blackmoore certainly wasn't a foppish dandy, she decided, his proximity making her slightly nervous. "Strangely enough they are, my lord," she replied in a very proper tone of voice.

Blackmoore was obviously at some sort of loss. He began to eat a tart, and, unexpectedly, commented, "You know, Miss Ravenwood, you certainly don't act like a proper heiress."

Jane stared at him in horror, almost dropping the tart. Who had told him her financial status? "I beg your pardon?" she managed to say, paling considerably.

At this point, it was obvious that Blackmoore was unaware he made a conversational blunder of momentous proportions. "I said, you don't act much like a proper heiress. They're usually quite stuffy and full of themselves," he replied, looking up at Jane. That's when he noticed that she had turned a rather unpleasant shade of white.

After what seemed to be an eternity, Jane managed to compose herself and asked, "May I ask where you received that information?"

"I have . . . friends in the Foreign Office. One of them knew your mother, actually," he said cautiously.

Jane once again stared at the ground, and replied, "If I'm not mistaken, an heiress in London is usually a female of marriageable age who has a sizable dowry. I have no dowry."

Blackmoore stared at her strangely. "You know your chance of finding a husband will increase dramatically if you let that bit of gossip reach the tabbies."

Her eyes widening most alluringly, Jane stared at him in dismay. "Lord Blackmoore, I certainly don't want a man who would marry me for my money, or for that of my family. I find that idea reprehensible. I'm simply in London to appease my father. *He* wanted me to have a Season. *I* didn't," she said passionately, now rigidly clasping her hands in her lap.

After a long, uncomfortable silence, he said, "Not every man in Town is an unscrupulous fortune hunter."

Jane still looked at the ground, silent for the longest time. Finally, she murmured, "It's difficult when all you have to offer Polite Society is a fortune."

If Jane had looked up, she would have noticed that Blackmoore was frowning at her. Again. "That's flummery if I ever heard it, Jane! You could be the toast of the Town if Lydia stopped treating you like a servant," he said passionately.

Jane looked up at him, convinced that he was only trying to make her feel better. Eventually she softly said, "I would be greatly indebted to you if you didn't spread the news of my . . . finances around Town. Aunt Lydia suggested the idea in the first place, to keep away the many gentlemen in Town who are strapped and need to exchange their title for a woman's fortune."

Strangely enough, Blackmoore was sympathetic to her situation. Mothers had thrown their green girls after him because of his title, and it took years of continually rude behavior to finally stop them.

Before he could reply to her request, Aunt Lydia and Charlotte returned, and Charlotte was suddenly the vision of a woman in love. "Richard, would you favor me with a short walk? There are the most beautiful flowers a little way away that I'd love to show you," she said in a cloying voice.

"Of course, Charlotte, but only for a short time. I'd like to finish off the last tart before Roger gets to it," he said as he got up from the blanket.

Roger returned, sat down next to Jane and muttered "So, do you think Richard is going to fall to his knees and beg for Charlotte's hand?" smiling a bit.

Aunt Lydia lit up and Jane unconsciously frowned. "I don't think Blackmoore would get on his knees, Roger," his mother replied with a broad smile. "Don't you think

Charlotte is going to make a splendid Marchioness?" she asked brightly.

Roger looked into the distance, toward the "happy" couple. "I don't know, Mama. I wouldn't order Charlotte's bride clothes just yet," he concluded in a sage voice.

"Richard, you don't understand the situation," Charlotte said harshly, almost hissing at him.

Blackmoore strolled beside her, not really paying much heed to what she was saying. "What, sorry?" he said, thinking about his talk with Jane. She was the most unusual female.

"Mother expects you to propose marriage to me. Today. Now. What do you plan to do?" she said, turning quite red with repressed anger. Richard wasn't taking the situation seriously.

CHAPTER TEN

Blackmoore stared at her as if she had run mad, his wavy ink-black hair blowing in the breeze. "Propose? I think not. You know I agreed to help you with your artist, but I'm certainly not going to marry you, no matter what your dearest mother says. I'm not going to propose either," he added.

"Well I don't want to spend my life leg-shackled to an ill-tempered recluse either," Charlotte declared, then paused. "I do honestly appreciate all of your help, Richard, but Mama has some sort of maggot in her brain, and now she's practically ordering my bride clothes," she finished breathlessly.

"Don't fret over it, child. Let's just rejoin this debacle of a picnic and I'll do my utmost to dissuade your mother," he replied, walking briskly back to the others.

Charlotte had to run to keep up with him, since her tiny, ladylike steps could not match his long, lanky stride.

Aunt Lydia smiled at the pair as they returned, since they were both smiling. *He's going to make the announcement that he offered for Charlotte,* she thought triumphantly.

Her mouth gaped open as Blackmoore cordially asked, "Miss Ravenwood, would you favor me with your company on a boat ride?"

Before Jane could answer, Aunt Lydia gasped a bit and said "Richard, why don't you take Charlotte? She adores boat rides and would welcome the opportunity to speak privately with you."

Blackmoore smiled at her, a smile that didn't reach his eyes. "Ordinarily that would be a magnificent idea, Lady Stockmorton, but I most certainly wouldn't want anyone to think I was favoring Charlotte over any other young lady, especially her charming cousin," he said smoothly, staring intently at Jane, who once again stared at the blanket.

"Jane certainly isn't a young lady," Aunt Lydia protested, completely shocked by this outburst from Charlotte's future husband.

Once again Blackmoore smiled, a look that quelled the harshness in his features. "Miss Ravenwood may not be a schoolroom chit, but she certainly possesses more intelligence and beauty than they could ever aspire to," he said smoothly. Turning to Jane, he asked, "Would you join me for a boat ride, Miss Ravenwood?" holding out his hand to her.

Jane looked up into his golden eyes, and became extremely confused. He actually seemed to want to go for a boat ride with her. She glanced over to Charlotte, who nodded a bit. "Of course, Lord Blackmoore," she replied, taking his large masculine hand in hers.

Soon they were gliding down the small river, enjoying the view of the English countryside. Blackmoore's gaze never left Jane, and Jane simply stared at the water.

"I'm sorry that I forced you into this, Miss Ravenwood. Your Aunt Lydia is convinced that I'm going to offer for Charlotte. We decided that it was best that I distance myself from her for a time," he said apologetically, his eyes roving over her svelte figure.

That explained this boat ride. She was his escape from the machinations of Aunt Lydia. Of course, she couldn't blame him. She would probably do the same exact thing in his position. "I understand the situation, Lord Blackmoore," she said softly, dipping her hand into the cool blue water as he casually rowed them along.

Much to Jane's surprise, Blackmoore seemed to completely lack conversation. She didn't want to raise his ire, so she remained silent.

Finally, after an interminable amount of time he said, "You mentioned that you're interested in accounts. How long have you been working on your father's books?"

Jane frowned. What a deuced odd question. But at least he was trying to be polite. "For a while. Our tutor gave my brother Jon and me lessons at the same time. Jon had no talent for numbers at all," she explained patiently.

Much to Jane's utter amazement, Blackmoore seemed interested. "It must have been difficult for your brother, having a sister who excelled at numbers."

Jane shook her head, relaxing somewhat. "Not at all. Jon is much more athletic than I am, and he taught me a number of horribly unwomanly diversions."

"Really? Like what?" he asked, a genuine smile on his face.

Talking about her home and family made Jane forget that she was supposed to be a simpering miss. "Oh, Jon helped me become a tolerable card player, how to fence, and of course we've gone hunting." She paused and added, "I don't particularly like to kill anything, so I tend to spend more time in the stables with our horses rather than in the field, actually hunting," she confessed. Jane was so at ease that she was oblivious to the rustling in the bushes, and the figure that watched them intently.

"I don't particularly care for hunting either, which is a great disappointment to my family. You won't tell anyone, will you?" he asked, with a wink.

Jane giggled. "Of course not."

Blackmoore continued rowing, his rather harsh features transformed by his smile. "I've seen you on horseback. Your father must have an impressive stable," he said casually.

"Yes, Papa has a few champions," she replied simply.

Blackmoore wasn't surprised. "You know, I think you're a strapping rider. Most men can't handle Diablo, yet you seem to be perfectly at ease on him," Blackmoore observed, laying down the oars for a moment.

"Oh, Diablo and I have an understanding. I know Diablo wants to run, and Diablo knows that I'll let him run each and every time we go out," she said simply, her eyes shining like veritable emeralds.

Blackmoore gaped at her, his air of indifferent sophistication deserting him. Jane blushed prettily, but said nothing.

"Did you know that you have a faint sprinkling of freckles across your nose?" he asked with a boyish smile.

Jane blushed even more and stared into the murky waters. "Yes, I know. Aunt Lydia insists that I use lemon water to get rid of them, but it's no use," she sighed. "I don't care for bonnets, so I'm plagued by freckles."

"I think they're beautiful," Blackmoore said, and began to lean toward her in the boat. They were in full view of Aunt Lydia, Roger, Charlotte, and anyone else who happened to be looking their way.

As he leaned over, Jane shifted position, and the small boat, which wasn't the most stable in the first place, quickly tipped, hurtling the pair into the chilly waters of the river.

Blackmoore, an experience swimmer and all-round athlete, came up from under the water in a panic. He looked around for Jane frantically, certain she didn't know how to swim.

Jane appeared a few feet away from him, drenched from head to toe, treading water. Her dress made swimming more than a bit difficult, but she could easily make it to the shore. "Jenny! Can you swim?" he called in an urgent voice, swimming towards her.

"Of course," she called, and began to make her way to the shore.

She was soaked when she walked onto the sand, her garments clinging to her in the most revealing way. No one noticed their spill, although they were still within view of Aunt Lydia.

Jane was wringing out her clothes when Blackmoore emerged from the water, rather reminding her of an extremely attractive sea god.

"Are you all right?" he asked, his face etched with worry.

Jane began to think that Lord Blackmoore was indeed a slow top. She was standing on the shore, wringing the water out of her dress. It was obvious she was quite safe.

As she looked at Lord Blackmoore, she noticed that his clothes hid a surprisingly muscular build, clearly outlined for all to see. In fact, Lord Blackmoore looked even more handsome all wet than he did respectably clothed, which was rather surprising.

After staring at Lord Blackmoore for a very long moment, she managed to blurt out, "Of course I'm all right. One of the other things my brother Jon did was teach me how to swim," and continued fussing with her skirts. She heard a rustle in the brush behind them, and, from the corner of her eye, saw the shape of a man. As she turned, the shape disappeared, and she decided that it was just her imagination.

Blackmoore wrung out his sopping wet coat with care, and when he judged it dry enough, placed it over Jane's shoulders.

When she silently looked up at him, her green eyes shining in the sunlight, he could only murmur, "The coat will keep you a bit more covered."

She looked down at herself, and turned a most delightful shade of red. "Gads, I'm quite a sight," she said, walking towards the picnic.

"Yes you are," Blackmoore said softly, trailing after her.

As they neared the picnic site, Jane quietly said, "Aunt Lydia is going to scold me."

On cue, Lydia rushed over to the pair and said, "Jane! What happened to you? Did you overturn the boat?"

Strangely enough, Blackmoore was smiling at Jane. Before Aunt Lydia could say anything more, Blackmoore stepped forward and intervened. "Actually it was my fault. I leaned over to shoo a bug off Miss Ravenwood's shoulder and upset the boat."

Aunt Lydia frowned at the pair, obviously not happy about the turn of events. Jane sneezed and Roger immediately walked over and replaced Blackmoore's wet coat with his. "Let's get you into the carriage, I think we have a blanket we can wrap in. Mama and Charlotte can get our things together and Blackmoore and I can see about the boat," he said, and took Jane over to the carriage and dutifully wrapped her in a blanket.

Needless to say, the trip back to London was less than pleasant. Aunt Lydia began lecturing Jane almost immediately.

"Jane, I took notice of your behavior today and you were much too forward with Lord Blackmoore," Aunt Lydia said sternly.

Jane was still new at the Stockmorton residence, so she didn't know how to answer. So she tried to be honest. "Really? How so?"

"You shouldn't have gone rowing with him. He's Charlotte's suitor, not yours."

"But he insisted," Jane countered.

"And a lady knows when to refuse."

"So I'm not allowed to spend time with Lord Blackmoore?" Jane asked in apparent confusion.

"Not alone. He's Charlotte's future husband."

Jane sighed. "Yes, Aunt Lydia."

"And he's quite above your touch," Aunt Lydia added for good measure.

Jane frowned and stared out the window.

Aunt Lydia then turned on Charlotte. "And you! I gave you ample opportunity to talk to Blackmoore. What happened?

"I don't know, Mama," Charlotte said softly.

"Did you tell him you admired him?"

"Yes, Mama."

"Did you compliment his looks, and his manners?"

"Yes, Mama," Charlotte answered, not looking up form her hands.

"Well, what happened?" Aunt Lydia asked, completely and utterly frustrated.

"I don't know, Mama," Charlotte said softly.

It's too bad that Aunt Lydia doesn't ask me what was wrong, Jane thought, with the hint of a smile. *I know exactly what's wrong with both of them.*

"Gwen, tell Aunt Lydia that I'm not feeling quite the thing today so I'm going to stay in bed. To get rid of my chills," Jane added hastily, sitting at the escritoire, writing a letter to her brother.

Gwen frowned at Jane. She didn't seem the least bit ill. "But Miss Jane, you don't have the chills, do you?" she asked, her blond curls bobbing as she moved around the bedroom, arranging Jane's clothes.

"I feel fine, Gwen. I just don't want to deal with Aunt Lydia and all of her fustian today. So let's just tell her that I have a chill, and I can spend the day up here," she replied simply.

"If you say so, Miss Jane," Gwen replied, and bounced out of the room in search of Aunt Lydia.

Moments later, Gwen appeared. "Miss Jane, Molly tells me that Aunt Lydia and Cousin Charlotte went to visit a Dowager Countess Marston, who is a connection on the other side of the family. They're not expected back until supper."

Jane smiled brightly. "Splendid! We can go out and visit Parliament today. No one will miss us!" Jane said, putting her writing away. She wanted to visit Parliament since she arrived in Town, but no one was keen on taking her. This was the perfect opportunity. Later they would stop at the lending library and tell Aunt Lydia that's where they spent the day.

Before Jane could go any further, Gwen handed her a small letter and said, "Jeffries said this came for you."

Jane opened the letter immediately, wondering who would send her a missive. It was an invitation to go riding next week with Lord Wilford. Since he was an amiable enough companion, and her outings convinced Aunt Lydia that she was being sociable, Jane quickly sat down and penned her acceptance. "Gwen, please see that this will get to Lord Wilford, and then come upstairs directly. I have to find something suitable to wear," Jane said, handing Gwen the note and wandering over to the wardrobe to look over her clothes.

"Yes, Miss Jane," Gwen replied obediently.

Jane continued looking through her wardrobe, disgusted. Everything that Madame Mimette created for her was so . . . frivolous. She had absolutely nothing to wear for a serious outing. Her entire wardrobe consisted of dresses that made her look stunningly attractive and beautifully hen-witted.

She was still looking at her dresses when Gwen returned and suggested, "How about the Bishop's blue walking dress? That would look right spanking for a visit to Parliament."

Jane looked at the dress that Gwen held out to her. It had long puffed sleeves, the neck was very high, and it was gloriously free of all decoration, except for some embroidery on the hem and the sleeves. The blue was so deep it was almost purple, and it was the most serious-looking dress Jane had in London. She would have preferred something in brown or black, but Aunt Lydia almost had a fit of the vapors when she suggested those colors. Moreover, she did have a matching pelisse and bonnet to add to the ensemble.

"The blue dress it is, Gwen," she announced, and, in no time at all, the pair came downstairs.

"Is Cousin Roger about?" Jane asked Jeffries, who looked a bit tired today.

"No, Miss Ravenwood. He's at Tattersall's inspecting some horses," Jeffries informed her stoically.

Jane smiled at him. She liked Jeffries. Gwen said he was always kind to her, and tried to help her fit in with the proper London servants. "I'd like a hackney coach. Gwen and I are going sight-seeing," she explained, and was soon on her way.

The streets of London were crowded, and Jane was glad that they didn't have a long drive. The poor and disabled lined the streets, and it hurt Jane's heart to see such misery. There was nothing like that in Swansea, the largest town near the Abbey. London was a stench-filled abyss that housed the most influential in the nation, as well as the most pathetic.

Gwen, knowing nothing of Jane's thoughts, occasionally commented on whatever sight struck her fancy, from the flowers being sold on the street to a good looking gentleman across the road. Jane knew that Gwen liked the lads and, to her, London was filled with opportunities for a sassy young abigail.

Finally, the hackney came to a lurching halt, and the ladies stepped out in front of the Houses of Parliament.

Westminster Abbey, an imposing structure that loomed above them, overwhelmed Jane from across the street. Before Gwen could comment on any more good looking men, Jane hustled her through the doors, and they were met by an official looking man of about four-and-forty who immediately asked, "Are you interested in a tour?"

Jane frowned a bit. She wanted to see Parliament in action. "Is either house in session today?" she asked, hoping she could at least see the House of Commons debate something.

"'Tis Wednesday. Neither house is in session. However, we do have a tour starting. Are you interested?" he asked, smiling at Gwen, who was grinning cheekily at him. Of course, Gwen smiled at every male above the age of majority.

"Yes, we'd like the tour," Jane replied, and soon they were on the official government tour of the Houses of Parliament. The group was small, and consisted of Jane, Gwen, two elderly ladies with their companions, and a governess with two young boys of about eight and ten. The boys were remarkably well-behaved and listened attentively, as did Jane.

As the group worked their way systematically through the rooms, Jane was deluged with historical information. She wasn't aware that the House of Commons was held in St. Stephen's Chapel, which, the guide informed them in a deathly serious voice, "Was deconsecrated after the Reformation of the sixteenth century."

How does one deconsecrate a chapel, Jane wondered, as they made their way through the halls.

Their guide also went into detail on the construction "Built in the year of our Lord 1050, by Edward the Confessor, later enlarged by William the Conqueror and William Rufus. Richard the Third later rebuilt portions after the dreadful fire in 1512," the guide intoned, rather like a grand Shakespearean actor.

Jane smiled at Gwen, who was mesmerized by the guide. "He belongs on stage, doesn't he?" Jane whispered loudly to Gwen.

Gwen smiled broadly. "He's not hard on the eyes either, is he, Miss Jane?"

Jane grinned. Gwen was nothing if not consistent.

The tour ended much too soon for Jane, who found it

mentally invigorating. Aunt Lydia would definitely have the vapors if Jane ever uttered that particular expression in front of her.

Gwen was chattering on about the guide while they headed for the door, when a familiar voice from behind them said, "Excuse me, Miss Ravenwood?"

CHAPTER ELEVEN

Jane turned and found herself facing Lord Blackmoore, once again dressed in black and looking splendid. His boots were shining black and his coat was obviously cut by Weston. The simplicity of his dress made every other gentleman in view look like preening fop. His wavy black hair, which was once again rather wild looking, gave him the romantic air of a gypsy.

Blushing, Jane all but stammered, "Lord Blackmoore," then lapsed into silence.

Blackmoore smiled at her, his features softening, transforming him into a very boyish looking four-and-thirty. "Good afternoon. Are you here for a tour?" he asked, noticing her smart blue walking dress.

"My maid and I have already completed the tour," Jane said a bit breathlessly.

"I was looking over some papers for a bill that's coming up later next week. Are you expected somewhere?" he asked, his eyes never leaving her face.

Jane noticed that he was studying her intently and she blushed even more. "Gwen and I are on our way to the lending library."

He smiled charmingly at her, and she noticed his nearly perfect white teeth. Yes, Lord Blackmoore was certainly the most attractive man in London. "May I escort you?" he asked in a very polite tone of voice.

Jane's confusion showed on her face. Why was Lord

Blackmoore being so convivial with her? It must be because he knew that she was an heiress, she decided a bit cynically.

While Jane was contemplating her answer and Lord Blackmoore was staring at her intently, Gwen took matters into her own hands. She looked at Jane and said, "It would be ever so nice to have an escort, Miss Jane. I get nervous on the streets and a gentleman would keep away any pickpockets."

The pair looked at Gwen in amazement. Jane's mouth dropped open in shock. Gwen knew better than to be so forward, and almost scolded her. Nevertheless, Gwen was right, and it would be nice to have an escort. They had a few blocks to walk, and it wouldn't be so awful to spend the time with Lord Blackmoore. So she smiled and said, "I fear Gwen is right. We'd welcome your escort, my lord."

They set out toward the lending library, and Jane immediately asked "Are you active in Parliament, Lord Blackmoore?" She was hard pressed not to stare at him, since he was such a commanding presence today, and seemed to stand a head higher than every man on the street.

"I've been active for a few months. I was doing work for the government and returned to England six months ago," he said casually, as if working for the government was the most common thing in the world.

"You're to be commended, Lord Blackmoore," Jane began, smiling at him. "From what I've been able to observe, you're one of the few men of the Upper Ten who are actually doing something useful. Everyone else appears to spend his time gaming and wenching," she said, and blushed. She really shouldn't use the expression "wenching" in front of him.

"You amaze me, Miss Ravenwood," he began as they continued down the street. "I've never had a woman commend me for taking my place in the government. Most of the time I'm chided for not attending enough social events," he replied.

A slight frown creased her brow. "London is a very curious place, my lord. The members of society are more interested in the latest scandal than the welfare of the less privileged. I find it rather sad and pathetic," she said harshly, shocked that she was so outspoken with him.

Blackmoore stared at her for a very long time as they walked, and Jane knew that something was bothering him. She knew she should tell him that she was from Wales, but Aunt Lydia was certain that letting that fact be known would put an end to her meager social life. She also knew that if Aunt Lydia found out she let her secret slip, she'd scold her until the end of time.

It was Gwen who brought their minds back to the matters on hand. "Miss Jane, look behind us near the hackney," she said in a very loud whisper. "That looks like Charley, my beau."

The trio turned around in unison and saw a handsome young man casually standing near a hackney. When he noticed that they saw him, he ducked into the nearest storefront.

Jane frowned. That was certainly strange, Gwen's current boyfriend ducking into a shop like that without even saying hello.

Blackmoore was frowning. He turned to Gwen and asked, "Are you sure that was Charley?"

Gwen blushed a bit. "I'm not quite sure, my lord. If it was, wouldn't he have said hello?" she asked.

"That would have been the proper thing to do," Blackmoore replied, still frowning. "Have you been seeing him for a long time?" he asked, much to Jane's surprise.

"A while, my lord," Gwen said very properly.

"He looks somewhat familiar to me. Does Charley know Lord Wilford?"

"I don't think so, my lord."

"What does Charley do?" he quizzed.

Jane was astonished. Blackmoore was interrogating her maid.

"I don't rightly know, my lord," Gwen answered, a little chagrined.

Before Blackmoore could come up with another question for Gwen, they found themselves on the steps of the lending library.

Jane turned to Blackmoore and said, "Thank you for your escort, Lord Blackmoore," and stepped into the library.

Strangely enough, he followed her and replied, "I don't have any pressing engagements myself, so I thought since I was here that I'd pick up something for myself. Then I could escort you and your abigail home."

Blushing, Jane replied, "Thank you," and the trio walked into the book-filled building.

A short while later, Lord Blackmoore found Jane in a small section of the library that he had never visited. She was reading a small volume and didn't even notice him.

"Have you found something, Miss Ravenwood?" he asked, wondering what she could be reading.

A look of alarm filled Jane's eyes and she snapped the book shut. Before she could thrust the book back onto the shelf, Lord Blackmoore asked, "May I see what book kept you so enraptured?"

Jane reluctantly handed the book to him, panic filling her eyes.

Blackmoore stared at the title in amazement, then began to flip through the pages. Miss Ravenwood was certainly full of surprises. "I didn't know that you were interested in Welsh poetry, Miss Ravenwood."

Jane frowned. She was obviously the queen of all bluestockings. "My lord, you know I'm the veriest quiz. Yes, I'm interested in Welsh poetry. Actually I'm fascinated by any number of obscure topics, which Aunt Lydia has told me is terribly shocking," she replied, a blush staining her cheeks.

Blackmoore's golden hazel eyes never left her. "It isn't particularly shocking at all," he said in a gentle voice.

They stood in the narrow aisle for a long time, just looking at each other. Finally Blackmoore said, "Are you ready to head back to the Stockmorton residence?"

"Lord Blackmoore, there's no reason you have to accompany us home. I'd be more than grateful if you just procured a hackney for us," Jane said calmly. "In fact, Aunt Lydia would probably have another seizure if she saw us alone and treat me to another dressing-down for trying to steal Charlotte's future husband," she said, walking toward the front desk.

Her statement stunned Blackmoore. Lydia actually thought he was going to marry Charlotte? What gammon!

As Jane checked her books out, he softly said, "I'm not going to marry your Cousin Charlotte."

Jane raised an eyebrow. "Tell that to Aunt Lydia. She's convinced that you're going to make Charlotte a marchioness."

The trio walked outside, and before he hailed her a hackney, he said, "I have a message from my mother. The poultice you recommended to her has all but worked miracles. She wanted me to thank you."

Jane lit up like a beacon in the night. "I'm so glad. A few of our tenants have the same problem as my father, and I was able to help them, too. They can't afford a proper doctor, so they're more willing to try something different," she finished breathlessly. Jane immediately forgot all of Aunt Lydia's lessons on how to be a proper young lady.

Blackmoore smiled back at her, definitely impressed with her concern for the people that lived on her land. If more landowners were conscientious about their workers, there would be much less civil unrest.

A hackney appeared out of nowhere, and Jane and Gwen found themselves leaving Lord Blackmoore. Before he shut the door he took Jane's gloved hand and lightly kissed it. "Thank you for your company today, Miss Ravenwood," and shut the door, watching them drive off toward Grosvenor Square.

As he briskly walked toward Bond Street and his tailor, he wondered about the enigmatic Miss Ravenwood. He knew that she was still hiding something from him, but he couldn't fathom what that might be. Certainly he had shown her in the past few weeks that he could be trusted and that he appreciated her straightforward demeanor. Of course, it probably didn't help that he was constantly trying to take liberties with her either. But she was a dashed beautiful woman, someone who possessed charm and intelligence. It was quite a mystery to him that some lucky buck hadn't already married her. Obviously all the men in her part of the country were complete flats. Of course, their loss was definitely his gain.

Life went smoothly for the next few days. Jane avoided the morning calls, and Blackmoore avoided Charlotte, much to Aunt Lydia's chagrin. In fact, Aunt Lydia and Charlotte were on one of their morning calls when Jeffries found Jane in the library and handed her a missive from her father.

As Jane read the letter, all of the color drained out of her face. There was no possible way this could be happening, she thought in anguish.

"The most wonderful news, Jane,"

her father wrote in his rather rambling and distinctive scrawl.

"The Earl of Pembroke was visiting Swansea with his daughter, and Jon met her at one of the assemblies,"

he began, making her head reel. Since when did her brother attend assemblies? Or dance? Or even appear interested in respectable young ladies?

The letter continued,

"To sum it up, they have become engaged and are planning to marry in the winter. Pembroke is actually in favor of the match, says his girl has been sought after by too many titled fortune hunters. I've invited them to live with us in the Abbey, and they've accepted."

The paper shook in Jane's hand as she held it. This was the most inconceivable circumstance. Jon and his new wife were probably going to move into the Abbey with her father. Jane would be displaced as the mistress of the house. Jon's new wife would naturally assume all of the household responsibilities, leaving Jane as an interloper in her own home. *I have to think up some course of action,* Jane decided in a panic. *I can't stay at the Abbey once Jon is married. That would cause too many problems, which no one needs,* she decided with a very serious frown.

Jane's heart was in her throat as she finished the letter

"Have you thought about your own plans? Things will be changing now that Jon is betrothed.
Enjoy London, love, Papa."

Things were going to change. *What a vast understatement,* Jane thought, completely at a loss.

Holding the letter in her hand, Jane went slowly up to her room, feeling a tiny bit sick to her stomach. Too many things were changing since she came to London, and she certainly didn't like it one bit.

Jane spent the morning pondering her situation. Her first and only idea was to set up her own establishment near the Abbey. It was something of a drastic solution, and it wasn't something that respectable ladies did, at least not in Wales. She needed some input, so she decided to tell James and Charlotte about the situation during their weekly portrait session.

After the lengthy explanation of why she couldn't still live in the Abbey, a situation Charlotte couldn't quite understand, Jane announced her solution. "I'll set up my own establishment," she said with more confidence than she felt.

James and Charlotte exchanged a meaningful glance, and Charlotte replied, "You know that's not really quite respectable, Jane. You'll need a companion."

"Nonsense," Jane replied, dismissing Charlotte's concern. "I'm of a certain age and don't need any type of companion."

Charlotte shook her head, her blond ringlets bouncing prettily. "Jane, it just won't do. It's not quite the thing."

"But Charlotte, it's the best solution of all. I'll have a place of my own, and Jon's new wife will take her place at home at the Abbey," Jane said, as if she was trying to convince herself.

James wasn't convinced. "I say, Miss Ravenwood, I'm sorry to speak out of turn, but Charlotte is right. Respectable women don't set up households alone in England," he said in a firm voice.

"Ah, but you see, James, I'll be in Wales, not in England," Jane concluded triumphantly.

"I don't think so, Jane. Isn't there another relation you could live with?" Charlotte asked curiously.

Jane sighed audibly. "Only Great-uncle Aubrey, and he's a bad-tempered recluse."

"You could always stay here," Charlotte suggested, much to everyone's surprise.

"I would love to stay here with you, Charlotte, but your mama is a bit much for me to take," Jane admitted.

That made James smile broadly, and the hint of a smile even appeared on Charlotte's beautiful face. "Yes, well, Mama takes a bit of getting use to, I suppose," Charlotte admitted.

Jane smiled weakly. "You see, I've found the only solution there is," Jane said, once again in a firm, convincing voice.

No one was convinced. However, Jane went ahead with her plans nonetheless.

"Your brother is marrying Lady Anne Pembroke, how absolutely delicious! You never hinted to me that this was coming about, you naughty minx," Aunt Lydia chided with a grin, most possibly the happiest woman in England. "Your side of the family is going to be aligned with the Upper Ten once again; this is the best news possible for you, my dear!" Aunt Lydia exclaimed, in alt.

Jane was not in alt. Her features were a bit more pale, and she looked like anything but a naughty minx. She felt like an aging spinster that no one wanted anymore. She sighed a bit and said, "I gather that it was a rather unexpected betrothal. I knew nothing about it until my papa wrote me," she said, delicately nibbling on a tea biscuit.

Aunt Lydia digested that bit of information. "Do you know where the happy couple will be residing?"

"In the Abbey. With Papa," Jane answered curtly.

"So Pembroke's daughter will become the new lady of the house," Aunt Lydia mused.

"Yes," Jane replied unhappily.

"So what are your plans, Jane?" Aunt Lydia inquired, her high state of jubilation dampening some.

Jane had no plans. Not any real concrete plans. However, she had ideas. So she simply replied "I'm going to set up my own establishment," to see what Aunt Lydia would say.

Aunt Lydia got up and began to pace the parlor. "That won't do, Jane. Spinsters, even those who have companions, are considered fast if they have their own establishment. No, that won't do at all, and I know your father won't approve. He certainly wouldn't want everyone in the area thinking that you're a woman of loose morals," she concluded dramatically.

"Why would they think that? I'm still the same person, I'd just be living somewhere different," Jane countered, hoping to persuade Aunt Lydia to her position.

Aunt Lydia was adamant. "It won't do, Jane, and that's final. I'll be writing your father and brother a letter of congratulations, and you, my dear, had better start looking for a husband. Is Wilford coming up to scratch?"

Jane groaned slightly. "No, Aunt Lydia, I don't expect him to offer for me," she said blandly.

A frown once again appeared on Aunt Lydia's brow. "If Middlemarch is in town, I'll see if I can arrange an introduction. He's still a good catch, even though he is two-and-fifty," Aunt Lydia concluded, sweeping out of the room.

A very audible groan escaped Jane's lips. A man of two-and-fifty! He was older than her father. Aunt Lydia was no help at all, she decided, becoming more blue-deviled by the moment.

Hyde Park was awash in riders who were doing much more socializing than riding, but Jane was oblivious. Lord Wilford was babbling about some thing or another, but she couldn't focus on his words. Jane was actually so preoccupied with the news of her brother's upcoming nuptials that she actually rode out on Buttercup, Charlotte's very docile mare.

Wilford, looking rather foppish in a striped green waistcoat with numerous fobs, could tell something was amiss. "I say, Miss Ravenwood, you seem out of sorts today," he said innocently, his voice filled with concern.

The frown deepened on Jane's forehead. Yes, she was very out of sorts. How much should she tell Wilford? He was only an acquaintance, but he could have another idea. In the end, she simply told him the truth. "I just found out my brother is going to be married in the winter, and I need to make some sort of living arrangements for myself."

Wilford looked at her intently. To each and every rider in the Park, he was the picture of concern. "May I ask your plans?"

Jane stared at the horses and the riders, all so carefree. She wasn't carefree at all. She had the veritable weight of the world on her shoulders. "I'd like to set up my own establishment, but Aunt Lydia says that's scandalous," she admitted with a sigh. She sighed a lot lately, she realized.

Jane glanced over at Wilford. He actually looked genuinely concerned, she realized. Maybe she did have another friend in London after all.

They rode a while in silence. Jane wished she had chosen Diablo to ride. He was a much more spirited mount than Buttercup, and she would have had to concentrate on her riding. One didn't have to think when riding Buttercup; one just spurred her on occasionally and Buttercup ambled forward listlessly.

Wilford had a solution that Jane didn't consider. "Do you have an old governess you could contact? They're usually quite helpful in these kinds of circumstances," he said.

Her eyes lit up. "Why, I never thought of Miss Bridgeson! She's the perfect answer. Thank you ever so much,

Lord Wilford, I'm going to write to her immediately," Jane replied, suddenly in a much more jovial mood.

"If you like, I'll frank the letter for you when you're ready to contact her, so you don't have to involve your family," he said, in a tone of voice that was almost uninterested.

"I wouldn't want to inconvenience you, Lord Wilford. I'm sure Roger wouldn't mind mailing it for me," she replied, somewhat surprised by his generous offer.

He shrugged. "I know your aunt is a high stickler, so she may get upset that you're contacting your former governess and realize that you're planning to stay with her for a time," he observed.

He was right. Aunt Lydia might have the most awful taste in clothes, in furniture, and in food, but she wasn't stupid. She would see through Jane's plans immediately. "You're probably right," Jane admitted.

"Why don't you just let me frank the letter for you so your relations don't have to be involved at all," Wilford suggested in the most mild of tones.

Something about what Lord Wilford was suggesting didn't sound quite right, but Jane couldn't put her finger on it. Aunt Lydia could very well forbid her to visit Miss Bridgeson, so it might be a better idea to hand her correspondence over to Lord Wilford. "You're probably right. I'll send the letter over to you when I've written it, if you don't mind," she finished, her voice tinged with uneasiness.

"That would be fine, Miss Ravenwood. Once you get it to me, I'll send it out posthaste. I know you're anxious to hear from your . . . Miss Fridgeson."

"No, it's Miss Bridgeson," Jane quietly corrected as they headed home. "But thank you very much for your help." Jane still didn't understand why he wanted to help her so much, but he did appear to be trying to be her friend, so she didn't want to refuse.

* * *

The next few days were very quiet for Jane. Aunt Lydia was still miffed that Jane was determined to set up her own establishment, and not concentrate on getting married. Both ladies stayed in their respective bedrooms, both suffering from the vapors.

After two days of basically sulking in her room, Jane woke up at dawn and realized that she would go mad if she spent one more moment indoors. She was feeling reckless and decided to take Diablo for an early morning ride.

Fog enshrouded the Park as she rode in the near darkness, the sun inching up into the sky. She was preoccupied, and didn't hear the horse approaching her from the rear.

"Good morning, Miss Ravenwood," Lord Blackmoore said, bringing a large white stallion beside her.

Jane looked over at him in surprise. He was the last person she expected to meet in the Park. In addition, every time she saw him he had a beast more magnificent than the last. He obviously had the best stable in all of London.

"Good morning, Lord Blackmoore. That's a noble bit of horseflesh you're riding this morning," she commented, noticing how wild his hair looked in the morning. He obviously had not run a comb through it, and it made him look rather dashing.

Blackmoore smiled easily at her. "This is Neptune. I like to keep an extensive stable when I'm in Town," he said, patting Neptune fondly.

Jane said nothing, thinking how regal he looked atop the white charger. *Lord Blackmoore would have made a jolly good knight in shining armor,* she thought, glancing casually over at him.

As they walked through the Park on their respective mounts, Blackmoore asked, "Is something bothering you, Miss Ravenwood?" he asked, seeming actually concerned.

Looking into the grayish mist, Jane decided she might as well tell him the situation. Goodness knew everyone else knew of her dilemma. "I received a letter from my papa. My brother is getting married," she stated simply.

"My felicitations. Is this a sudden betrothal?"

"Very much so. He is engaged to Lady Anne Pembroke, the daughter of the Earl of Pembroke, and my father asked them to live with him. They said yes, of course," she said, wishing she could ride Diablo off into the mist forever.

"Have you met Lady Pembroke?" he asked curiously.

Shaking her head, she replied, "Not at all. They were visiting the area and I suppose it just happened. Lord Pembroke is agreeable, since my brother is also as rich as the Golden Ball. Apparently Lord Pembroke spent an entire Season warding off fortune hunters, so he's happy with the match," she said dispiritedly.

Blackmoore nodded slightly. "I know Pembroke and his daughter. I believe she's in her second Season, and is a very charming young lady. She has red hair and a lively disposition. In fact, she's rather like you, except not quite as bookish," he finished, and Jane groaned inwardly. She always enjoyed having handsome men call her "bookish."

"Once they're married, Lady Pembroke will become the mistress of the house, so I'm planning on setting up my own establishment," she said quickly, before he called her an heiress or a spinster.

They continued through the Park and he asked, "Are you planning on staying with another relative?"

"No. I'm going to write my former governess in Cornwall. I know I can't stay at home any longer," she said in a desolate little voice.

"Have you spoken to your father?"

Jane stared at the trees and the flowers, but didn't notice the rider in the distance, watching them. "No. I've talked to just about everyone else, though. Lord Wilford is the person who suggested contacting Miss Bridgeson," she said, waiting for his lecture on how she shouldn't associate with Lord Wilford.

Thankfully, he spared her that particular lecture. Instead, Lord Blackmoore, as curious as Lord Wilford, focused on her impending trip. "Are you going alone to visit Miss Bridgeson?" he asked casually.

"No, I'll take Gwen with me. I certainly won't leave her alone in London or send her off by herself. She'll definitely be accompanying me," Jane said firmly, wondering why Blackmoore was so interested in her plans.

"Are you staying until the end of the Season?"

Jane shrugged. "I suppose. Aunt Lydia is trying desperately to find a husband for me, and Papa would be disappointed if I came home early."

They continued to navigate their mounts through the early morning mists, watching the sunrise over the lush, green trees.

Finally, after a long silence, Blackmoore said, "I hope you feel you can call on me if you have any sort of trouble, Miss Ravenwood. And I do wish you would call me Richard."

If Blackmoore would have been paying more attention, he would have noticed the slight blush that stained her cheeks. Aunt Lydia would definitely not approve of Charlotte's beau calling her, the spinster cousin, by her Christian name. "I'm sorry, my lord, but I couldn't call you by your given name. It would cause too much fuss, especially with Aunt Lydia," she said regretfully.

Blackmoore smiled brilliantly at her. "If it would bother your aunt so much, then I'll be sure to address you as Miss Ravenwood in public. That doesn't mean we have to be so formal in private," he replied in a very persuasive tone.

Jane relented without much of a fight. She had already begun thinking of him as Richard, so there could be no harm in calling him by his first name. "I suppose that would be all right, Richard," she replied, blushing even more.

He favored her with another dazzling smile, one that Jane was certain had stopped the hearts of many young ladies.

"You'll find, Jenny, that I usually get my way in most matters," he said with a very definite dash of arrogance.

Jane continued looking forward, afraid that if she looked at him she would blush even more. Jenny. Where did that come from? No one ever called her Jenny. "May I ask why you insist on calling me Jenny? I've always been simply Jane," she replied, wondering what cock-and-bull story he would create to appease her curiosity.

"No one ever called you Jenny before? You must be from a singularly backward family, since almost every female in England named Jane is called Jenny by her close family," he replied, walking toward the gates with her, Jane's groom trailing behind.

If she were English, she would be a Jenny. But she wasn't. She was Welsh and a simple "Jane." She smiled at him, amused by the endearment. "If you insist on calling me Jenny, I suppose I can accommodate you," she said, a warmth spreading throughout her body. She was certain that he liked her. Or else he had monumental gambling debts and planned to borrow some blunt from her.

She was enjoying her newfound camaraderie with Lord Blackmoore so much that she hadn't realized what was happening. He became more cordial at exactly the same time he found out she was an heiress.

"Oh, Jane, Mama is never going to permit me to marry James," Charlotte wailed, completely oblivious of the rest of the patrons of Almack's.

Jane surveyed the room. Thankfully, no one, most especially Aunt Lydia, noticed Charlotte's impassioned outburst. "Charlotte, you know very well that this is not the proper time or place to discuss your problems with James," Jane gently scolded.

Charlotte's eyes glistened with unshed tears. She looked

even lovelier than ever. "But, Jane, Mama is continuously plaguing me! All she talks about is the day I'll become a bride to some lord or another; I don't think she even cares who it is, as long as he has a title," Charlotte blurted.

Jane frowned. She knew that once Aunt Lydia got an idea in her head, she was as tenacious as a bulldog. Thankfully Mr. Middlemarch was suffering from some sort of awful ailment, and wasn't seeing visitors, or Aunt Lydia would have already been posting the banns for Jane's wedding. Oh yes, Jane knew about Aunt Lydia's stubborn streak. "Have you talked to Roger about the situation?" she asked the now delicately sniffling Charlotte.

Charlotte shook her artfully dangling ringlets. "No." Sniffle. "But I know that Roger likes James, he's spoken with him several times on his way out of the house after one of my sittings," Charlotte explained.

Jane noticed those moments, and it was a good sign. But then again, Roger was incredibly cordial to everyone, and one of the most popular men in Town and at home, with the servants. As Charlotte sniffed discreetly into her handkerchief, Jane glanced over at Aunt Lydia, who was seated across the room. She was engaged in what appeared to be a very intense conversation with one Lady Thornhill. From what Jane heard, Lady Thornhill was quite the gossip.

It was scant moments after Jane spied Aunt Lydia and Lady Thornill that Lord Bilkinshire, a rather squat, spotty fellow, strolled over, lemonade in hand.

"I say, Miss Ravenwood, would you care for a lemonade?" he asked, holding out the glass to her.

Jane frowned. Bilkinshire had all but ignored her after he found out her age. "No, thank you," she replied, puzzled.

"Might I claim a dance with you later, then?" he asked, cordially.

"Of course," Jane replied, frowning a slightly.

Lord Bilkinshire made his exit, and Lord Filmore appeared. He was tall, thin, and rather gangly. And also rather let in the pocket.

"I say, Miss Ravenwood, I was wondering if I might call on you this week," he said in the most amiable of tones.

Jane frowned. He had never even bothered to speak directly to her when she met him in the Park with Roger. "Perhaps next week, Lord Filmore, my schedule is rather tied up," she said mildly.

And so it progressed. The ever-so-proper lords that wouldn't even speak to her in the Park, or in Aunt Lydia's sitting room, were now paying court to her.

Jane found out the reason when she was going back to her seat after a particularly lively reel. A group of men in their cups were chatting a bit too loudly. And she heard the dreaded words: "Stockmorton's cousin. Quite the heiress." It explained everything.

A long while later, after Jane decided to placate Aunt Lydia by dancing several reels with several completely ineligible men, Lord Blackmoore arrived. He had no idea what compelled him to attend the Marriage Mart that night, and scanned the crowd for someone he knew. He thought Roger might be about, with one of his adoring chits, Charlotte and the delectable Jenny. As he scanned the room, he noticed the most attractive woman standing near a potted palm, talking earnestly with an elderly man. Her emerald silk gown was completely unadorned, except for the Grecian style gold braid at the neck and sleeves. Her skin was glowing, and her hair was the color of the sky on a stormy night. She stood as erect as a soldier, and when she turned and laughed, it was as if someone had landed him a facer. The goddess was none other than Miss Ravenwood. The on-the-shelf spinster cousin. He began to part the crowd, heading her way, without even realizing that he was doing so.

* * *

Jane saw Richard the moment he entered the room. That wasn't any particular feat, since he stood a head taller than almost every man in the room.

Being a veritable giantess, she also towered over most of the ladies in the room, so watching the door wasn't a problem for her. When she saw him gazing about the room, her heart leapt in her chest. Maybe he was looking for her. Before she could really take hold of the idea, her common sense broke in and asked: why would a handsome titled lord be interested in an aging spinster whose only benefit was a hefty purse? As far as she knew, he wasn't let in the pockets, unless he was incredibly discreet about his debts. That was probably the answer. The only reason he sought her out was because he needed money.

Major Something-Something, who had a habit of mumbling, retreated rapidly when he saw Blackmoore approaching, leaving Jane alone.

"Good evening, Jenny. You're in fine looks today," Blackmoore commented, eyeing her green silk dress.

Jane blushed. He looked absolutely regal in his black coat, gleaming Hessians, and white silk cravat. He towered over every man there and made the rest of the male patrons look like costumed, foppish boys. "Thank you, my lord," she replied, then corrected, "Richard."

He smiled at her, which made almost every dowager in the room take notice. Lord Blackmoore rarely showed up at Almack's and didn't spend much time chatting with anyone other than Charlotte Wyndmere. Yet here he was, smiling at her rich cousin as if she were Venus. It was all very unusual.

"May I see your dance card?" he asked very properly, deciding he must waltz with Jane.

She blushed. "It's quite astonishing, Richard. I appear to be rather popular as a partner today."

Blackmoore felt a stab of jealousy. "Really?"

"Oh, yes. Perhaps it's because Aunt Lydia has made it public that I'm an heiress," Jane stated simply.

Blackmoore was dumbfounded. "She hasn't."

"Unfortunately she has. Aunt Lydia appears rather desperate to fob me off on someone, and I just wasn't taking. I rather think this was her last resort," Jane added bluntly.

Blackmoore was stunned. "So I suppose you're going to be deluged by fortune hunters," he said with an edge to his voice.

Jane sighed. "Of course. But it's well known that the food at the Stockmorton residence doesn't agree with me, so I'll be able to avoid most of them," she added with a small smile.

Blackmoore favored her with a smile that illuminated the room. "You must promise me at least two waltzes, and let me get some lemonade for you, since this place is like a hothouse."

"All right," she softly murmured, wondering what had caused Lord Blackmoore to act so . . . cordial toward her. It was most unusual, she mused, as he sauntered off to get her lemonade.

Blackmoore was at the very crowded and very paltry refreshment table when Roger appeared.

"Richard, what are you doing at Almack's?" Roger asked casually, getting himself a glass of lemonade.

Blackmoore smiled a bit, and replied, "I promised my mother that I'd attend tonight, and you know that she'd hear about if I didn't. I knew you were attending tonight, so I thought it would be an ideal evening."

"I noticed you were talking with Jane," Roger commented, in the most casual of voices.

"Yes."

"Mama is trying to find a match for her," Roger commented.

"Why?" Blackmoore asked curiously.

"Her brother is getting married. Won't be mistress of her house anymore. Needs a husband," Roger said.

"And so your dearest mama has decided to try and sell her to a fortune hunter?"

"So you heard."

"Yes. Why did your mama make public that Jane is an heiress?" Blackmoore asked moodily.

Roger frowned. "Why? She's dashed old. Mama has tried to curb her tongue, but the chit has opinions about everything. Tends to be headstrong. Reads too much. Mama thought it would help Cousin Jane find a husband," Roger concluded.

Blackmoore raised an eyebrow sardonically. "Your cousin Jane doesn't simper and is quite the entertaining companion. She'll find a husband in her own good time," he concluded.

Roger sighed. "That could take an eternity, Richard. Mama did the right thing. Now that some of Jane's finances are known, she'll get to meet more eligible men and her problems will be solved," Roger explained.

Blackmoore tugged at his perfectly tied Waterfall. "Roger, I would take it personally amiss if you encouraged Jane in a relationship with someone who was less than top of the tree," Blackmoore advised.

That caused Roger to frown. Severely. "Jane's not your problem. She's ours," he stated simply.

"Roger, Jane is definitely not anyone's problem, and I certainly don't appreciate the fact that you're treating her like some poor relation that needs to be sent away at the first possible moment. She's a charming, intelligent young woman and any man would be lucky to call her his wife," Blackmoore declared dramatically.

A look of shock spread across Roger's face. "Of course,

Richard," he said, and watched in horror as Blackmoore took a glass of lemonade over to his now very eligible cousin.

The rest of the evening was like a dream to Jane. Blackmoore stayed at her side almost exclusively throughout the evening, charming her with his amusing anecdotes on society. They waltzed in perfect unison and were undeniably the most handsome couple in the room.

The dream ended abruptly when Jane inadvertently heard some of the dowagers gossiping; "Blackmoore's paying court to the Stockmorton heiress, he must be let in the pockets," one woman mused. Another was less tactful. "Blackmoore must be so tired of the opera singers and Cyprians that he's moved on to seducing ape leaders," another dowager, dripping in jewels, speculated. Jane was horrified.

Jane tried to erase their cruel words, but they kept running through her mind over and over again. The only real reason Blackmoore was paying any attention to her was that he felt sorry for her. Or needed money.

So when he bid her adieu and gently kissed her hand, Jane knew that every eye in the room was on her. And it was. She knew that there was no possibility that Blackmoore was interested in being anything but her friend. Or possibly borrowing some ready to stave off the moneylenders.

The drive home was exceptionally quiet. Charlotte was the one who finally broke the oppressive silence. "Did you enjoy yourself, Jane?"

Jane looked out into the London night. *If only I had remained stubborn and defied my father, I'd be home right now,* she thought wistfully. "Yes, I had a nice time, Charlotte. It was very kind of Lord Blackmoore to whisk me away from the . . . suitors I now seem to have acquired," she finished, feeling very blue-deviled.

"Jane, you must defer to my better judgment," Aunt

Lydia intoned. "You know you didn't take, and you can't set up your own establishment, so I had to drop a few hints about your father's income."

Charlotte frowned at her mama and turned to Jane. "If Richard didn't want to dance with you he wouldn't have," she said softly.

"Charlotte, he's an old friend of the family. He was just trying to be . . . helpful," Jane concluded, hoping they would get home soon so she could cry herself to sleep.

"Jane, Charlotte is right. If Richard didn't want to spend time in your company, he wouldn't," Roger said simply.

Jane remained silent, thoroughly confused by Lord Blackmoore's actions.

"And would it be possible for me to join you in Cornwall for an extended visit?"

Jane wrote in her very precise handwriting.

"I know you've invited me dozens of times, and I've cried off. I'm in London right now, and the journey isn't so far. Please let me know your immediate plans,"

Jane concluded.

That should do it, Jane thought, as she signed her name to the missive. Lord Wilford is a godsend. Miss Bridgeson will more than likely rejoice at the thought of a visit from Jane, and that would give her time to figure out a permanent solution to her problem. Jane sealed the envelope and headed out to the kitchen.

Jane found Gwen giggling with a crowd of servants, eating some pastry.

"Gwen?" Jane said softly, not really wanting to interrupt her abigail's lunch.

Gwen sprung to her feet. "Yes, Miss Jane?" she said in her most proper voice.

"Please come out to the hallway, I have something to discuss with you."

Gwen followed Jane out into the dark hallway, frowning slightly. "Is something wrong, Miss Jane?"

Jane glanced at the letter in her hand. "Not at all, Gwen. I have an errand for you to run. I need you to take this to Lord Wilford; I've written his address on the envelope. Do you think you'll be able to find it?"

Jane handed her the envelope and Gwen studied it. "Yes, Miss Jane, it's not far from where I meet my man Charley for an ale," she said lightly.

"Good. If you leave now, you can be back here before supper," Jane said calmly.

"Of course, Miss Jane."

"And, Gwen? No one in the household needs to know about this letter," Jane added cautiously.

"Yes, Miss Jane," Gwen replied obediently, sauntering down the hall.

Well, it's done, Jane thought with a sigh.

"Release my daughter at once, you blackguard!" Aunt Lydia shrieked, as she glared at Charlotte in the arms of her artist.

Lydia was purple with rage, and her mustard colored turban toppled to the ground, unnoticed.

Charlotte was visibly trembling when James released her, but she didn't back down from her formidable and enraged mama. "Mother, it's time you know. James and I have been seeing each other for a few months now, and we plan to be married."

Before Charlotte could explain further, and as a vein popped in Aunt Lydia's forehead, Jane stepped into the room, innocently munching on one of cook's scones. She was the next victim of Aunt Lydia's very considerable wrath. "You! You were supposed to chaperon them and stop this from happening, you encroaching little nobody. I never should have invited you into my house!" she shouted, her temper running amuck.

"Mother, Jane has nothing to do with this," Charlotte said resolutely, glancing at Jane.

Without uttering a word, Jane retreated to a corner, turning a bit pale. Her eyes moved from Charlotte to James, but she held her tongue as Aunt Lydia continued her tirade.

James was the next target. Aunt Lydia looked at him and shrilled, "YOU! I want you out of my house this instant! And you will never see my daughter again!" she yelled, her face now bright red.

James looked from Charlotte to Aunt Lydia and back again, without saying a word. Aunt Lydia was in a white-hot rage, and appeared to be on her way to an apoplexy. He silently began gathering his paints together.

Aunt Lydia turned to Charlotte. "You will stay in your room, reading the Bible until I call you for an interview," she commanded, motioning to the door.

"But, Mother . . ." Charlotte entreated.

"Now," Aunt Lydia said in a frightfully loud voice, and Charlotte and James both skittered out of the room like frightened puppies, with Jane in tow behind them.

Jane sat quietly in her room, reading. She locked her door; she didn't want to talk to anyone at all. *If only Jon wasn't getting married, I'd go home right this instant,* she thought, trying to concentrate on anything but the present situation. The words blurred in front of her eyes, and she began to feel even more despondent. Her own flesh and blood didn't even care for her.

A small rap came on the door, and Jane heard Charlotte say in a loud whisper, "Jane? It's Charlotte. Can I come in?"

Jane sighed, walked over to the door and unlocked it.

Charlotte stole into the room, closing the door silently behind her.

"Molly says that Mother is having an episode and is sleeping. She had to be given some laudanum to calm her nerves," Charlotte explained.

Jane studied Charlotte. Her eyes were red from crying, and she looked more pale than usual. It was obvious to the entire world that she was quite upset. "Are you all right?" Jane asked quietly, wondering what plans Charlotte had.

Charlotte sat down on the bed and stared at her hands. "I wish I knew. If Papa were still alive, he'd set things straight," she replied softly, despair written on her features.

Jane sat down on the bed next to Charlotte, and patted her delicate hand softly. "You'll see, Charlotte, everything will turn out fine," in her most reassuring Welsh minister's voice. "Did you talk to James?"

"Just for a moment," Charlotte said, a tear slowly trickling down her pale cheek. "He . . . he said Mama is a Bedlamite!"

Jane had to stop herself from smiling. Aunt Lydia was acting like a Bedlamite. But she was certain that Charlotte didn't want to hear that fact.

"What am I going to do?" Charlotte wailed, the tears falling freely down her cheeks.

Jane sighed. "That's a very good question, Charlotte," she replied in a resigned voice.

Across Town, Blackmoore sat once again in the Foreign Office with Castlereagh, discussing his current assignment. His mission was to observe and collect information on bootleggers outside of Dover, which was, in Blackmoore's mind, simplicity itself. Blackmoore would be away for three days, and he welcomed the chance to do something that would occupy his mind. Lately he had found himself daydreaming about Miss Ravenwood, of all people, and that could not be healthy or normal.

"Are you clear on all the details?" Castlereagh asked, frowning at Blackmoore, who was staring vacantly out the window.

"Details?"

Castlereagh shook his head a bit. "Yes, the details for the mission. Do you need any more information, or do you have any questions?"

"No, no questions about the job. I was wondering though, have you spoken to Pembroke lately?" he asked, looking intently at Castlereagh.

"Pembroke? Isn't he in Wales, looking at coal mines?" Castlereagh replied, a puzzled look on his face.

For one brief moment, Blackmoore's mind spun, then came to a dizzying halt. Everything now made sense. Jenny's strange accent. It wasn't French, it was Welsh. The book of Welsh poetry she was reading in the lending library. *That's why Lydia wouldn't talk about her background,* he realized with a start. No one of any consequence was Welsh and connected to trade. That's why Lydia was so vague with talk about Jane's fortune.

Blackmoore leaned back in his chair ever so slightly and said, "I found out this week that Miss Ravenwood is quite the heiress. And it appears she's Welsh as well. Is her father in trade? Coal mines perhaps? Is that her secret?" he asked, wondering if Castlereagh would admit the facts.

Castlereagh ran his hand through his straight blond hair, his agitation very apparent to Blackmoore. "Who told you about Miss Ravenwood?"

Blackmoore relaxed and smiled slowly. Obviously, that was the bit of information Jenny was terrified to let anyone know. As if he would care that she was Welsh and involved in trade. That was tame compared to some of the scandals in his family history. "Her aunt is trying to buy her a husband. In addition, Miss Ravenwood told me her brother is marrying Pembroke's daughter. I just inferred the rest," he answered simply, a wave of relief coming over him. Jenny wasn't some traitorous doxy with a child born on the wrong side of the blanket; she was Welsh.

A small sigh escaped Castlereagh. "I forgot you're a bit quicker than some of our other operatives. Yes, you're right, she's Welsh and her father owns a number of mines outside of Swansea, among other things. He's quite the nabob, but I didn't want to tell you the rest of the facts since Miss Ravenwood obviously didn't want her background known around Town."

Blackmoore smiled easily at him. "I've been acting like a sapskull for weeks," he admitted. "I thought she was working for Napoleon. Or trying to embezzle money from Roger. Or a half dozen more scandalous ideas I'd rather not admit," Blackmoore said with a wry smile. "And, in the end, her grand deception is that she's Welsh and connected to trade! What a glorious letdown," he concluded.

"But those pertinent facts would shut the door at some of the better residences, even though she is the grand-daughter of a Duke," Castlereagh countered.

"True, but we both know that the *ton* is filled with complete half-wits. And I know that it doesn't matter to me that she's Welsh and connected to trade," Blackmoore finished with a tinge of passion in his deep voice.

Frowning, Castlereagh still had one question. "Why is Wilford hanging about her though?" he asked, sipping his brandy.

"I have no idea. I just hope he isn't up to anything nefarious, or he will have to face my wrath," Blackmoore stated succinctly, making Castlereagh take notice.

As both men finished their brandy, Blackmoore couldn't take his mind off Jane. Or her connection with Lord Wilford.

"But Jane, I can't let Mama control my life any longer," Charlotte proclaimed in a wavering voice.

Jane paced the room. This was quite a fix. Charlotte was ready to pack her bags and travel to Gretna Green this very night. It was only Jane's attempt at logic that held her to the house.

"Charlotte, you don't want to do anything rash," she said calmly, feeling the hypocrite, since she wanted to bolt home immediately and escape Aunt Lydia's tantrums.

"There must be someone who could help me," Charlotte wailed, her dainty upper lip trembling in consternation.

"Charlotte, just try to have a good night's sleep and we'll talk about it tomorrow," Jane advised calmly.

Inspiration struck Charlotte. "I know! You can write a note to Richard. He'll know what to do," Charlotte said brightly.

Jane frowned. Why should she write to Richard? Why couldn't Charlotte write her own letters? "Charlotte, Lord Blackmoore is a busy man, and I honestly don't know what he could do," Jane reasoned, pacing the room.

"Jane, Richard's been a friend of the family for years, and he's always helped me out of one scrape or another. Like the time I was caught in the rain in the Park without a bonnet or an umbrella."

"This is much more serious than being caught in the rain, Charlotte," Jane said rationally.

The tears began anew. "Oh, Jane, you just don't understand. Would you please write Richard for me?" she implored passionately.

"Charlotte, why don't you write to Lord Blackmoore? You know him much better than I do," Jane stated flatly, her head beginning to throb.

Charlotte waved her hand. "I'm much too upset to write a letter. You'll write Richard and ask him to come to see me immediately, won't you? Please?" she asked in a pleading voice, making Jane feel incredibly guilty.

Jane sighed. "I'll send him a note later today," she conceded, wondering why she bothered to get involved in the entire situation.

* * *

Blackmoore began his journey to Dover, strangely uninterested in the entire affair. He actually wanted to talk to Jenny and let her know that he didn't care where she lived or how her family came about their vast fortune. Her Aunt Lydia was wrong when she thought everyone would judge Miss Ravenwood harshly, and it was obvious that Jenny wasn't happy with her deception.

This is going to be a very long journey indeed, he decided, watching the sun sink on the horizon.

"My dear Lord Blackmoore,"

Jane wrote, and crumpled up the piece of paper. This was not a simple task, she decided in frustration. She had tried writing Blackmoore a note several times, and each time she put her thoughts to paper they sounded contrived and witless.

Finally, completely frustrated, she forced herself to write the most direct letter possible.

"Lord Blackmoore,"

her letter began,

> *"Charlotte's deception with James has been discovered and she has asked me to contact you. Please call on us as soon as possible.*
>
> > *Your servant,*
> > *Jane Ravenwood,"*

she finished, stuffing it into an envelope. *Blackmoore isn't going to be able to help at all,* Jane decided, angry for agreeing to bother him. However, Charlotte was adamant, and she did promise.

Jane rang for Gwen, and moments later her ever cheerful abigail appeared, a ready smile on her face. "Yes, Miss Jane?"

"I want you to personally take this to Lord Blackmoore's residence," she directed tensely, handing the letter over to Gwen.

Gwen stared at it reverently. "Is everything all right, Miss Jane?" she asked curiously, her eyes never leaving the missive in her hand.

"Charlotte and Aunt Lydia have had a disagreement, and Charlotte wanted me to write Lord Blackmoore for her. She thinks he'll solve all of her problems, but I have my doubts."

A short time later, Gwen appeared on the doorstep of Lord Blackmoore's very elegant house. A very starchy old butler greeted her.

"You should be using the servants' entrance," the elderly, disagreeable man said, standing to his full height and looking mightily superior to Gwen.

Gwen would not be deterred. "My lady has a note for Lord Blackmoore," Gwen said, holding her chin high.

"I'll be sure he receives it when he returns home," the butler intoned, haughtily looking at the letter in his hand.

Gwen decided she didn't like Lord Blackmoore's stuffy butler. He never smiled and seemed to think he was better than all the other servants in Town. "You'll see that he gets it as soon as he gets home? It's very important," she added, hoping this rude man would indeed deliver the message.

The butler stared at her. "Of course. As soon as he returns," he concluded, slamming the door in Gwen's face.

Gwen was halfway home when she realized that she didn't know when Lord Blackmoore was due to return home.

CHAPTER TWELVE

Jane managed to avoid the household until supper. Then she found herself alone with Roger, since Charlotte and Aunt Lydia were too stubborn to leave their respective rooms.

"I hear that I missed quite the drama this morning," Roger commented, filling his plate with some sort of horrible, grayish meat.

Jane stared at the meat in horror, and decided to concentrate on the braised asparagus. That didn't threaten her existence like the grayish meat had in the near past. "Yes, Aunt Lydia was quite upset," she commented, washing her food down with a glass of claret.

"I hope Mama didn't blame you for any of this. When she loses her temper, she tends to vent her wrath on anyone who happens to be near. So if she offended you, I do apologize," Roger said carefully.

Jane sighed. "I understand. I just feel sorry for Charlotte. I believe she does have a genuine tendre for James, and nothing her mother says is going to change that."

Roger attacked his meat enthusiastically. "The strange thing is that I like James. It's too bad they couldn't work something out," Roger noted, helping himself to another plate of gray roast meat and congealed gravy.

"At one point Charlotte thought that Lord Blackmoore could help her," Jane said cautiously, drowning the taste of her food with the claret. When she got back to the Abbey, she was going to make sure cook got an increase in her salary.

"Charlotte has plagued Richard with favors ever since Papa died. Seems to think he's her knight in shining armor," Roger commented, helping himself to another glass of claret. "Blackmoore's a busy man. Can't rely on him for everything," he said simply.

Jane nodded her head in agreement. Lord Blackmoore was definitely too important to help an old friend in need.

Charlotte was desperate. Blackmoore didn't answer her summons, and her mother wouldn't let her out of the house alone. Or with Jane. Therefore, she resorted to desperate means.

Before Roger went out for the evening, Charlotte cornered him in the library.

"Roger, you have to help me," she pleaded, her eyes welling up with tears.

Roger tugged at his cravat and frowned. "Charlotte, I don't want to be involved in this fracas with Mother. You shouldn't have been embracing James in the first place," he admonished.

"But Roger, I love James," Charlotte confessed, her tears flowing like a river of despair.

Roger got up from his seat and began to pace the room as Charlotte wept. After an interminable silence, he said, "Charlotte, I have no objection to James at all. He seems to be a nice enough cove. If you want to marry him, I certainly won't stand in your way," he said with a sigh.

Charlotte continued to cry. "But James won't marry me till his finances improve. And Mama will disown me," she wailed.

Another sigh escaped Roger as he sat back down and faced his errant sister. "What would you like me to do Charlotte?"

"Could you go see James? And talk to him? Please?" she pleaded.

Roger considered the idea for a moment. "All right. Maybe we can sort out this mess. Hate to see you so blasted miserable," he added.

The tears slowly stopped, replaced by the hint of a smile. Perhaps there was hope for Charlotte and James.

The next afternoon, Roger sat on the small chair in the dingy white office, watching James pace in front of him.

"I never wanted it to come to this," James said in a desperate tone. "Unless I get a patron, I would never even consider marrying Charlotte, and she knows that," he finished, obviously distraught over the situation.

"If it makes you feel any better, I don't have any real objections to the match. Of course Charlotte would have to live more economically, but you could live well off her allowance," Roger said in a level tone of voice.

"I won't live off a woman," James declared passionately, holding his chin high.

Roger stared at the dust on the floor, unsure of his course of action. Finally, he said "Why don't you just stay away from Charlotte for a time, until my mama calms down. Then we can discuss things."

Frowning, James replied, "I don't want to abandon Charlotte right now, but I fear that it's the only logical solution for now. Will you tell her that I send my love?" he asked, his voice rife with despair.

Roger smiled and stood up to leave. "I'm sure we'll eventually get this mess sorted out," he said in a voice that projected much more confidence than he actually felt.

Dinner was once again a private affair between Jane and Roger. The menu offered poultry that Jane guessed might be pheasant, with a creamed vegetable that was possibly carrots. Jane wasn't sure. She devoured the carrots and drowned the taste with her port. She never drank this much alcohol at home, but it was a necessity in Town, since the food wasn't to her liking.

"Talked to James today," Roger mentioned, eating his dinner with zeal. "He has more character than most of the bucks in Town."

"What did he have to say?" Jane asked curiously, pushing the meat around on her plate. Gads, the food was horrible tonight, she decided.

"Won't marry Charlotte till he gets a patron. Doesn't want to live off of her blunt."

"Did you make any plans?" Jane said, hoping that dessert was edible.

"I told him to keep out of sight for a while, until Mama gets over her episode. Then we should be able to reason this out," he said without much conviction.

"I hope you're right, Roger," Jane said, thinking about her own impossible situation. Miss Bridgeson must write soon, or she would certainly go mad, she mused, finishing her glass of port.

"James won't be coming to see me for a while?" Charlotte said in a pathetic little voice from her chair in the library.

Jane sat in a chair next to her and Roger paced the room. Actually, it wasn't proper for Jane to be embroiled in such a Cheltingham tragedy, but Roger insisted that she was present when he spoke with his sister. "For moral support," he explained.

"Charlotte, that's the best idea. Hopefully your mother will become. . . accustomed to the situation, and then you can make your plans," Jane said logically, as Roger fixed himself a rather large glass of brandy.

"But, Jane, I'll wither away and die if I don't see James," Charlotte said dramatically, a tear running down her slightly flushed cheek.

"If you insist on seeing James, and Mother gets wind of it, she'll send you off to the country to rusticate," Roger pointed out.

Charlotte's eyes widened in horror. "Mother would never do that! Not at the height of the Season!"

"I wouldn't wager against it. Mother is quite miffed, my dear," Roger said calmly.

"And wouldn't it be better to be in Town and not see James instead of being in the country without him?" Jane added for good measure.

Charlotte sighed. "I suppose. If only Richard were here, he'd know what to do."

"Charlotte, Richard has his own life, he doesn't need to be dragged into our intrigues," Roger said harshly.

"Roger is right. This is something you have to handle yourself," Jane chimed in.

Charlotte sniffled. "Richard will eventually come and help me, I know he will."

I wouldn't wager on it, Jane thought cynically, utterly disillusioned with the handsome lord.

Alone in the comfort of his study, Blackmoore freely admitted that he was glad to be home. The mission was simple and had come off quite well, but he had other things on his mind. He planned to meet with Castlereagh the next day after a good night's rest. *Then maybe I'll visit Mama,* he decided with a smile. *There were a few decisions that I made under the night sky in Dover that she would be interested to hear.*

He was still ensconced in his study, sipping his port, when Harris arrived in the room, carrying the salver that held his messages.

Blackmoore looked up at the retainer that had been a member of his household since he was a child. "Anything interesting happen while I was gone?" he asked, smiling.

He was rewarded by a small smile from Harris, which was an achievement. Harris was the most serious of servants, and had no discernible sense of humor. He was kind hearted but gruff, and Blackmoore knew it would be impossible for him to adjust to another household.

"Yes, my lord. A cheeky young wench came by not long after you left, bearing a message from her mistress. She requested that I bring the note to your attention immediately," he said, handing Blackmoore the note from Jane.

Blackmoore was stumped. Who would send a maid with a note? Something was certainly amiss, which he confirmed when he read the note. He could tell that Jane was at her wit's end, and had to restrain himself from going to their house immediately. He had been unaware of her message for three days. Now it was after eleven, and he most certainly couldn't call at such a late hour. *Jane must be beside herself,* he thought with chagrin, *since I've left her high and dry.* He'd guarantee that Harris didn't tell Jane's maid that he wasn't in Town, since he gave explicit directions that no one was to know he was leaving London. Gads, what a bramble.

"Sir, you cannot enter the house and search for Miss Ravenwood. She is not at home to callers," Jeffries intoned with a frown. It was apparent that Blackmoore would not take no for an answer, and Jeffries was frail. And old. No one could expect him to stop the strapping Lord Blackmoore.

Blackmoore smiled gently at him and replied, "Don't worry, Jeffries, I'm just going to speak with Miss Ravenwood for a moment. Would she happen to be in the library?"

Jeffries looked at the floor, and coughed slightly. However, he said nothing.

Once again, Blackmoore smiled. "Thank you," he said simply, and headed down the hall.

Jane was alone in the library, perched on a rather large and rather uncomfortable brown chair, reading the latest novel from Mrs. Radcliffe. It was a tolerable gothic and it did succeed in taking her mind off the myriad problems she was facing. She thought she heard the door open, but must be mistaken. The library was the least-used room in the entire house, so it was unlikely that anyone was visiting it.

"Good morning, Jenny," Lord Blackmoore said, coming up beside her.

Jane all but jumped out of her chair in surprise. "Lord Blackmoore. Who let you in? I am not at home today," she stated firmly, trying to stare him down.

He smiled benignly at her. Jane blushed when she realized that she was wearing her oldest and most unattractive high-collared brown muslin dress. *All I need is a mob-cap!* she thought in horror. *Then I'd pass for a dowdy governess,* she thought with a blush.

"Of course you're at home, you're here, aren't you?" he said with a smile.

Jane didn't reply.

His eyes swept over her body, and, much to her chagrin, he had to comment. "That's quite a dowdy dress. Are you trying to frighten off suitors?" he asked, his hazel eyes dancing with mirth.

Jane stood up and strode purposely to the library door and opened it. "I'm sorry, Lord Blackmoore, you must leave. I do not wish to speak with you," she said dramatically, her whole posture reflecting her hostility.

Of course, with that order he sat down and crossed his

legs. "You know, you're frightfully beautiful when you're angry, Jenny," he remarked calmly.

Jane could not fathom this mood at all. Lord Blackmoore was the most vexing man! So she sighed and simply sat down on the chair next to him. "Since you're obviously not going to be a gentleman and leave, may I ask the reason for your visit?"

Once again, Blackmoore smiled, his entire countenance transforming into that of a carefree young lad. "I'm here to answer your summons. You did ask me to come by to talk about Charlotte's situation."

"I really don't want to speak of it now. Perhaps you could have helped a few days ago, but not now. Thank you for coming," she said, her voice laced with anger. "You may leave now," she added, waving her hand toward the door.

Blackmoore laughed heartily. "Jenny, you make a duchess look like a peasant. 'You may leave now.' That may work for the callow youths that hang about Charlotte, but I certainly won't be summarily dismissed," he said firmly. "Now, what is the problem? I would have come sooner, but I was out of Town."

Jane walked across the room and stared out the window and commented, "No doubt tending to one of your mistresses, while poor Charlotte was waiting for your help," she said recklessly.

"I was certainly not visiting a mistress, for goodness' sake! How dare you imply such a thing," he retorted, following her over to the window and staring at her.

"Then let me guess. You were on a secret mission or some such flummery. Isn't that the popular thing for men to say when they're unavailable?" she replied, angry that he would deny having a mistress. From what Aunt Lydia said, every man in London had one, if not more, and she was convinced that Blackmoore had a woman somewhere. Or perhaps more than one.

Blackmoore's anger flared. He grabbed her shoulders harshly and turned her to face him. "If you must know, I was doing some work for the Foreign Office. It's all very classified, but if you doubt my word, you can ask Roger. He also is involved in certain activities. If I had been in Town, I would have been here earlier," he finished, staring into her luminescent green eyes.

"You work for the Foreign Office?" she asked in a small voice, wondering if he was lying.

He eased his grip on her arms, and pulled her closer to him, so they were almost embracing. "Yes. That's how I found out you're an heiress. The Foreign Secretary, Castlereagh, knew of your family," he said in a soft voice, his eyes searching hers.

A feeling of despair washed over Jane as she looked down at the floor. If he knew of her father, he knew everything else. Castlereagh probably told Blackmoore the rest as well, she realized in horror.

Blackmoore gently took her chin in his hand and forced her to look up at him. "And yes, I know you're Welsh and that your family is in trade. And Castlereagh didn't tell me, you did," he concluded mysteriously.

Jane frowned. "No I didn't. Aunt Lydia would banish me from London if I ever admitted that I was from Wales. How did you find out? "

His smile was as gentle as a summer breeze. "I deduced it when you told me your brother is marrying Pembroke's daughter."

She broke away from his grip, and crossed the room, sitting back down on the chair. "Aunt Lydia told me Society would undoubtedly reject a spinster from Wales who was connected to trade. I had no choice," she said in a very soft voice.

Once again, Blackmoore amazed her. He walked over to Jane's chair and sat down next to her, his hazel eyes glimmering with something she couldn't define. He softly replied, "I wouldn't care if you were a demi-rep with a child born on the wrong side of the blanket. Your status in Society means nothing to me," he proclaimed in a husky voice.

She looked up into his golden hazel eyes and really wasn't sure if he leaned toward her or not. Once again, she found herself entwined in his arms, his lips moving fervently over hers. They were both so lost in their passionate embrace that they did not hear the door to the library creak open.

Roger strolled into the library, looking for Richard. Jeffries informed him that Blackmoore had shown up in search of Jane, and would not accept her pat answer that she was not at home. According to Jeffries, Blackmoore was in the library alone with Jane, where they had been for an inordinately long period of time.

When Roger spotted Jane and Blackmoore locked together in a lover's embrace, his mouth dropped open. Roger's suave and debonair friend was embracing his dowdy cousin. And not only was he embracing her, but he was practically treating her like a bird of paradise in his library. Roger simply stood dead in his tracks, gaping like a sapskull.

Finally, after the shock wore off, the gallant in Roger won out. "Unhand my cousin," he ordered loudly, in his most authoritative voice.

Jane and Richard sprung apart as if they had been doused with cold water. They looked guiltily at each other, and Jane turned a deep shade of red.

"Jane, please leave the room," Roger asked, tugging at his cravat. Jane scurried out quickly, her eyes cast to the floor in shame.

Roger studied his friend, who had walked over to the window and was obviously composing himself. There was a long pause before Roger finally said, "So, Richard, am I going to have to call you out?"

Blackmoore turned around and faced him, his face a mask. "You wouldn't call me out, Roger. You know I'm a much better shot than you are," he answered calmly.

Roger frowned. "It won't do, Richard. As her nearest male relative, I have to provide her some sort of protection," he said, tugged even more at the cravat that was choking him.

Blackmoore shrugged. "What would you like me to do Roger?" he asked in a voice filled with resignation.

Roger began to pace the room. "I don't know, Richard. I'm not going to demand that you marry her. I suppose an apology will have to suffice. I'm having enough problems with Charlotte. I don't need to add to my worries," he said.

A slight sigh of relief escaped from Richard. "I'll send my apologies," he said calmly. "Now what's going on with that scapegrace sister of yours?" he asked, changing the subject neatly.

"Wants to marry James. He needs a patron. He won't marry her until he can support her. Not much else to tell," Roger finished, falling into a large, overstuffed chair.

Jane paced in her room, her agitation quite apparent. *Richard obviously thinks I'm open to some sort of flirtation,* she thought in horror. *He undoubtedly thinks of me as some sort of loose screw that he can trifle with, and who is he to blame? I've behaved abominably,* she mused, almost regretful of the time she spent in his arms.

Aunt Lydia told her repeatedly that she was on the shelf, and that no eligible man would be interested in a bluestocking of her advanced age. Yet, their longtime friend was interested, but Jane was certain that marriage wasn't on his mind.

So she sat down at her escritoire, and began a letter to

her papa. It was time to tell him that she was planning a visit to Miss Bridgeson as soon as she received a reply from her former governess. In fact, she wrote her papa that she was probably going to stay in Cornwall for an extended visit. *Until I can set up my own establishment. And forget Lord Blackmoore,* she added mentally.

Blackmoore paced his mother's sitting room, still agitated from the events of the morning. He let Roger think that the episode with Jane was a once in a lifetime occurrence that was meaningless. That was far from the truth. However, he didn't want Roger to know his plans.

His mother was perched expectantly on a lavishly carved rosewood armchair, waiting for his news. News that he told her would be important. Finally, after an interminably long silence, her patience ran out. "You have something to tell me, Richard?"

Blackmoore stared out the window, not really noticing the variety of English flowers in full bloom. He dreaded telling his mother the news. *She has so many ambitions for the family, and now I'm going to crush every one of them,* he mused. But she did have to know, so he began gradually. "Do you remember Miss Ravenwood, Lord Stockmorton's cousin? You met her briefly at our rout." he said, his brow furrowing into a frown.

"Yes, of course. The charming young woman with the poultice. Is she in some sort of trouble?" she asked, a look of concern appearing on her classical features.

"No, why do you ask?"

The Dowager Marchioness paused for a moment apparently thinking over what she was going to say. Finally she commented, "I'm sure Lydia doesn't want this known about Town, but her niece is half Welsh and connected to trade. I thought someone might have found out and was causing trouble for her," she said softly.

Blackmoore's jaw dropped open. "You know? How did you find out?" he demanded.

"Maria Sefton knew her mother, and I just asked a few people the right questions. Miss Ravenwood is also quite well off. It's not too difficult to find information, if you know whom to ask," she concluded in a sage voice.

Blackmoore was stunned. "You amaze me, Mother."

She smiled softly and never took her eyes from his face. "And now you're going to tell me you're going to offer for Miss Ravenwood, but you're certain I won't approve."

Blackmoore chuckled as he strode over to the chair and sat down next to her. "You're exactly right, Mama. How on earth did you know? It's not something that I've even discussed with Miss Ravenwood."

"Gads, Richard, I'm not as cork-brained as you think. I know about the incident at Almack's, and I know about the argument you had with her at Drury Lane. I also know you were closeted with her in our library during my rout," she concluded triumphantly.

"Have I been that obvious?" he asked, a slight blush staining his tanned cheeks.

Thankfully, his Mother decided to let him keep the remnants of his dignity. Finally, after another long pause, he asked, "Will it bother you so much if I marry Miss Ravenwood?"

The Dowager Marchioness smiled enigmatically. "How long have my hands been bothering me?"

"Years," he replied, utterly and completely confused.

"And in that time, no one in Polite Society asked about them. Except my physician. People in the *ton* care only about themselves, you see," she explained simply. "And then, the first time I met your Miss Ravenwood, she noticed my fingers were twisted. And tried to help. That's when I knew you should marry her," she concluded softly.

Blackmoore beamed at her. "Thank you, Mama. I would

have proposed to Jenny regardless of your answer, but I appreciate your support."

The Dowager Marchioness stared at him for a long while, her eyes sparkling with mirth. "I know. The question is, will Miss Ravenwood have you?"

Blackmoore turned away, almost blushing. "I really don't know. I plan on writing her father this afternoon."

The Dowager Marchioness smiled. "You know Richard, you could make the most spectacular match in Town if you wanted, but I'm sure that you would drive most of the milk-and-water misses insane within the first six months of your marriage. Strangely enough, I don't think your Miss Ravenwood is in that category," she concluded.

Blackmoore smiled hesitantly. "Jenny is quite the handful and will make a splendid marchioness. Undoubtedly the tabbies in Town will be aghast at her connections, but she cares less about Society than I do, so I don't foresee any problems," he finished, anxious to get the letter off to Mr. Ravenwood.

"I hope for your sake it does go smoothly, Richard," the Dowager Marchioness commented.

Blackmoore got up and paced the room again. There was something else he was going to ask his mother about, but he couldn't quite recall what it was. His eyes fell on the picture of his great grandfather, and the request popped into his head. "Mother, I know of a talented artist who is looking for a patron. Do you know of anyone who might be interested?" he asked, wondering if his mother could save Charlotte from an elopement.

His mother frowned at bit, and appeared to be deep in thought. "I'll ask around. Is this artist actually talented, or just someone you want to help?" she asked directly.

Another smile appeared on Blackmoore's striking face. "A bit of both. I'd act as his patron myself, but I'm sure that he would think it was charity," he finished, hoping there was someone who could help James and Charlotte. They certainly deserved a chance at happiness.

"Dear Mr. Ravenwood,"

Blackmoore began, staring at the piece of paper. *My handwriting is dreadful,* he thought, crumpling up the paper and starting over.

"Dear Mr. Ravenwood,"

he began again.

"I've come to admire your daughter Jane and I think she holds me in similar regard."

Perfect, except that Blackmoore had no idea if Jane cared for him or not. He crumpled up the paper.

He started again.

"Dear Mr. Ravenwood.
I'm writing to request permission to address my suit to your daughter Jane,"

he wrote, then crossed it out. Egads, this was tedious work, he thought in dismay.

He was having a dashed difficult time, so he tried a different tactic. *What does Jane's father want to hear from a prospective son-in-law,* he wondered, pen in hand. *If only I could tell him I loved his daughter and didn't want any of her money. And that I won't beat her, or keep a mistress. That might quell any fears Ravenwood might have,* Blackmoore decided. But it would be terribly crass and ill bred to write any of those sentiments.

Therefore, he began again.

"Dear Mr. Ravenwood.

I'm writing to inform you that I plan to ask your daughter for her hand in marriage. Although she has reached the age of majority, it would be my greatest wish to have your approval. I have no need of Jane's portion, and upon Jane's acceptance, will have my solicitor contact your solicitor to discuss the marriage settlement.

> *Your servant, Richard Hughes,*
> *The Marquess of Blackmoore,"*

he concluded, and sealed the envelope.

It was done. *I hope that her father doesn't think I'm a fortune hunter out to dupe Jenny,* he thought, a weight lifting off his chest. *Now all I have to do is ask Jenny,* he thought with a smile. Jenny. My beautiful half Welsh Marchioness.

CHAPTER THIRTEEN

Jane stared at the letter from Miss Bridgeson with mixed emotions. On one hand, she wanted to leave London and all of the problems that it represented. On the other, she had become rather enamored of Lord Blackmoore, rake that he was, and knew she would miss his company.

Miss Bridgeson was going to send her carriage for her as soon as possible. *How odd,* Jane thought with a frown. Miss Bridgeson never even rode in a closed carriage in the past, since she routinely got sick in them. But, closed carriage or not, at least Jane would be putting an end to this farcical Season that her papa insisted upon, and that was a relief. She was deuced tired of pretending she wasn't from Wales and that she was a proper lady who was frivolous, uneducated, and completely useless. *It will be nice to be myself for a while, and Miss Bridgeson will help me until I sort out this mess,* Jane thought with a sigh.

For the first time in days, supper was a family affair. Aunt Lydia and Charlotte joined Roger and Jane, and Aunt Lydia began the meal by announcing, "We won't be speaking of the unfortunate incident that occurred with the artist. Life will resume as it was before, or there will be dire consequences," she predicted, staring at Charlotte.

Roger sipped his claret. "May I ask what these dire consequences may be, Mama?" Roger asked, a mischievous smile on his face.

Frowning fiercely at him, Aunt Lydia replied, "Certain members of the family would be sent to visit Aunt Honoria." Charlotte gasped audibly, and gazed down at her plate of indefinable meat.

Jane looked questioningly at Roger who grinned at her and whispered, "Aunt Honoria is a Methodist and spends most of her time contemplating the Bible. She's rather fervent about religion, you see," he concluded, and Jane realized that a visit to a woman of that ilk would make Charlotte a candidate for Bedlam in no time.

"We will also be attending a masquerade at Vauxhall Gardens at the end of the week. I thought you might enjoy that, Jane, since it will be different from any other function you've attended in Town," Aunt Lydia said, in the most placid of tones.

"What does one wear to a masquerade at Vauxhall, Aunt Lydia?" Jane asked, hoping to keep the tension at the table at a minimum.

Aunt Lydia began attacking her large portion of meat with relish. "A mask and a domino. You can purchase both this week," she said, between bites. "And you will both enjoy yourselves," Aunt Lydia ordered, glaring at both of her recalcitrant charges.

"Your correspondence, my lord," Harris announced in dramatic tones, handing Blackmoore his mail.

Blackmoore was looking increasingly unkempt these days. He was actually anxious about the situation with Miss Ravenwood, and was at that very moment writing her a note of apology. Of course, he wasn't sorry at all for what happened, but he did promise Roger he would apologize for his behavior. "Thank you, Harris," he replied, and stared back down at the paper.

"Dearest Jenny,"

he began, becoming heartily sick of penning missives to everyone in his acquaintance.

> *"This note is to formally beg your forgiveness for my reprehensible behavior in the library. As you must know, I hold you in the highest regard and would never intentionally offend you.*
> > *Your servant, Richard Hughes,*
> > *The Marquess of Blackmoore,"*

he finished hastily, hoping the missive would appease Roger. *It's dashed hard writing a letter of apology when one isn't a bit sorry,* he decided, sealing the missive.

He smiled slightly, and wondered what was running through Jenny's mind. *She's probably convinced I'm a rake of the highest degree, since I'm always trying to take liberties with her,* he admitted to himself. He would right that situation soon enough, and would get down to the business of setting up a nursery.

Blackmoore thumbed through his correspondence, finding it as unexceptional as usual, except for a letter from his mother. He opened it and a wide smile broke out on his face. His mother had actually found a patron who was interested in James and wanted to see his work. A Lady Morrison. He penned a brief note to his mother, giving her the pertinent information regarding James Clayton. *I definitely need a servant to do this sort of work for me,* he decided. Writing missives all afternoon was dashed dull and rather reminded him of his seemingly endless days in the schoolroom.

"Miss Charlotte is waiting for you in the study. She also requested the presence of your abigail," Molly said in a soft voice, cowering in the doorway.

Before Jane could answer the poor girl, Gwen said, "Thank you, Molly. We'll be downstairs directly," virtually dismissing the girl.

Jane grinned. Gwen was not a proper abigail at all.

Molly shut the door behind her, and Jane ran her hand through her ink black hair nervously. "I don't know if I told you, Gwen, but I received a note from Miss Bridgeson. She's sending her carriage for us, so hopefully we'll be leaving soon," she said, walking toward the door.

"Very soon, Miss Jane?" Gwen asked, a bit on edge.

Jane smiled reassuringly at her. "You'll like Cornwall, Gwen, and don't think for a moment that you're not going. I'd turn into a virtual quiz if you weren't around to help me," Jane said, hoping to ease Gwen's fears.

Smiling slightly, Gwen replied, "Thank you, Miss Jane," and trailed behind Jane as they headed downstairs.

When they reached the library, they were both in for a surprise. Charlotte quickly shut the door and whispered, "Mama is joining us. Could Gwen deliver a note for me? I'd ask Molly but she's so afraid of displeasing Mama that I know she'd refuse."

A letter. To James, no doubt. Jane looked over at Gwen and asked, "Would you like to deliver a letter for Cousin Charlotte?"

Before Gwen could answer, Charlotte added, "I'll give you money for a hackney. All you have to do is deliver the letter to the person at the address without my mama knowing. That shouldn't be hard, since she pays no attention to you at all."

Smiling easily and always ready for an adventure, Gwen answered, "I'll deliver your letter, Lady Charlotte."

"Thank you, Gwen. Here's the note and the money for the hackney. Leave after we do, and be sure to be home right away. There's a shilling in it for you when you get back."

"Thank you, Lady Charlotte," Gwen said, heading out of the library.

* * *

Gwen delivered the message with alacrity, and was cheerfully walking up to the house from the hackney, when, as if by magic, Charley appeared in front of her.

"Good morning, Gwennie," he said cordially, looking remarkably handsome in his buff breeches and brown jacket.

"Morning, Charley. What are you doing here?" she asked curiously, trying to smooth down her blond locks.

"I had an errand to run down the street. How are things going?" he asked casually, hoping no one else from the house noticed him talking to Gwen.

"A bit better. The family is going to the masquerade at Vauxhall Gardens on Friday," she replied, frowning down at her dowdy dress.

"Is your Miss Jane attending?"

Gwen nodded. "She really doesn't want to go, and said she was going to buy a black domino to wear." Gwen shrugged and added, "At least everyone will be able to find her in the crowd, since ladies never wear black dominos, or at least that's what Molly says," she finished, moving towards the house. She really did have to go inside before the rest of the family returned from their various excursions.

Charley seemed dashed interested in Jane's arrangements. "I'll see you next week, Gwennie, maybe we'll have an ice at Gunther's," he called, smiling as she rounded the corner to the servant's entrance.

James stared at the letter from Charlotte with interest.

> *"My darling, please don't forsake me because of my family,"*

Charlotte pleaded.

*"I beg you to meet me at Vauxhall on Friday. I'll
be with Jane, who will be wearing a black domino,"*

Charlotte concluded dramatically.

He glanced at his calendar. Friday was, of course, open.
He was obviously going to Vauxhall.

Blackmoore bustled into the studio, once again looking as if he had forgotten to comb his hair. The bell on the
wooden door tinkled as he walked in, and James appeared,
as if by magic.

"Good day, James," Blackmoore said cheerfully, obviously in the best of spirits.

"Good day, m'lord," James replied.

"Wanted to give you some good news. Lady Morrison
is coming by next week. Wants to inspect your paintings,"
Blackmoore explained.

James was a trifle confused. "Is she interested in pur-
chasing something specific?"

Blackmoore smiled. "No. Lady Morrison is great patron
of the arts. She's actually looking for new talent to sponsor."

James gaped at him. "She's looking for new talent?"

"Yes," Blackmoore replied simply.

"If she became my patron . . ." James began, then just
trailed off.

Blackmoore smiled broadly. "Yes, well, don't put the
cart before the horse," and strolled out of the gallery.

A few days later, Jane sat in her bedroom, staring at the
black domino. *It certainly fits my mood,* she thought. *Damn
Lord Blackmoore. Trying to make me fall in love with him,*
she mused. *Now I am in love with him and he thinks I'm a
spinster with loose morals,* she thought in despair.

She continued staring at the domino, dreading the masquerade for no particular reason, when a knock came at the door. Before she could reply, Gwen bounded in cheerfully.

"Miss Jane, you've received a letter. I found it downstairs," she said, handing the letter in question to Jane. Jane frowned. It wasn't from her papa or Jon. Who would be sending her a missive? Deciding on some privacy, she said quickly, "Thank you, Gwen," and looked expectantly at the door.

Gwen frowned in consternation but replied, "Yes, Miss Jane," and disappeared out the door, closing it behind her.

Jane fumbled with the letter, and finally ripped it open in the most unladylike way, staring at the signature. Richard? Why would he write to me? she wondered.

A strange feeling came over her as she read his missive. *One would almost think that Lord Blackmoore has developed a tendre for me. Of course, that idea is totally ridiculous,* she immediately decided.

Then the reality of the situation hit Jane. This was what he was discussing with Roger. This missive was Blackmoore's punishment for their scene in the library. He was placating Roger by writing an ever so proper letter of apology.

Staring at the words and reading them over and over, Jane sighed with unfulfilled longing. *If only he did hold me in the highest regard,* she thought wistfully. If only he wasn't a peer and she wasn't a completely ineligible dowd.

Charlotte sat next to Jane in their closed carriage, and squeezed her hand for reassurance.

"The masquerade isn't going to be that awful," Charlotte said in a whisper.

Jane shrugged slightly. Her mood was as black as her domino.

As usual, Aunt Lydia was immune to the feelings of everyone around her. She sat across from Jane in a bright Pamona green domino, complete with a matching jeweled turban, and wondered out loud, "Why did you ever buy a black domino, Jane? You look rather like you're in mourning."

Jane decided to try and shake off her dark mood and make the best of the situation. "I thought it would be original, Aunt Lydia," she said liltingly in her natural Welsh accent.

"Well, I suppose we'll have no problem finding you in the crowd. But you would have done better to emulate Charlotte, who looks like a princess tonight."

Charlotte did look like a princess. As usual, her golden locks were coaxed into perfect ringlets, adorned by pearl-encrusted combs. Her domino was in a shimmering gold silk that made her look ethereal. Undoubtedly Charlotte would be the most attractive female at the masquerade.

Jane, in contrast, had won a slight battle with Aunt Lydia. Tonight she was clad unassumingly in black, not because she wanted to be original, but because it suited her mood. For one evening she was in a mask and she could be herself, not some vapid society tabby who only cared about her clothes and the latest gossip. She would simply be herself tonight, instead of the artificial role that her Aunt had cast her in for all these weeks. So tonight she wore black, because she was Miss Ravenwood with no expectations, a connection to trade and finally, because she was naturally unassuming in large public functions.

"Jane, you're gaping," Roger said with a bright smile, scanning the crowd for a familiar face.

Jane blushed under her black mask. "Roger, this place is indecent," she hissed, staring at the unclothed marble statues surrounding them.

Roger chuckled. "It is rather . . . unique, isn't it?"

"Scandalous is a better word," Jane said, trying not to

focus on the well-formed statuary in front of her. "I'm surprised Aunt Lydia approves," she added.

"Just make sure you stay off the darkened paths," Roger warned. "It can be a bit dangerous there," he added for good measure.

Jane watched several half-naked merrymakers skulk off into the night in shock. Vauxhall Gardens was nothing like she expected and she was surprised that Aunt Lydia approved.

"Why don't you go join Charlotte? She's getting a glass of champagne. I'm going to pay my respects to Lady Martinwood," Roger said, his eyes moving to the chestnut-haired beauty.

Jane glanced toward the refreshments. There was a huge crowd of obviously drunken fops hovering around, and she had no idea if she could even locate Charlotte. But she saw the gleam in Roger's eyes, and didn't want to ruin his romantic assignation. "Of course, Roger," she replied, and began to work her way over to the crowd of masked revelers.

Blackmoore strolled through Vauxhall, in search of Jenny. Roger assured him that his mother was forcing her to attend the masquerade, and that she would definitely be there. So Blackmoore made an exception to his rule to avoid the Gardens, and put on a simple mask and domino. To see Jenny.

Scanning the crowd, his eyes settled on an incredibly lovely young woman with flowing red hair trying to discourage a persistent suitor. If he became more aggressive, Blackmoore decided that he would go over and intervene on behalf of the lady. She seemed to encourage the man though, so he probably wouldn't have to play knight-errant.

His eyes returned to the crowd, in search of his Jenny.

He was so absorbed in his task, that he didn't even notice the fact that Charlotte had come up next to him.

"Good evening, Richard," Charlotte said casually, following his gaze.

Blackmoore immediately focused on the lady at his side and favored her with a winning smile. "Good evening, Charlotte. Is Miss Ravenwood with you?" he asked cordially.

Charlotte laughed, a wonderful tinkling sound. "You know, Richard, you may have the rest of polite society fooled, but I know the truth. Why don't you just offer for Jane and be done with it?" she said boldly.

To her utter astonishment, he laughed heartily. "Dearest Charlotte, I commend you on your powers of observation," he commented, but didn't elaborate further on his plans.

A smile remained on Charlotte's face. "Why thank you, Richard. By the by, I don't know where Jane is. I've been looking for her myself for a quarter of an hour," she explained, studying the crowd.

Blackmoore smiled down at her. "Then we most certainly must locate her. Do you think she may have found James?" he asked with an enigmatic smile, as Charlotte gaped at him in surprise.

James stood in the darkness, watching the most unusual event unfold in front of him.

He had spent most of the evening looking for Miss Ravenwood. Charlotte informed him that she would be with Jane, who would be dashed easy to spot. She would be in a black domino. And Jane would probably be the tallest lady at Vauxhall.

And sure enough, after searching for almost and hour, he spotted a lady. A tall lady in a black domino. Probably Miss Ravenwood.

Miss Ravenwood, if indeed it was Miss Ravenwood, was

off to the side of the crowd. She was speaking with a handsome young man who looked like a coachman. They chatted for a moment, and Miss Ravenwood followed him into the darkness of the gardens.

James frowned. Even the most slow-witted miss knew that it wasn't appropriate to go off into the darkness with a stranger. But perhaps Miss Ravenwood didn't know better.

Sensing something was amiss, James followed them through the winding paths, keeping a steady eye on their progress. The lady in the black domino followed the man through the entire Gardens, until they were outside, at a servants' entrance. A closed carriage stood secluded behind a huge tree, and the pair stopped.

James hovered in the shadows, waiting to see what would happen next. The pair exchanged heated words that James couldn't discern, but he could tell by the lady's posture that she wasn't happy. The lady in the black domino turned around abruptly and began to walk briskly back to the masquerade, her arms folded in front of her.

Much to his surprise, the coachman didn't let Miss Ravenwood, if indeed it was Miss Ravenwood, return to the rather debauched festivities. Instead, the coachmen skulked up behind her and struck her on the back of the head with some sort of object. James squinted. The object was a small handgun. The lady in the domino fell to the ground with a thud.

James was paralyzed. The coachman threw the lady in the domino over his shoulder like a sack of potatoes and took her over to the carriage. Then he simply opened the door, spoke to someone inside and thrust in his victim. James strained to hear their voices, and could make out one word. Milford. Or perhaps Silford. Or something of that sort.

The coachman closed the carriage door, and in an instant, the horses were off, as if the hounds of hell were on their heels.

James knew he just witnessed a kidnapping, possibly of Miss Ravenwood. He knew ladies never wore black dominos, so he was fairly certain that it was Miss Ravenwood. He turned back toward the festivities, determined to find one of her relations and let them know what he witnessed.

Charlotte and Richard stood together under the Chinese lanterns near an almost naked statue of a Greek man. They barely conversed, since Charlotte was searching for James and Richard was looking for Jane. In fact, they were both so busy scanning the crowd before them, they didn't notice the man with the short brown hair and maroon domino that came up along side of the pair.

"Lord Blackmoore?" James asked hesitantly, obviously uncertain if the man in front of him was indeed Blackmoore.

"Oh James," Charlotte cried, and immediately embraced him.

James held her for a brief moment, then pushed her away. "Charlotte, you must excuse us. I have something important to discuss with Lord Blackmoore," he said in a deadly serious tone.

Charlotte frowned but replied, "Of course, James," and joined some ladies she knew a few feet away. Her eyes never left her beloved, though.

Blackmoore knew instantly that the artist wanted to talk to him about his potential patron, Lady Morrison. "How can I help you, James?" Blackmoore asked casually, still in the most cordial of moods.

James frowned and a very intense expression settled on his face. "My Lord, I feel something very bad may have happened to Miss Ravenwood," he said in a serious voice.

Stiffening, Blackmoore instinctively grabbed James by the arm and led him away from the crowds. "Miss Ravenwood? What?" he said in a clipped tone, his heart lurching in his chest.

"I was to recognize Charlotte by Miss Ravenwood's black domino," James explained. "Well, I spotted a lady in a black domino talking to a rather handsome coachman. Something just didn't seem right, so when they walked off together, I followed them. They went around the back side of the Gardens, where a closed carriage was waiting. They argued, and the lady began to walk back toward the crowd. She walked only a few feet before the man came up behind her and hit her on the head with the butt of a pistol," James concluded, watching Blackmoore pale.

"And then?" Blackmoore asked in a hushed voice, ready to seek out and kill anyone who would harm Jane.

"He dragged her over to the carriage and put her inside. Another man was waiting there, and they spoke briefly. I couldn't really hear anything, but I did hear a name. It sounded like Milford. Or Silford," James said, with a frown. "When they drove off at breakneck speed, I knew something was amiss," he finished.

A black scowl settled on Blackmoore's face. Milford. Or Silford. "Could it have been Wilford?" he asked intently, staring at James.

"It could have been, but I'm not certain."

Blackmoore sprang into action, his military training taking over. "Follow me," he commanded James, and strode purposefully over to Charlotte. He pulled her away from her lady friends and asked, "What was Jane wearing tonight?"

Charlotte frowned. "I told you, Richard, a black domino; she was the only one here in black that I noticed. She had a black mask as well, with the most enchanting feathers on the sides," Charlotte added.

Blackmoore's golden eyes bored a hole through her skull. "Was she carrying anything?"

"Of course. She had a small black reticule with tiny golden beads on it."

Blackmoore turned his attention to James. "Does Charlotte's description of Miss Ravenwood match that of the woman you saw with the coachman?"

James gulped. "I didn't notice her mask or a reticule," he said in a barely audible whisper.

Charlotte was utterly confused. "What's wrong, Richard? What's happened?"

"It would appear that Jane may have been the victim of foul play. When was the last time you saw her?" he asked succinctly.

"About an hour ago," Charlotte replied simply.

Blackmoore turned to James. "There's no time to waste. Start searching Vauxhall for Miss Ravenwood. Meet me at the refreshment stand in exactly one quarter of an hour," he ordered.

James, still pale, disappeared into the glittering crowd.

"And Charlotte. You will locate your mother, Roger, and my mother and search for Jane for a quarter of an hour. Then you will all meet at the refreshment stand. Hopefully you'll have Jane with you," he concluded, his eyes glinting like molten gold.

"Yes, yes, Richard," Charlotte stuttered, and headed out in search of her mama.

Blackmoore strode toward the group of people that awaited him at the refreshment table. While the merrymakers danced and laughed, the ladies in their party were pale, and Roger had a deep frown etched into his usually easy countenance.

He approached them confidently and began asking questions he didn't want to address. "Is Jane still missing?"

Roger nodded. "We've covered every inch of Vauxhall. She isn't here," he said in a deadly serious voice.

Blackmoore paled behind his mask, but his confidence didn't waver. He was a born leader and knew what had to be done. "Then we must assume the worst. We'll return to your house, to see if there is any message. From Jane or her abductor," he added hastily.

"Shouldn't we go after the carriage?" Roger suggested.

Blackmoore shook his head. "If she is indeed missing, and I'm not wholly certain that she is, they will undoubtedly leave a note with instructions." Blackmoore then turned to James and said, "You will accompany us. You can ride with Lady Stockmorton and my mother. Roger will accompany me."

Before James could utter a single word, Aunt Lydia chimed in. "I must protest. I'm not sharing a carriage with this fortune hunting puppy," Lydia said, staring at James.

A hard glint appeared in Blackmoore's golden eyes, and he replied sternly, "If it wasn't for James, we would not even be aware of the situation. You will ride home with him in my carriage and cease your complaining," he said harshly, tired of Lydia and her scenes.

Strangely enough, that quelled her protest. The Dowager Marchioness whispered something to Lydia that made her shake her head in agreement. It was settled.

Blackmoore's carriage was silent as they headed back to Roger's house. Roger was wrapped up in his thoughts, and Blackmoore was beside himself with worry. In fact, he could barely breathe, despite his apparent calm. *Oh God, please let Jenny be home,* he prayed, his heart lurching in his chest. But, deep in his heart, he knew he wasn't wrong. He also knew he would kill anyone who harmed her.

CHAPTER FOURTEEN

When they arrived at the Stockmorton residence, Jeffries was indeed in possession of a letter from Jane. Actually, Jeffries found the letter shoved under the door, so he wasn't actually certain that the letter was delivered by the lady in question. Before anyone could say a word, Blackmoore took it out of Jeffries's hand.

"My Dearest Aunt Lydia,"

the missive began,

> *"I'm leaving for Cornwall for an extended visit with Miss Bridgeson, my former governess. She has sent her carriage for me.*
>
> *Your niece, Jane,"*

it concluded, and Blackmoore stared at it, raising his eyebrow. This didn't sound like a letter Jane would write.

Lydia, James, and his mother hovered around him in the library, and finally Lydia asked, "What does it say?"

Blackmoore continued to study the letter. *It looks nothing like the note she wrote me to ask for help with the Charlotte situation,* he realized in shock. In fact, he was certain it wasn't the same writing. "The letter says Jane has left to see a Miss Bridgeson in Cornwall," he stated, then commanded, "Bring me her abigail. I wish to speak to her."

Lydia frowned. "If Jane left to see Miss Bridgeson, then this half-wit imagined the whole abduction," she said, giving James a hostile stare.

Before James could reply, Gwen entered the room. "Can you read?" he asked succinctly.

"Yes, m'lord," she said as he handed her the letter. Gwen gazed at the letter for a long moment. "Miss Jane didn't write this," Gwen said firmly, handing the missive back to him.

"How can you be sure?" he asked, wondering if this abigail could be trusted. She certainly didn't appear to be the most intelligent female in the house.

"Miss Jane taught me how to write herself, and her writing is . . . pretty and loopy. This writing is thick and doesn't look right," she replied confidently.

A plan was beginning to form in Blackmoore's mind but he needed all the information he could get. "Is there any other information you might know that could help us in our search for Miss Ravenwood?"

"Miss Jane was taking me with her. She told me so. She'd never leave for Cornwall without taking me or any of her clothes," Gwen finished, raising her perky chin in defiance.

"Thank you. You may go," Blackmoore commanded with a wave of his hand.

Blackmoore turned to the trio awaiting his next move. "I'm going to Devon. James mentioned that he heard the coachman address a man in the coach as Wilford. Or something of that sort. Wilford has a hunting box in Devon," he explained.

He then turned to Roger. "I need you to come after me with the Runners," he stated simply. Roger nodded in agreement.

It was then that Aunt Lydia spoke up. "Lord Wilford has Jane?"

"He's our most likely suspect." Blackmoore noticed that Lydia refused to meet his eyes.

"Well, this may not be important, but, well, years ago, Jane's mother was connected with Wilford's father," Lydia said, still not looking at him.

"That's hardly a reason to abduct someone," Blackmoore countered, ready to jump on Diablo and head for Devon.

"Yes, you're right, of course. But, well, the late Earl was rather unstable in his later years, and it was rumored that he was a bit of a Bedlamite. You see, Wilford's father believed that Jane's mother Sara would marry him. When she didn't, the tabbies said he didn't take it well," Lydia concluded, looking at a potted fern behind Blackmoore's head.

The anger welled up inside Blackmoore. "And you encouraged Jane to associate with his son?" he said, his golden eyes glaring at her. "If anything happens to Jane because of your grasping search for another title in the family, I will personally hold you responsible," he finished, his threat very apparent to all in the library.

The trio paled, and Blackmoore turned to Roger. "I'm taking Diablo, is that a problem?"

Roger shook his head. "Of course not."

"I'll need one of your pistols," Blackmoored said decisively.

"Of course," Roger replied.

"I'll find her before they get too far," Blackmoore added, striding out of the room like a general preparing for battle.

The first thing Jane could sense was the swaying of the carriage, and the sound of the horses' hooves on the firm earth. The sound echoed in her ears, and made her head hurt even more than it already did.

She opened her eyes, only to find that she was blindfolded. The rope that bound her hands behind her back was cutting into her flesh, as was the rope around her ankles. She had a rag her in mouth, so she couldn't call out for help. *So, this is what it's like when one is abducted,* she thought distractedly.

The to and fro rhythm of the carriage didn't really agree with Jane, and her stomach began to rebel. *It would serve whoever is kidnapping me right if I was sick all over their carriage,* Jane thought angrily.

She, of course, knew there was someone else in the carriage with her. She could hear the person moving around in their seat. *Who would want to abduct me?* she wondered, trying to free her hands.

Of course, the plan was admirable. Obviously she wasn't in Miss Bridgeson's carriage. That was why the coachman had knocked her over the head when she left to go tell Aunt Lydia that she was leaving Vauxhall. Her relations weren't supposed to know that she was missing. They were probably still swilling warm champagne and enjoying the party, completely unaware that she was gone.

The carriage hit a rut in the road, and Jane hit the side of the door, groaning. *Gads, my head hurts,* she thought, feeling absolutely wretched. *Obviously, the novels have it all wrong,* she decided. *Getting abducted is rather dreadful.*

"So, you're awake. You've slept through a good part of our journey, Miss Ravenwood," the Earl of Wilford said.

A wave of confusion passed over Jane. *Lord Wilford? Why is Lord Wilford kidnapping me? What's happening?* she wondered, her head suddenly engulfed in a fog.

"As I'm sure you know, Miss Ravenwood, I'm abducting you. It's going rather well, don't you agree?" he said with an evil chuckle. A chill ran down her spine.

"You might want to know why, I'll explain. Your mother, the harlot, was supposed to marry my father. When she ran off with that vulgar Welsh tradesman, it devastated my father, and he never recovered. Her betrayal haunted him for the rest of his life," he said dramatically.

Jane continued to struggle with the ropes that were wound around her wrists, listening intently to Wilford. *He's mad,* she thought in a panic.

"And then my father died. His last request was vengeance against Sara Ravenwood. I promised that I'd do all in my power to grant his dying wish," Wilford said, his voice tinged with utter hatred.

Jane continued to squirm, working on the ropes on her ankles. None of the ropes were loosening at all.

"I must say, your maid was a great help to me," he began calmly. "My man has been dallying with her. She told him your every single move. When he wasn't with her, he was watching you. Every single day. I knew your every move. And of course, you told me all of your plans. Not very bright, Miss Ravenwood."

Jane's mind began to spin. *No one will believe that the Earl of Wilford kidnapped me. I left Vauxhall voluntarily and I know no one saw me,* she realized in horror.

"Don't worry, Miss Ravenwood, I'm not going to kill you," Wilford explained, licking his lips. "Not at first. But, when I'm finished with you, you'll probably wish you were dead," he giggled insanely.

He's obviously mad, she thought, knowing that her chances of escaping from this lunatic were very slim. He was a Bedlamite, but he was a thorough, intelligent one. She was likely doomed to whatever he had planned.

"I don't want to ruin the surprise and tell you all the plans I have for you, my dear. Suffice to say that it will be quite different from your night at Vauxhall," he added calmly.

Try not to listen, Jane admonished herself. *Think of a plan.*

But Wilford wouldn't stop talking. "Of course, when

I'm finished, I'll be leaving for France. No one will ever know what happened to poor Miss Ravenwood."

The sweat on Diablo was glistening in the moonlight, and Blackmoore knew he was straining the magnificent creature. He let Diablo run free on the road to Devon, thinking of nothing but Jenny. And letting Diablo run was the quickest way to get to her. He knew they were traveling by coach, and he knew the roads were dreadful outside of London. Their progress would be slow; his progress would not be slow.

The full moon shone above them, and he felt as if he had been riding forever. But whatever anxiety he was going through, would be nothing compared to a lone female who was abducted. His heart ached for her, and he silently prayed that she was safe.

He tried to concentrate on the recent weeks, trying to solve the mystery of her abduction. Wilford was assuredly the man who held her, and Lydia's information sealed his conviction. But how did he know her actions? Obviously he had an accomplice. Someone who was watching Jane's every move, who might even be working in the house. *But who?* he wondered, wracking his brain for the answer.

The lone figure on the gigantic black horse continued riding hell-bent for leather across the countryside, determined to reach Jane before she left the coach. Although there were two of them, Blackmoore was certain that he could subdue both men and rescue his beloved. He didn't really care if he was injured in the process. The thought of a woman, any woman, being abducted by a lecher like Wilford sickened him, and he lost all thought of his own safety. He was an experienced operative, and, for the most part, one of the most successful. In the mind of Lord Blackmoore, there was no possibility of failure.

The journey was endless; he knew they had approximately a half-hour start. Blackmoore knew the roads outside of London better than most men, and rode Diablo like the Devil through several unmarked paths that would save him immeasurable time. Yes, he had a chance. Obviously, his work for the government was coming in handy, since it was giving him an edge in finding Jenny.

Stay safe, Jenny, he thought wildly. *I won't let him hurt you, I won't,* he promised, praying for her safety.

Then he saw it. On the horizon, a closed carriage rode along at an alarming rate. The air was still, and the moon hung over him lighting his path. James gave him a slight description of the carriage, as well as the driver. If this was the carriage holding Jenny, he would get her out safely.

As he approached the carriage from the rear, he saw the driver turn and stare at him, then whip the horses. He didn't want to be caught, Blackmoore realized instantly. This was the correct carriage. His plan of action began.

What's going on? Jane wondered, as her fragile body was thrown around the interior of the carriage. The carriage was careening out of control, but Wilford didn't notice. He simply continued his evil diatribe, and Jane tried to shut out his dreadful words.

Then she heard a noise, somewhere in the distance: hoofbeats. A rider, or riders, were approaching the carriage. Wilford was oblivious.

When the carriage came to a jolting halt, and there was some sort of scuffle outside, Wilford seemed to be utterly surprised. "Charley! What in damnation is going on?" he yelled, banging on the interior of the carriage. There was no answer.

Actually, there was no sound at all for what seemed to be the longest time to Jane. Of course, she was bound, gagged, blindfolded, and didn't feel quite the thing. A minute felt like a quarter of an hour to her.

Then, as they waited in the oppressive silence of the carriage, Jane heard the door swing open. In desperation, she tried to scream as much as her gag would let her, which didn't amount to much noise at all.

Wilford swore when the door opened, and when no one appeared, said, "Who's there?" in anger. When silence was his only answer, he leaned out of the coach to look.

Jane heard the carriage door slam shut and a definite crunching sort of noise. A loud groan followed, and then she heard the door open again.

It sounded as if someone dragged Wilford out of the carriage and was thrashing him soundly. At least Jane hoped someone was thrashing him soundly, since he certainly deserved that punishment. The thuds stopped, and then there was silence.

Anxiety engulfed Jane. What if it was a highwayman? *What if he is going to abuse me worse than Wilford?* she thought wildly. She had no money or valuables to give him.

Once again Jane began to feel dizzy and her stomach was tied in knots. The inside of the vehicle was stiflingly hot, and she feared she was going to disgrace herself by throwing up. If one could throw up while wearing a gag.

Finally, the door opened again, and a voice said, "Oh God, Jenny, are you all right?" and began untying the ropes.

Relief flooded through Jane. Somehow her prayers were answered and Lord Blackmoore had found her. She didn't know how he found her, but he did. She was safe now. Her body sagged in relief.

His large fingers fumbled behind her as he worked on her gag, finally getting the material out of her mouth.

Jane coughed, and said in a small, shaky voice, "I don't feel well," ashamed of the tears that were welling up in her eyes.

Blackmoore struggled with the knots, and finally the

blindfold came off, and Jane found herself staring into Blackmoore's golden hazel cat-like eyes. Before she could stop herself, she flung her arms around him and began to weep.

Blackmoore held Jenny gently in his arms, stroking her short black hair in the moonlight.

"It's all right, my dear," he whispered into her ear, gently kissing her neck. "I'm sorry I took so long. I have tied up the driver and Wilford. He may require some medical attention when we get to the inn. I was vexed at him for abducting you, and got a bit carried away," he said lightly.

She held onto him even tighter and said in a rough, wavering voice, "I don't think he was going to kill me. Not right away," she said between sobs.

Blackmoore gritted his teeth. "Don't worry, love. He won't hurt you ever again, I promise," he said, moving her out of the carriage into the moonlight.

She clung to him, breathing in gulps. "They hit me on the head and I don't feel well," she said in a tiny voice, before she collapsed and lost consciousness.

The horrible throbbing in her head finally woke Jane up. She was having the most awful dreams, about Lord Wilford taking her to his house and torturing her. She forced herself to awaken, to make the dreams go away, only to find herself reaching for a level of consciousness that included an incredible amount of pain.

She turned her head and moaned, the ache in her head becoming worse every time she moved.

A male voice she didn't recognize said, "She appears to be waking up."

Jane felt someone take hold of her hand, and heard Richard say, "Come on, Jenny, wake up. The doctor says you have to wake up. Please," he beseeched.

The urge to go back to sleep came over Jane like a wave

and she wanted to ignore Blackmoore. *I'll talk to him later,* she decided groggily.

But he wouldn't stop talking to her. "Come on, love, wake up. If you want to get better you have to open your eyes," Blackmoore pleaded, kissing her hand.

Using all her willpower, she forced her eyes open, and moaned once again. Her head hurt abominably.

Richard was sitting next to her, worry etched on his face. He looked tired, and his clothes were dirty and torn. She managed a small smile. "Thank you, Richard," she said, staring into the golden eyes of the man who risked his life for her.

A smile crept onto his face. He kissed her hand again, and held it firmly in his. "I wouldn't let anything happen to you, Jenny," he said in a voice thick with passion.

"Excuse me, if you'll leave the room for a moment, Lord Blackmoore, I'd like to examine the patient," the doctor said, moving to the bedside.

Jane smiled weakly as Richard kissed her hand again. "Don't worry, Jenny. The magistrate has Wilford and his accomplice, and Roger is coming with a Bow Street Runner. You're safe now," he said, still gazing protectively at her.

"Please come back after the doctor has gone," she said softly.

Blackmoore reluctantly let go of her hand and said, "Of course, Jenny. I won't leave you alone," and walked out the door so the doctor could examine her in privacy.

Jane gave the doctor a brave smile. "Will my head ever stop hurting?"

The doctor, an elderly man with white hair and pink cheeks, smiled back at her. "Of course it will. You know, you gave your husband quite a scare. He was beside himself when you wouldn't wake up. I thought I was going to have to give him some laudanum to calm him down. Can you sit up, please?" he asked, standing next to her bed.

Jane sat up and got a bit dizzy, but didn't succumb to the

vapors. *What is the doctor talking about?* she wondered. *My husband?*

The doctor began to gently explore the bump on the back of her head, which was rather unpleasant looking. "Does this hurt?" he asked, pressing various areas of her head and neck.

"Only the bump hurts. And I have a dreadful headache. And I feel dizzy," she added, grateful that she didn't feel nauseated.

The doctor continued to examine her, then finally said, "Try to rest for the next week, and call your doctor if you have any unusual symptoms. I don't see why you can't have a complete recovery if you have plenty of rest."

Jane scanned the rest of the bedroom, noticing that it didn't appear to be a top of the tree inn. "Where are we? What inn is this?" she asked, wondering if she could go home in the morning. Or sooner.

"This is the Cock and Bull Inn," he replied, gathering his instruments together.

"Can I return to London tonight?" she asked wistfully, knowing the answer was going to be "No."

The doctor chuckled heartily. "Lady Blackmoore, you certainly have a sense of humor. No, you need to rest tonight. If you're not dizzy tomorrow morning, you can leave then," he concluded, shuffling out of the room.

Jane stared at the blank, washed-out gray wall in front of her. *Blackmoore obviously told the innkeeper and the doctor that I'm his wife,* she realized in shock.

She had only a moment to reflect on her situation, when Blackmoore came back into the room, a weary smile on his face. He looked exhausted. But his smile was sincere, and she felt her heart lurch inexplicably when he sat down next to her bed and said, "You did very well, Jenny. You didn't succumb to the vapors until after you were rescued, and then only because of your head injury. Most females would have been hysterical after what happened, but here you are in bed, perfectly quiet and smiling. You're quite the woman," he said, the admiration he felt apparent in his voice.

Apparent to everyone but Jane. In her mind, he was still trying to be nice to her, for whatever reason. She stared at the almost white coverlet over her, and then finally said, "None of this would have happened if I had avoided Lord Wilford. Everyone said he wasn't respectable."

Blackmoore stared at her, his mouth dropping open in shock. "Jenny, none of this is your fault. You couldn't have known his plans," he said in a soft, caressing voice.

"But I made it so much easier for him. I told him all of my plans. His man, Charley, followed me and I never noticed. And I knew Miss Bridgeson would never send a closed carriage," she said in anguish.

Blackmoore frowned. "I know, Jane. While I was tying up Charley, I recognized him. I saw Wilford talking to him one night. We also saw him across the street that afternoon, when he ducked into a shop," he said calmly.

"I should have suspected Wilford. Everyone else did," she said with a sigh.

Blackmoore sighed. "You couldn't have known, Jenny."

Jane stared at the faded painting on the wall of the room. Once, it was a rather nice oil of the inn. Now it was faded and gray. "I just want to go home," she finally said in a soft voice.

Blackmoore frowned. "To London?"

"No. Home. To the Abbey. I don't care if Jon is getting married and I'll lose my place in the house. I just want to be back with people who care about me," she replied, her voice drifting off.

Blackmoore sat at her bedside for the longest time, watching her sleep. Finally, he got up and walked over to the window, looking for Roger. He paid one of the stable boys to intercept them on the main road and bring all of them to this awful inn. *Where are they?* he wondered irritably.

Jane moaned slightly as she tried to turn in bed, and he realized that it wasn't proper to be alone with her. "Jenny?" he said softly, his voice filled with emotion.

She didn't open her eyes. "Yes?"

"I'm going to go down to the public rooms. The inn is booked solid you see, and you have the last room," he explained. Her face was pale and bruised, yet she had never looked so beautiful to him.

Jane opened her eyes and saw a larger chair in a corner. "If you'd like you can stay here. You might be able to get some sleep in the big chair; you must be exhausted," she finished, her eyes closing again.

"All right," he replied, shocked by her generosity. She was obviously nothing like Yvette. He moved over to the chair in the corner and settled in.

Blackmoore began to drift off into a light sleep himself when an unsteady little voice asked, "Wilford and his driver can't get away, can they?"

His eyes snapped open and he was instantly awake. Poor Jenny. *It must have been unspeakably horrible for her,* he mused. "The magistrate has them both locked up, and they're waiting for the Runners. And, if it makes you rest easier, I do have Roger's gun. You're safe here with me," he said in a steady voice, hoping to reassure her.

She gingerly turned over in bed, and moaned a little in pain. "Thank you, Richard," she said in a tiny, childlike voice and drifted off, asleep.

The sleep that engulfed Jane was as welcome and as comforting as the thin blanket that covered her on the very lumpy mattress of the Cock and Bull Inn. Although she was loathe to admit it, she was tired, and was happy to

have the opportunity to rest before the journey back to
Town. Blackmoore convinced her that Wilford wouldn't
try to harm her again, so her sleep was genuine.

She was dreaming about riding Sage, her favorite mare,
by the sea, at the Abbey. Her beloved mastiff, Chaucer,
who died when she was a child, was running alongside
them. The breeze was ever so slight, and she could all but
smell the salty air.

Then, someone began talking in her dream, which was
most unusual, since she was alone on the beach. In fact,
there were several people holding a very loud discussion,
which was confusing, since they didn't belong in her
dream at all. As she tried to determine where the sounds
came from, she heard a door open, and Cousin Roger's
voice. "My God, what's going on?" he asked in a shocked
voice.

Jane's eyes fluttered open, and there was Cousin Roger,
dusty and tired, standing at the foot of her bed, staring at
her in disbelief. *No, he isn't staring at me,* she realized instantly. His was gaping at Lord Blackmoore, who was
sleeping soundly in the chair in the corner.

Jane sat up in bed at bit. "Roger, you finally arrived. Do
you have a Runner with you?" she asked in a sleepy voice.

Roger shifted his gaze from the sleeping peer to his very
unkempt cousin. "The Runner is down in the public room.
What's been going on here?"

"Richard, Roger is finally here," Jane said in a clear
voice, finally becoming a bit more coherent.

Blackmoore stirred from his slumber. "Eh, what?
Roger?" he said, opening his eyes.

Jane tried again, noticing how boyish the usually severe
Blackmoore looked while he was sleeping. "Roger is here
with the Runner," she explained. "The Runner is downstairs," Jane added, for good measure.

"Richard, what's going on?" Roger said, pacing the
room.

Blackmoore focused on Roger, and demanded, "What took you so bloody long? We could have been dead by now."

Roger frowned. "I would have been here hours ago if it wasn't for the Runners. You see, the bucks at Oxford have been misusing their services lately, and they didn't believe my story. I had to go find Castlereagh to verify my identity," Roger finished with a sigh. "Do you know how many functions Castlereagh and his wife attend in one evening?"

"Probably more than a few," Blackmoore replied, his eyes darting back to Jane's rumpled form.

"Seven. The clerk from the Runner's office and I went to seven different routs," Roger complained. "And then, once they were convinced my story was genuine, it took ages to find an available Runner. I finally ended up riding out here with Old Tommy. I was on Satan, so I could have arrived in record time. Old Tommy was on a worthless nag that should have been sold to the knackers years ago," he concluded.

"I'm sorry I was so much trouble, Roger," Jane said in a trembling voice.

Roger shrugged, and sat down on a chair in the corner. "It's not your fault. You're all right, aren't you?" he asked in a voice laced with concern.

"I suppose. Richard had a doctor look at me last night because I have a nasty bump on my head."

Roger turned to Blackmoore. "So it was Wilford? You captured him, I assume?"

"Oh yes, and he has more than a few bumps himself," he explained, rising and walking towards the door. "I'll take you to the magistrate. He has Wilford and his accomplice."

Blackmoore gazed at Jane, curled up on the bed. "Jenny, you're going to have to talk to the magistrate and Old Tommy before you leave. You'll be all right, won't you?" he asked softly.

Jane nodded, and the two men left the room. As they walked down the hall, Jane could still hear their voices. The words "utterly compromised," and "must marry her," floated into her room as she fell back into a troubled sleep.

CHAPTER FIFTEEN

"Oh my heavens! Jane!" Lydia exclaimed before she succumbed to a fit of vapors and collapsed on a rosewood chaise.

Charlotte exchanged a look with James, who was sitting next to her on the settee, then turned to the Dowager Marchioness of Blackmoore. "Do you think we should use hartshorn?" she asked casually.

"I'm sure your mother will recover in due time," the Dowager Marchioness replied calmly.

Jane sighed, and walked slowly over to a free chair near the window, sitting down. Aunt Lydia and her hysterics were getting on her nerves.

"You were not injured, Miss Ravenwood?" the Dowager Marchioness asked, concern riddling her features.

Jane glanced around the room. Blackmoore was hovering near her chair, a strange expression on his face. Charlotte and James were on the settee. Roger was fixing himself a drink on the other side of the room, while Lord Blackmoore's mother sat next to Aunt Lydia's prone form. Everyone was waiting for her to confirm that she was, in fact, unharmed. "Yes, I'm all right," Jane said simply, staring at her bandaged wrists.

"What happened?" Charlotte asked with a frown.

Jane glanced at Blackmoore, who looked startlingly handsome, travel dirt and all. "Well, from what Lord Blackmoore tells me, Mr. Clayton should get a fair amount of credit. He was the one who noticed my abduction," Jane began, wondering when tea was going to arrive.

James smiled at her. "I didn't do anything that anyone else wouldn't have done," he said modestly, blushing a little.

"I don't think so, Mr. Clayton," Jane said, giving him a warm smile.

"Well, what happened next?" Charlotte prompted, leaning forward in her seat.

"Well, after Mr. Clayton saw me thrown into the carriage, we headed towards Devon. I was unconscious for a long time, and when I finally woke up, I was bound, gagged and blindfolded," she said in a strangely calm voice. "Needless to say, they weren't the most delicate about it, and I didn't help any by trying to escape. You see, Lord Wilford was intent on avenging his father. His father never forgave my mother for not marrying him. Since Mama has passed on, he had to find someone else to punish. Namely, me," Jane added with a slight shiver.

Before Jane could continue, Blackmoore took up the story. "I caught up with their carriage, and then there was a bit of a scuffle. I managed to . . . subdue the driver and then Wilford without much trouble. Neither were particularly adept at hand-to-hand fighting. After I untied Jane and found out that she wasn't seriously injured, I took her to the nearest inn," he concluded.

"What did you do with Wilford and his driver?" the Dowager Marchioness asked curiously.

"Oh, Wilford. I tied him and his coachman up and brought them to the inn as well. I didn't want them to escape because of my negligence. After I got a room for Jane I had the inn keeper call the magistrate. The magistrate kept them both in jail until Roger arrived with the Runner."

No one really noticed, but Lydia had recovered and was listening to the story intently. "But how did Wilford know that Jane was going to be at Vauxhall? Or that her governess was in Cornwall? He was the one that sent the note to the house, wasn't he?" she asked, her chartreuse turban tilting forward as she inclined her head towards Blackmoore.

"Wilford had an accomplice who was involved with Jane's maid, Gwen. He got information from Gwen, and followed Jane as well," Blackmoore replied, glancing over at Jane.

Charlotte was transfixed by the story. "When did you arrive, Roger?" she asked, and Roger frowned.

"I arrived with Old Tommy, the Runner from Bow Street, near dawn. I found Jane and Richard asleep," Richard said, a vague statement at best. "I woke them and Blackmoore took the Runner over to the magistrate," Roger said, as everyone in the room frowned.

"You did have separate rooms," Lydia commented with a fierce scowl.

"Well, not precisely. But Lord Blackmoore did tell the doctor I was his wife," Jane explained softly. *Here it comes,* she thought nervously. *Aunt Lydia is going to insist that I am hopelessly compromised.*

"What does 'not precisely' mean, Jane?" Aunt Lydia asked in a firm voice. "Where exactly did you sleep and where did Lord Blackmoore sleep?"

Jane sighed. Every eye in the room was upon her. "Well, I slept on the bed, you see, I wasn't feeling quite the thing at all. I had that horrid blow to the head," she said in a rush. "And then Lord Blackmoore was going to spend the night downstairs in the public rooms because there weren't any rooms at the inn, but I couldn't let him stay there all night and not get any sleep after he rescued me. So I said I wouldn't mind if he slept in the chair on the other side of the room," she concluded breathlessly.

The Dowager Marchioness turned to her son. "Richard, you've compromised Miss Ravenwood. You're going to have to marry her."

Jane's jaw dropped open in shock. "No, no, there's no

need," Jane said quickly. "No one will know. Really," she added for emphasis.

It was as if Jane hadn't spoken. "Of course I'll marry Miss Ravenwood," Blackmoore said calmly, smiling at his mother.

"We'll announce it in the paper at the end of the week," Lydia said brightly.

"No!" Jane exclaimed vehemently, losing all color in her face.

Every eye in the room was on Jane.

"Dear, you must marry my son. He's compromised you. There is no other way," the Dowager Marchioness intoned in a sage voice.

Jane began to think quickly. *If I can delay the announcement of the engagement, maybe I can bolt home and avoid it all together,* she mused. Finally she said in docile tones, "Can't we wait to announce this until I'm feeling more the thing?"

Lydia was obviously beside herself, but Blackmoore gave her a fierce look and she replied, "Of course, Jane. Lord Blackmoore can stop by in a few days to discuss everything."

A sigh of relief escaped from Jane. She was undoubtedly in love with Blackmoore, but she knew he didn't return her regard. She wouldn't force him to be leg shackled for life to someone he didn't love.

But Aunt Lydia unwittingly saved her. She gave Jane the opportunity to leave London rather than be forced into a sham of a marriage. *And if he does propose before I manage to reach the Abbey, I'll simply jilt him,* she decided. A decision that made her very unhappy indeed.

Jane knew that something was very definitely wrong when Molly, Charlotte's abigail, appeared to draw her bath.

"Molly, where's Gwen?" Jane asked curiously as Molly helped her into her dressing gown.

"Gwen is downstairs talking to a man from Bow Street about her boyfriend, Charley," she replied in a meek voice.

Putting a single finger into the tub, Jane found the water to be pleasantly warm. The bath would be heaven sent after the past twenty-four or so hours. Turning to Molly, she said, "Thank you, Molly. I'll send for you when I'm through with my bath," and waited for her to leave. The thought of the maid watching her bathe made her cringe in embarrassment.

Molly opened her mouth as if to say something, thought better of it, and hurried out the door.

Every muscle in Jane's very sore body seemed to relax in the warm water, and she managed to clean herself up rather nicely. She was shocked to notice the bruises on her legs and wrists, and decided that this was the last time she would leave Wales without her father or her brother.

As she washed her hair and tried to get rid of most of the caked blood that had become a permanent part of her head, she did have to admit one thing. If it wasn't for Lord Blackmoore and his tenacity, she would probably still be in Wilford's clutches.

She forced Wilford out of her mind as she got out of the tub and began to dry herself off. *I hope Richard understands why I'm going to jilt him,* she thought. *It isn't fair that he should be forced to marry me because of that silly incident at the inn,* she decided firmly.

Jane slipped into her dressing gown and rang for Molly, or whoever might show up, to dispose of her bath water. The bath had made her incredibly sleepy, so she curled up on the bed and decided on a short nap.

A few moments later there was a knock on the door and Jane called, "Come in."

A very subdued Gwen appeared, looking down at the floor, her eyes brimming with tears. "Miss Jane?" she began in a soft voice. Jane looked over at her but didn't get up. She was too tired to sit up. "Yes, Gwen?" she said, frowning. Gwen was acting deuced odd.

Gwen continued to stare at the floor. "With all that's happened, you know with Charley and all, I'm here to give my notice," she finished abruptly, heading towards the door.

"Gwen, wait a moment."

Gwen stopped at the door, and turned to Jane, tears in her beautiful blue eyes. "I'm sorry, Miss Jane. I would never do anything to hurt you. But everyone downstairs says that all of this is my fault and the only thing I could do is quit, since you're going to fire me," she finished with a sob.

"Gwen, do you want to quit?" Jane asked softly.

Gwen began to sob in earnest. "No, Miss Jane," she said between sobs. "I want to go home. I never want to come to Town again."

Jane finally took pity on her maid, and went over to her and put her arms around her. "Gwen, I wasn't going to let you go. You couldn't know what was going on," she said softly.

Gwen stopped sobbing, but was still breathing in irregular gulps. "But I should have noticed that Charley was always around. The gentleman from Bow Street said that Charley was following us, and I never noticed. It's my fault you got kidnapped," she concluded, moving away from Jane.

Jane walked back over to the bed and sat down. "Gwen, did you learn anything from this whole unfortunate episode?" she asked.

Gwen finally met her eyes. "I learned that because someone is nice to me it's not always because they like me, it may be because they want something. And I learned that it's not right to tell outsiders what's happening in the house."

"Gwen, if you would like, you can remain my abigail until we get back to Wales. Then, if you want to search for a different position when we're home, you know you're free to do that," Jane concluded, not really wanting to lose

Gwen. She was a bit wild, but she was good hearted and performed her duties perfectly.

She received a slight smile from Gwen. "Thank you, Miss Jane. I don't think I'll be wanting a new job though. Before we came to London, we got on well, didn't we?" she asked, blushing a bit.

Jane smiled. "Yes, we did, Gwen. I would hope though, in the future, that you would be more careful about who you see and what you tell them."

"Oh yes, Miss Jane," Gwen said sincerely, and proceeded to attend to the bathwater and tub.

The family left Jane to her own devices that night, and Jane was happy to have supper alone in her room. As a surprise, Cook made Jane some picnic chicken, which was actually quite tasty. Jane was something of a heroine belowstairs, and they thought she was ever so brave.

Jane was still asleep at around noon when the knock came on her door. She sat up in bed and groggily said, "Come in," and was once again awed by how beautiful Charlotte looked, especially that morning.

Her golden hair was fashioned into dozens of perfect ringlets that framed her vibrant blue eyes and her perfect pale English complexion. Her dainty mouth seemed to be in a perpetual smile since Jane returned from her impromptu trip to Devon, and Charlotte wore an air of contentment about her. Today she was clad in a peach muslin gown adorned with tiny bows at the hem and a more revealing décolletage than she usually wore. Charlotte was a vision.

"Good morning, Jane," she said, walking over to the chair next to the bed and sitting down. "How are you feeling today?"

Propping herself up on her pillows, Jane looked over at her radiant cousin and smiled. "I'm feeling better. I've been having a hard time sleeping, though," she said, not wanting to admit to the nightmares that had been plaguing her every time she closed her eyes.

Charlotte reached out and patted her arm in a way that was very reminiscent of Jane's mother. "They'll go away in time. I know that whole experience must have been awful, but something good did come out of it. You see, James and I are engaged," she said, holding out her hand and showing Jane a modest diamond ring.

Truthfully, Jane was impressed. She didn't think that James had the wherewithal to purchase any kind of ring, let alone an almost respectable diamond. "That's a beautiful ring, Charlotte. What made your mother change her mind?" she asked, thinking that a direct order from the Prince Regent couldn't change Aunt Lydia's mind on her potential marriage to James.

"Well, it was James who saw that you were being kidnapped, and he had the foresight to immediately tell Richard. When Richard and Roger left, the Dowager Marchioness insisted that James be allowed to wait with us. She then started talking about Lady Morrison, who was interested in being James's patron. In fact, she said that she had seen his work and if her friend wasn't interested, then she would be. Then she started speaking to Mother about the problems a family has when a young lady or young man is disowned, and listening to the Dowager Marchioness lecture her about it all night, Mother finally relented. "Lord Blackmoore's mother can be very convincing you see, even more so than Mama. And now James has a regular income, and my dowry is enough to keep us living in a modest style," she concluded, fingering the ring.

"Are you going to be able to adjust to living less . . . frivolously?" Jane asked, wondering how Charlotte was going to be able to live without a dozen new gowns a month.

Charlotte surprised her. "I don't really care about gowns and routs and all of the trappings of Society. When James and I marry, I'll be able to pursue my painting. Mama is the one who's always insisted I participate actively in Society. I don't think I'll miss it at all," she replied with an impish grin.

Jane grinned back at her. "I'm glad, Charlotte. You deserve to marry the person you wish," she finished and stared at her covers. Her own situation was such a joke. She was being forced to marry a man she was wildly in love with who didn't think of her as anything but a friend.

The ladies sat in silence for a moment, until Jane said "Charlotte, could I ask you a favor?"

"Of course. Anything."

"Charlotte, I just want to go home. I don't want to marry Lord Blackmoore, and I don't want any fuss. Could you help me arrange for a carriage back to Wales?" she asked in a small, desperate voice.

A frown marred Charlotte's perfect features and she seemed deep in thought. After an interminably long period of time, Charlotte said, "Of course, Jane. I think going home is a good idea."

Jane's mouth dropped open. She didn't expect Charlotte to agree with her at all. This was like a miracle. "When do you think Gwen and I can leave?" she asked, afraid to leave and afraid to stay. *It would be so easy to stay and marry Blackmoore,* she thought with a sigh. *But I can't spend the rest of my life with someone who was forced to wed me because he had the temerity to take his life in his own hands and rescue me,* she decided sensibly.

Charlotte thought for a moment. "I can probably arrange for you to leave Wednesday morning. Before dawn. Would that be acceptable?" she asked hopefully.

A weak smile appeared on Jane's face. "That would be fine, Charlotte. But please don't tell anyone. I don't want to argue with your mother or Roger or explain to Lord Blackmoore that I'm leaving London so I don't have to jilt him," she concluded, feeling very tired all of a sudden.

Charlotte stood up and moved towards the door. "Don't worry, Jane, I'll take care of everything. I'll even talk to Gwen and help oversee your packing. All you have to do is get well," she finished, and regally swept out of the room.

Jane was completely overcome. She didn't realize that Charlotte had enough backbone to defy her family and help her with her flight from London. But then, Charlotte was engaged and Aunt Lydia could hardly change her mind about the situation, not with someone like the Dowager Marchioness voicing her approval.

She was glad that Charlotte had finally found a solution to her problem with James, and wished that it would be as easy for her to get on with her life. Or lack of one.

Blackmoore and Castlereagh sat over their glasses of brandy, both men in excellent spirits. They were in Castlereagh's office, and had due cause to celebrate. Wilford was being exiled from England, which Blackmoore opposed. He would have enjoyed watching him visit Jack Ketch, but the government decided that a public hanging of a member of the peerage would be a bit disgraceful. Instead, he was off to America, far, far away from Miss Ravenwood.

As Castlereagh sipped his brandy, he ran his fingers through his straight blond hair and frowned a trifle. "You did say you were forced to spend the evening in that awful inn—what was the name? The Cock and Bull, right, that was it. You spent the night with Miss Ravenwood, correct?" he finally finished, the frown marring his handsome features.

"Yes," Blackmoore answered simply, wondering if his valet was going to lecture him again. He was a good man, and it wasn't his fault that Blackmoore was too busy to worry that his cravat wasn't tied in the most fashionable mode or that his hair was much too long.

Castlereagh looked at him in abject amazement. "So, tell me why haven't the banns been published? Isn't that what usually happens to gentlemen who have unchaperoned adventures with unmarried females?"

The hint of a smile appeared on Blackmoore's strong features. "Actually, you can congratulate me. The announcement will be placed at the end of the week," he finished simply, noticing how unmanly Castlereagh looked with his mouth gaping open in shock.

"You mean you're actually going to marry her? Do you want an assignment out of the country so you don't have to go through with it and she'll be forced to cry off?" he said helpfully.

A large, definite smile took its place permanently on Blackmoore's face, transforming him from an arrogant nobleman to a charming young man. "No, I don't want to bolt to the Continent. I was actually planning to offer for Jenny before this episode occurred, so although Society may think she's been compromised, I wrote her father a while back and informed him of my intentions," he explained in his most reasonable tone of voice.

"So you're going to leg-shackle yourself for life to the daughter of a Welsh tradesman and make her your marchioness? You know that's just not done."

Blackmoore sipped his brandy and regarded Castlereagh. He was an incredible Foreign Secretary, but occasionally he was quite the flat. "Robert, Jenny will make a more admirable marchioness than any of the milk-and-water simpering little misses I've met in the past fifteen years. She's intelligent, charming, and doesn't care a whit for Society. We'll get on famously," he finished in a decidedly firm manner.

"You must introduce me to this paragon. Of course, knowing you, I don't doubt that Polite Society will embrace her, only because she will make you as rich as Croesus," he concluded.

"I'll bring her to the office after the official announcement," Blackmoore said casually.

Castlereagh leaned forward and stared intently at Blackmoore and asked cautiously, "Does she still remind you of Yvette?"

A slight smile appeared on Blackmoore's face. "It's the strangest thing. I can't see any resemblance at all between them now," he said honestly.

Castlereagh finished off his brandy. "So am I to assume that you'll be ending your association with the Foreign Office?"

Blackmoore nodded. "Unfortunately. I'll be taking up my seat in Parliament on a regular basis from now on, and I'm sure Jenny will have some projects for me as well," he finished, wondering what mischief she would get them into once they were married.

"Would it be possible for you to go back to Dover for about a week to tie up all the loose ends there? I'd consider it a personal favor."

Blackmoore drained his glass of brandy and considered the idea. It would be his last work for the government, and it was part of his current mission. *I'll just pen Jenny a note and let her know I'm going to be gone on government business for a week,* he thought. She would undoubtedly understand the circumstances. "I can leave when need be," he announced, much to Castlereagh's obvious delight.

"Let me fill you in on the details," Castlereagh began with a smile.

The journey back to Wales was accomplished with amazing efficiency. Charlotte consulted Roger, who agreed that Jane should return to the Abbey when she desired without the interference of his mother. So, after a brief discussion with Jane, he arranged for her transportation while Charlotte helped Gwen with her packing.

A subtle transformation had come over the usually bubbly Gwen since she had unknowingly betrayed her mistress. She was now a bit more serious, a bit quieter, and, most amazing of all, a bit more proper. In fact, in the space of few days, Gwen had become the epitome of a ladies' maid. The entire staff was awed by the transformation in her, in much the same way that they worried about poor Miss Ravenwood.

On early Wednesday morning, Jane was on her way back to her beloved Wales. A heaviness she had never experienced before nearly devoured her heart.

That very afternoon, the letter from Blackmoore arrived for Jane at the Stockmorton residence. There was much debate on what should be done with it, and, in the end, Charlotte had the last word. She decided to mail it to Jane at her earliest opportunity.

"Really Papa, I'm fine, except for the bump on my head," Jane reassured her father once again.

Jane had been in the study with her father for almost two hours. He demanded a full explanation of everything that happened, which took Jane a prodigiously long time. She also purposely downplayed Blackmoore's involvement, simply referring to him as a friend of the family.

As Jane related the story to her papa, she realized how strange it sounded. She focused mainly on the episode with Lord Wilford, the kidnapping, her rescue, and her return to London. She haltingly admitted her compromise, and informed him that Society expected her to wed Lord Blackmoore. Jane liked Lord Blackmoore well enough, but she didn't want to force him into a marriage because he had the courage to rescue her from a deranged Bedlamite. So, in the end, she had to leave Town.

Jane squirmed a bit in the rosewood chair. Jon was visiting the country home of Lord Pembroke, so she couldn't share her fears and concerns with him. Gwen was trying to be helpful, but she felt so guilty about her involuntary involvement in the plot that she wasn't much help. Although Jane was home, she was still very much alone.

That night, her father found her alone in her room, a dozen candles blazing. It was well past midnight, and Jane was sitting at the window, staring outside.

"Jane, are you feeling well?" her Papa asked with a frown.

"I'm fine, Papa. I haven't been sleeping much lately."

He entered the room and sat down on her bed. "Not sleeping? Why?" he demanded, leaning forward in concern.

Jane looked away and stared at the familiar carpet on the floor. "I still have the most dreadful dreams about the night I was kidnapped," she said softly, feeling very embarrassed. She should be above having nightmares. She was a Ravenwood. She was brave.

Her Papa walked over to the window and put his hand on her shoulder. "It's nothing to be ashamed of, Janie. Would you feel better if I put a footman outside of your room?" he asked, the picture of parental concern.

She smiled. This time it was genuine. "No, I don't think I need a guard outside of my door. Roger tells me that Wilford is already half way to America," she said, feeling very glad to be home.

Gareth Ravenwood frowned. "Is there anything else I can do, Janie?" he said softly.

Jane shook her head. "No."

Ravenwood studied his daughter, a worried expression still on his face. "You know, Janie, you never did tell me why you found it necessary to go to visit Miss Bridgeson in the first place."

Jane looked down at her hands. "I knew that when Jon got married, his bride would be mistress of the Abbey. I wouldn't be needed, or wanted here," she replied simply.

"Balderdash!" her Father replied. "Pembroke's daughter is an only child. She wanted you to live here, she already sees you as the sister she never had," he explained.

A huge sigh escaped Jane. "So I don't have to leave the Abbey? My plans were all for naught?"

"You should have written me, my dear. We could have sorted though this mess," Ravenwood commented.

Jane was silent for the longest time. "If I wouldn't have tried to see Miss Bridgeson, perhaps none of this would have happened with Lord Wilford," she remarked.

"Janie, Wilford was deranged. His father sent your mama letters for years, horrible, threatening letters. I never suspected his son was of the same ilk, or I would have never sent you to London."

"I didn't know," she said simply.

"No one knew, Janie. You're lucky that you escaped with just a few bumps and bruises. From what you tell me, Wilford would have tried to hurt you before the Season is over. What happened wasn't pleasant, but you didn't get hurt. That's all that's important," he added calmly.

Jane stared into the darkness outside her window. "You're right," she said, a slight chill running down her spine. Broken heart and all, she was indeed glad to be home.

CHAPTER SIXTEEN

"What do you mean she's not here?" Blackmoore asked, a black rage encompassing him. His friends, or his supposed friends, had let his fiancée bolt back to Wales without a by your leave.

Charlotte smiled docilely. "She left you a note. Would you like to see it?" she asked in a level voice.

"Of course I want to see it," he growled at Charlotte, who handed him the missive.

As he stared at the letter, a sinking feeling came over him. This was in Jane's writing.

"Dear Richard,"

she began,

> *"I'll be forever in your debt for your intervention with Lord Wilford. If it wasn't for your foresight and daring, undoubtedly I'd be dead by now."*

He frowned. This was not what he wanted to read.

> *"I know your actions compromised me, and that Society expects you to marry me. Unfortunately, I don't believe that you should be punished by being forced into a marriage simply because you acted with courage and concern,"*

it read, and he became frightened. Jane didn't love him at all.

Blackmoore tugged at his cravat, which was now impossibly tight, and continued to read.

> *"So rather than go through with a fake engagement which would end with my crying off, I thought I would simply go home and release you from any obligation you may feel as a gentleman. I enjoyed our friendship and will always think of you in the most complimentary way.*
>
> *Your servant, Jane Ravenwood,"*

it concluded, and Blackmoore sat down in the nearest chair. This was a disaster.

"What did the letter say?" Charlotte asked innocently. Blackmoore looked up, a dazed expression on his face.

"What?"

"What did Jane say in her letter?"

He continued staring at the letter. She didn't want him. She ran away to escape their marriage. He was a marquess. He was rich and thought to be the perennial catch of any Season. And she didn't want him.

The words on the letter seemed to run together on the page when he finally said, "Jane said she didn't want to force me into a marriage I didn't want only because I helped her. She's released me from all obligations," he said, feeling as he had gone nine rounds with Gentleman Jim. No, worse than that. This pain was deep inside him and wouldn't heal as easily as a bruise.

"So what are you going to do?" Charlotte asked, sitting primly on the satin-covered rosewood chair.

"Charlotte, she doesn't want to marry me. What can I do?" he asked in a tormented voice.

Charlotte sighed, and addressed him as if her were a rather slow child. "Richard, does Jane ever say in that letter that she doesn't want to marry you?" she said, becoming impatient.

Blackmoore was rather irritated with Charlotte. "Of course it says that. She doesn't want me to be forced into a marriage because I stopped that madman from abducting her," he said, his mood swinging from desolate to angry.

Charlotte sprang up from the chair and moved to the window. "Richard, you are definitely cork-brained. Did it ever occur to you that you didn't make your feelings clear to Jane? And instead of declaring yourself, you simply accepted a forced marriage. If I remember correctly, there has been more than one incident when you've been caught embracing her. Do you think she's a wanton who behaves like that with everyone?" she said sternly.

The frown lining Blackmoore's brow became deeper. "No, I don't think she's a wanton," he said, hope flaming in his heart. Maybe Jenny did love him.

He stood up from his seat and strode purposely toward Charlotte. He put his large, capable hand on her dainty shoulder and said, "Thank you, Charlotte. I've must go now."

Charlotte turned and smiled up at him. "May I ask where you're going, Richard?" she said .

A devilish smile appeared on Blackmoore's face. "I hear Wales is beautiful this time of year," he replied, and left the room, ready to confront Jenny and get this situation settled.

Jane stared at the letter her father showed her, wondering why Charlotte and Roger posted it to her. So Blackmoore was going to be out of Town for a while, what concern was it of hers? She was in Wales. Charlotte knew that she all but jilted Blackmoore.

Her papa stared at her. "Is it bad news, Jane?" he asked, obviously curious about the letter she was holding.

"It's nothing, Papa. I don't even know why Charlotte sent this to me," Jane replied blandly, staring blankly at Blackmoore's strong, definite strokes.

"What was the message?" he asked again, persisting.

A sigh escaped Jane. Her papa was nothing if not curious. She didn't want to talk about the entire episode with Lord Blackmoore, and consequently her father wouldn't stop plaguing her about it. "This is just a note from Lord Blackmoore. He was supposed to come visit me at the end of the week to discuss our engagement. He just wanted to let me know he'd be a few days late since he had to go to Dover," she finished, wondering if her papa would accept that explanation.

"So he was going to actually marry you?"

"Lord Blackmoore had no choice. That's why I left Town now, rather than go through with a phony engagement then cry off later," Jane explained patiently.

"If he didn't want to marry you, it seems that this lord of yours would have been smart enough to find a way out," her papa commented.

Jane considered the comment, but had nothing to say.

The sun was just dipping below the horizon when Blackmoore turned onto the road to the Abbey. The medieval structure was well known, and he would have saved some time if he had spoken the native tongue. It took him a deuced long time, but he finally found someone in town that was able to give him directions to Jane's home that he could actually comprehend.

He was on the road for at least an hour, and was thankful that the road was well-maintained, since he could barely see where he was going. The fields were lush and green, and the air smelled much better than the stench that filled London.

The outline of a giant stone building dominated the dark

horizon, rising up from among the neat looking cottages that were undoubtedly Ravenwood's tenants. Blackmoore quickly counted the cottages and was surprised. The Ravenwood estate supported more tenants and had more land than his own estates, and he was the holder of a respectable old title.

As he neared the castle-like structure, he gasped. This was no shabby former monk's dwelling; it was a gigantic medieval fortress. It loomed above him, making his properties look positively modest. Another leveling thought.

As he neared the front door, a young boy appeared to wait for him. He called to the boy, "Is this the Ravenwood house?"

"Yes, m'lord," the young boy replied in perfect English.

So he tossed the reins to the dark haired imp and approached the tall, imposing structure in front of him. If the inside was as impressive as the outside, he could see why Lydia didn't want anyone to know Jenny was an heiress. She was obviously from one of the wealthiest families in existence.

He knocked on the sturdy wooden door that looked as if it could have easily repelled a cannon shot, only to be faced with a very respectable looking butler.

"May I help you, sir?" the aged servant said in a very disapproving tone, since it was much too late to be calling on someone. This wasn't London, it was the country, and gentlemen didn't call unannounced after dark.

Blackmoore tried to be polite. "Good evening. I'm Richard Hughes, the Marquess of Blackmoore. I'm here to see Miss Ravenwood," he replied, somewhat surprised that another of Ravenwood's servants spoke perfect English.

The butler frowned and appeared to consider several options before answering. Finally he replied, "Follow me, sir," in the haughty tones of a London butler. After a rather long walk through numerous dark hallways, Blackmoore found himself in a rather impressive library.

Jane was in a small study in the west wing of the Abbey, reading. Two gaslights illuminated the room fairly well; in fact, they were the first in the area to have them in their home. Papa heard about them in the textile factories and decided to try them in some rooms of the Abbey.

Jane heard some sort of a commotion outside, but ignored it, uninterested. If there was an emergency with one of the tenants, the staff knew very well where to find her.

She was trying to read the same page for quite a while, utterly unable to concentrate, when Gwen burst into the room.

"He's here, Miss Jane! Lord Blackmooore is here, with your papa, in the library," she announced, all but bursting with excitement.

Jane's stomach lurched. "Why? Why would Lord Blackmoore come here?" she asked, not really expecting a reply.

Gwen giggled. "He's here to offer for you, Miss Jane. I've been expecting him for days!"

Oh no, Jane thought in horror. *I'm going to have to refuse him in person!*

Blackmoore studied the portrait of a delicate woman with lively eyes and sandy brown hair above the mantle. *Jane has her eyes,* he thought abstractedly, waiting. He had been waiting for a quarter of an hour, and he never enjoyed waiting.

Finally, the heavily carved mahogany library door creaked open. A gentleman, undoubtedly Jane's father, appeared.

The gentleman seemed to be about eight-and-forty years old, was on the tall side, and had short curly dark hair flecked with gray. He eyed Blackmoore warily, as if they were combatants.

"Good evening," he began, and extended his hand to

Blackmoore. "I'm Gareth Ravenwood," he said as he shook hands with Blackmoore.

"I'm here to see your daughter," Blackmoore said impatiently.

Ravenwood motioned for him to sit down in a plush chair near the fireplace, and then went over to the decanter of claret that he kept on hand for special occasions. "May I offer you some claret?" he asked casually.

Blackmoore was getting more annoyed by the moment. He was tired, dusty, hungry, and wanted to speak with Jane. "No, thank you. I'm here to speak with your daughter," he said stiffly, straightening to his full height.

Ravenwood poured a glass of claret for himself, and walked over to a chair near the fireplace. Blackmoore sighed, and sat down in the chair opposite him.

"I realize that you're here to see my daughter. Jane is very dear to me. What do you have to offer her?" he asked in the firm tone that confirmed his reputation as an astute and unyielding businessman.

The blood began to course through Blackmoore's veins in anger. Who was this man to treat him like some caper merchant?

He stiffened and announced, in his most lordly tone, "I am the Marquess of Blackmoore. I possess one of the oldest titles in England and have vast holdings across the country. I'm not some fortune-hunter out to bilk your daughter."

A slight smile appeared on Ravenwood's face. "I've found that most members of the Upper Ten are wastrels, gamblers, half-wits, or womanizers. Which are you?" he said, obviously trying to bait Blackmoore.

Blackmoore was never one to shrink from a challenge, and this man was most definitely challenging him. He turned his icy golden gaze on Ravenwood and said, "You know nothing of me, and you dare to insinuate that I have a disreputable background?" he said, his anger apparent in his clipped speech.

Ravenwood sipped his claret. "May I ask your business with my daughter?" Ravenwood asked cordially.

"I have some unresolved matters to discuss with her," he replied, his common sense strengthening him and calming him down a trifle.

Gareth Ravenwood stared at the portrait on the wall and wondered what Sara would do. He paused and eventually said, "Am I correct in assuming you're going to discuss the letter you wrote me a while ago? Janie isn't aware of it, you know," he said calmly.

A frown appeared on Blackmoore's weary features. "Why didn't you tell her about it?" he asked curiously.

"If you changed your mind and never came to Wales to seek out Jane, the knowledge that you wrote to ask permission to address her and then decided against it would have only hurt her. I suppose I might have told her about it some day, but there was no need to let her know now."

Strangely enough, Blackmoore actually followed his logic. "I know my own mind, Mr. Ravenwood. My feelings for your daughter won't change, even if she refuses me," he said, stretching out in the chair.

"You are aware that my daughter isn't an acceptable wife for you. She is half Welsh and much too intelligent to waste her time in London attending endless routs and gossiping," Ravenwood said harshly.

A smile escaped Blackmoore and he relaxed even more. "Yes, Jenny is completely unacceptable. She speaks several languages—of course, not as many as I do—abhors Society as much as I do, and actually has the audacity to argue with me. She will make a magnificent marchioness, since she has more bearing than a princess and more sense than any other woman I've met," he said.

"What can you offer her?"

"Jenny will live a life of rank and privilege. She will want for nothing, and will be free to use my title and fortune to whatever ends she wishes. I have to be in London for Parliament. The rest of the year we will live together wherever she wishes. I have no idea of her dowry, and, on principle, refuse it. If you will any money to Jenny, I'll make sure that the solicitor sees to it that it is her income, not mine," he finished dramatically.

"And after you have your heir? Will you leave Janie and keep a mistress?"

A slight chuckle escaped Blackmoore's lips. "You're a very thorough businessman, Mr. Ravenwood. I'll not have a mistress, and my wife will not have a lover," he finished in a confident tone of voice.

Ravenwood stared at him, as if they were involved in a game of cards and the stakes were particularly high. "Your family line will be forever tainted by trade and your heir will be part Welsh."

A wide smile spread across Blackmoore's face. "I have a variety of rogues in my family history, including a great uncle who was a pirate and another who was a Catholic monk. I would much rather taint my family blood with Welsh trade than marry a simpering schoolroom miss and have a passel of brats who are half-wits," he concluded, all hostility gone from his eyes.

A smile slowly appeared on Ravenwood's face. "I have no doubt that you truly want to speak with my daughter, and will do so, regardless of my actions. But you've been patient enough to answer my questions, and you've impressed me with your sincerity. Unfortunately, I cannot guarantee that Janie will wish to speak with you," he commented in a level voice.

Blackmoore's heart lurched in his chest. He had not considered that she wouldn't see him.

* * *

Jane was still sitting in the small study, staring at the same page. It had been over an hour since Gwen interrupted her silence. Once again, she had the urge to avoid speaking with Blackmoore. She didn't have the will to turn down an offer of marriage, and she was completely unsuitable as a wife. Goodness knew Aunt Lydia had told her that at least a dozen times.

So she just sat and waited, her nerves on edge. What could Blackmoore be talking about with Papa for so long? What was Blackmoore doing in Wales in the first place? It was all very vexing and part of her wished that he had never appeared at her front door. The rest of her had been waiting for his arrival since she left London.

The door finally swung open, and she looked up expectantly, only to find her papa smiling at Blackmoore and Blackmoore smiling back at her papa as if they were bosom bows.

"Jane, dear," her father began, "Lord Blackmoore wishes to speak with you," he announced with a smile.

Jane stared up at Blackmoore, transfixed. "Of course, Papa," she heard herself saying, as if she were in a play.

"When you're finished, ring Grayson to take him up to the guest room in the north wing," he said, calmly, as if visitors from London appeared on his doorstep on a daily basis.

"Yes, Papa," she said, amazed that her papa not only let Blackmoore in to see her, but was now leaving and closing the door behind her. *I'm in a dressing gown,* she thought distractedly. *This is most improper,* she decided, with a frown.

"Good evening, Jenny," Blackmoore said, sitting in the chair next to her.

Lord Blackmoore was the most handsome man in all of England, Jane decided with a blush. Even with more than a little traveling dirt on him he still looked elegant and confident, she thought, finally remembering her manners.

"Good evening, Lord Blackmoore," she said in a soft voice.

"You left London without saying good bye," he commented, his eyes taking in her delicately flowered dressing gown.

"I know," she said meekly, not meeting his eyes.

"Tell me, Jenny, how many hearts have you broken in your life?" he asked in a husky voice.

Jane looked up at him with a frown. *What is he talking about?* she wondered. "I don't believe I've broken any hearts, my lord," she replied stiffly.

He shook his head. "You're wrong, my dear. When I came back from Dover and found you were gone, you certainly broke mine," he said softly.

Jane's mind was in a whirl. She stared down at her hands for a long time, trying to sort out her thoughts. "My lord," she began, "I . . ."

"Richard. Can't you call me Richard?" he asked, seductively.

"Richard. I left London without consulting you because I didn't want you to feel obligated to marry me," she explained calmly. "I thought I explained that in my note," she added.

"Yes, your note. That was certainly an unpleasant surprise," he said in a deadly serious tone.

Jane was heartbroken and frustrated at the same time. "I wanted to do the right thing. It's not fair that you should have to marry me because of what happened at the inn. So instead of announcing the banns and then crying off, I simply left. Can't you understand?" she asked, on the verge of tears.

Blackmoore gazed at her intently, a strange look in his golden eyes. "No, my dear Jenny, I most certainly cannot understand. But then, as Charlotte pointed out, that in itself is my fault."

Jane frowned at him, utterly confused.

He sighed. "Yes, I know, I'm not making much sense. So let's start at the beginning. Do you recall that night at Almack's that I scandalized all of proper society by very pointedly showing you my attentions?" he asked in a matter of fact tone.

Jane nodded. "They said you felt sorry for me," she said in a tiny voice. "They said you were tired of opera singers. And you needed money."

"Oh God, Jenny, I'm sorry. I never knew you were subjected to that," he replied, his voice thick with emotion.

Jane stared at her hands, ashamed to meet his eyes. "I knew it wasn't true. I just thought you were trying to be nice to me. To make up for those times you . . . accosted me."

Blackmoore was shocked. "Just being nice to you? Balderdash. I spent time with you because you're the most enchanting female I've ever met. Not to be polite. Not because I need money. For goodness' sake, Roger and Charlotte should have told you that my manners are abysmal. I don't do things just to be polite," he explained.

Jane continued to stare at her fingernails, and wouldn't meet his eyes.

So he plunged on, running his hand through his ink black hair. "In any case, a short while after that, I wrote your father. To inform him that I was going to ask you to marry me," he said quietly.

Jane's head snapped up. "What? Papa never said anything about that to me."

"Your papa is a very shrewd man. When you didn't come home engaged, he wasn't certain that I would ever appear and propose properly, which I should have done in London," he admitted freely.

Jane finally looked up at him, her green eyes large and luminous. "You can't want to marry me! I am the daughter of a Welsh tradesman. My kind cannot marry into proper society! If I learned anything in London, it was that fact," Jane said harshly.

Blackmoore leaned forward in the chair and rested his elbows on his knees. "Let's see, I've already had most of this discussion with your father. I've managed to convince him that I don't care about your lineage. Or your fortune," he added for good measure.

He's making this so difficult, Jane thought in agony. *Even if he does care about me, just a little, I can't marry him. It would ruin his life in polite society,* she decided, on the verge of tears. She didn't say anything for the longest time, then finally said, "I'm sorry, Lord Blackmoore, I won't marry without affection."

Blackmoore leaned back in the chair and stared into her luminous green eyes. "Well, Jenny, my affections have been engaged for some time now. I hope yours are engaged as well," he asked in a soft voice, his eyes never leaving her green gaze.

Jane looked up at him, her eyes large with disbelief. "You don't care for me, Richard. You can't," she said softly.

And to that he laughed, a rich, hearty laugh. "I've been in love with you for ages, probably from the first time I saw you in the Park on Diablo. Why do you think I kept trying to molest you, my dear? Why do you think I went after Wilford when he abducted you? Why do you think I didn't protest when your family announced I had to marry you? I was planning to marry you no matter what happened. Being compromised made it easier for me, since I didn't have to actually ask you. Once I found out that you weren't involved in any nefarious activities, I couldn't stop thinking about you. Or wanting to be with you. When I found out that you had left London, it felt like I was shot in the chest," he declared passionately.

It was as if a giant weight had lifted from Jane's shoulders. The man she yearned for, cared for, and wanted to spend the rest of her life with didn't care about her heritage. Or money. He loved her. "You love me?" she said in a tiny voice, barely believing that it could be true.

Blackmoore gave her a devastating smile as he got up, walked over to her chair and took her hand, pulling her up and into his arms. "Yes, I love you and wish to marry you, and be with you for all of eternity," he said huskily into her ear as he pressed her warm, supple body to his.

He began with feather-light kisses on her neck, and, when she didn't answer him immediately, he said, "You haven't answered me yet, and I really don't want to go down on my knees and beg you. Of course, if you don't give me the answer I want, I suppose I'll have to, although I won't particularly enjoy it, since I'm not used to begging for anything," he said.

Her heart was soaring, and Jane knew the answer to his question. She wound her arms even tighter around his tall, masculine frame and replied, "Begging might be good for you. It could help you get rid of that awful arrogance," she said playfully.

Blackmoore answered by kissing her soundly.

"Your family won't approve of me you know," Jane said, her head resting on his broad shoulder.

He chuckled and brushed back a lock of her curly black hair. "You forget, my love, that I am the head of my family. I've already spoken to my mother, who thinks that our marriage is a dashed good idea, but she doesn't think that you'll accept me," he said.

Jane gazed at him in amazement. "Really?"

"Really. Mother decided that I should offer for you when she met you at our rout. And she spoke to Maria Sefton, who was a friend of your mama's. With my mother and Maria as your champions, you'll have no problems at all in London," he concluded warmly.

A small smile crept onto her face. "I hated gulling everyone," she admitted. "But Aunt Lydia said I wouldn't be accepted by Society if they knew who I was and where I was from."

Blackmoore smiled down at her, perfectly contented. "I know. But from now on, you don't have to pretend to make your way in Society. The Blackmoore name will protect you," he said firmly. "If you'll have it," he added in a soft voice.

Jane was filled with joy, and happier than she ever thought possible. "Yes, Richard, I'll have the Blackmoore name. For if I don't, my papa will undoubtedly call me out, since we've been alone for such an interminably long . . ."

Blackmoore's silenced her with a kiss that engulfed her senses.

"Gwen, what are you doing?" Gareth Ravenwood asked in a hushed voice. He knew exactly what Gwen was doing. She was listening at the door. That's exactly the thing he wanted to do, but he was the head of the house and really couldn't be seen engaging in such infantile behavior. Luckily, Gwen didn't have any such qualms, so he could find out what was happening in their south parlor.

"They're going to get married!" Gwen exclaimed in an excited whisper. A deep sigh of relief came from Ravenwood. He thought that Jane probably had a tendre for the gypsy-like lord, but one never knew with women. Why, he hadn't thought he had a ghost of a chance with his Sara, but she defied her family and married him. And claimed she never regretted it. "Did they say anything else?" he asked curiously, almost feeling guilty for eavesdropping.

In the past, Gwen would have told him every single thing she heard at the door. But London changed the pert young abigail, for the better. "I really didn't hear anything else, sir," she said in the most proper of tones.

Ravenwood smiled warmly. "You knew about this, didn't you, Gwen? About Blackmoore and Janie?"

Gwen grinned cheekily. "I knew all along he was the man for Miss Jane. He was the most handsome lord in all of London, and was always ever so nice to Miss Jane," she said merrily. "But his butler is a bit starchy," she added, practically bounding down the corridor toward her own room.

It was a very long time before Jane retired that night.

BOOK YOUR PLACE ON OUR WEBSITE AND MAKE THE READING CONNECTION!

We've created a customized website just for our very special readers, where you can get the inside scoop on everything that's going on with Zebra, Pinnacle and Kensington books.

When you come online, you'll have the exciting opportunity to:

- View covers of upcoming books
- Read sample chapters
- Learn about our future publishing schedule (listed by publication month *and author*)
- Find out when your favorite authors will be visiting a city near you
- Search for and order backlist books from our online catalog
- Check out author bios and background information
- Send e-mail to your favorite authors
- Meet the Kensington staff online
- Join us in weekly chats with authors, readers and other guests
- Get writing guidelines
- AND MUCH MORE!

**Visit our website at
http://www.kensingtonbooks.com**